Dream of a Spring Night

I. J. PARKER

I • J • P
2018

Published 2018 by I.J.Parker and I·J·P Books
3229 Morningside Drive, Chesapeake VA 23321
http://www.ijparker.com
Cover design by I. J. Parker.
Cover image by Ogata Gekko
Back cover image: Heike Monogatari scroll
Publisher's Note: This is a work of fiction. Names, characters, places, and incidents are a product of the author's imagination.

Dream of a Spring Night 3rd edition, 2018
ISBN -13 978-1726352031

Author's Note

This novel has undergone more than its share of revisions. Originally conceived as a single, albeit very long tome, I decided to break it into three parts to make it more manageable. This version went up on Kindle and had a nice success. But the more I considered the novel, the less I liked the way Hachiro inserted himself into the story of Toshiko and Sadahira. Clearly, he wanted to control the novel. I decided to give Hachiro his own book, *The Sword Master,* published earlier. With him taken care of, the story of Toshiko and Sadahira can be told separately. This is the first volume.

I. J. Parker August 2018

Characters

(* marks a historical character)

Oba no Toshiko
Fourteen-year-old daughter
of a Taira vassal

Lady Sanjo
Senior lady-in-waiting to
Emperor Go-Shirakawa's Consort

Go-Shirakawa*
The Retired Emperor

Taira Kiyomori*
Chancellor and clan chief of the Taira

Otomae*
Famous singer and performer of *imayo*

Lady Shojo-ben
Lady-in-waiting

Oba no Hiramoto
Toshiko's father

Oba no Takehira
Oba no Yasuhira
Toshiko's brothers

Yamada no Sadahira
Physician

Otori
His housekeeper

Togoro
His servant

Hachiro
Sadamu
Orphan boys adopted by the physician

Master Soma

A teacher of swordsmanship.

1168 - 1169

Even the jeweled throne,
Shining in the morning sun,
Partakes of darkness
When unrequited lust
Regrets the pleasures of the night.

Daini Takato Shu

Aloeswood

It was spring when the perfumed darkness swallowed her.

From the moment her parents told her that she must serve the Emperor, the palace seemed to her a huge maw to suck her in and consume her entirely. She struggled - weakly, for how do you disobey your parents who have given you birth, raised you, and now depended on you?

Already on the journey to the capital, the darkness embraced her. She was confined inside the elegant palm leaf carriage sent for her, behind reed curtains that were woven with crimson silk threads and securely fastened to all openings. Hemmed in by cushions, curtains, and her many-layered silk gown, she was aware of the outside world only through muffled sounds: the creaking of the carriage, the grinding of gravel under the huge wheels, the shuffling of ox hooves, the driver's shouts to make way, and the hoof beats and clinking of bridles and stirrups of outriders. Later there were the sounds of the capital, of many people, of tradesmen hawking their wares, of temple bells, of other carriages and horsemen. All belonged to the world of light she had left behind forever. She wanted to peek out, but that was strictly forbidden, and so she entered the maw blindly.

They backed the carriage up to a raised veranda, and when they lifted the curtain at its back, she saw a dim tunnel made of draped cloth held by many hands. Other hands reached for her and pulled her up and out, drawing her into a large, dusky room filled with the heavy scent of aloeswood.

A sort of birth – into darkness and whispers.

A woman's voice: "Let's have a look at her."

Blinding light from a candle thrust toward her face made her close her eyes. Indrawn breaths. A giggle. A cough. The first voice: "Well, at least she is young."

She was fourteen.

And her life was over.

But of course she did not die then. The women—scented shadows in a large room—took her in hand, removing most of her clothes, washing her face and hands before applying the heavy paste to her face, then painting her nails while the paste dried on her skin; they blackened her teeth, painted her moth eyebrows, outlined her eyes, rouged her lips, and oiled her hair; and finally they dressed her in layer after layer of silk. Each color had a name, but she was too dazed to pay attention. She was thinking of the maw, of being dressed like a dead pheasant or duck her father or brothers tossed at the cook to be plucked, drawn, and prepared for consumption.

And then it was time. One of the shadows took a candle and motioned her to follow. There were sighs and whispers from the others. The flame threw shadows on screens, grotesque distortions of female forms with elongated bodies and misshapen heads, thin, claw like hands gesturing, reaching.

"Hurry!"

She obeyed and began to walk, her own shadow gliding along beside her, a companion until it, too, was swallowed by the darkness.

She followed the flickering light along a corridor with floors so highly polished that they looked like black ice. The flame of the candle split in two, dancing both above and below the black ice until she no longer knew which light she followed. The cold crept up through the silk socks on her feet. She shrank away from it, shrank into herself trying to vanish into insubstantiality.

Someone was singing - a male voice - the tune strangely familiar but dreamlike. She floated toward it like a petal on a stream.

When she had almost achieved the state of notbeing, two wide doors parted before her and she came into a large room. On a raised platform in front of painted screens, a man sat at a desk. He was the one singing. Between snatches of song, he made notations on a scroll.

"The girl, Your Majesty," said her guide and knelt.

With that simple announcement, Oba no Toshiko, fourteen years old, rematerialized and became "the girl."

The singing stopped.

Oba no Toshiko's knees turned to water. She collapsed in a rustle of silks and lay face down on the black ice, wishing it would melt and swallow her.

"Ah, Lady Sanjo!" said the male voice. And then, "Yes. The wild goose. So she is here. It is good. You may leave."

Leave? A wild hope kindled and was instantly extinguished when he said, "Come here, little goose. Let me look at you."

For a moment, she toyed with a foolish thought: What if she pretended a fainting spell? Or better yet, death? From an excess of awe.

But she remembered that she was Oba no Toshiko, daughter of warriors, and got to her knees to look up at him.

For a Son of Heaven he looked quite ordinary. Not handsome at all. A broad face and small eyes that studied her. He smiled, and she saw that he was her father's age and had bad teeth.

"Come closer," he said again, waving a hand, and she got to her feet. Somehow the fact that he looked so ordinary gave her knees the strength to support her as she crept up to the dais. He made room beside himself, and she sat down on the high, thick grass matting.

"Do you know any *imayo*?" he asked.

She was startled. *Imayo* were popular songs sung by women of questionable virtue. Of course she knew them, but a lady could not admit to such knowledge. She shook her head.

"Ha, I thought so." He sighed, rinsed his brush in the water container, and laid it aside. "I had hoped," he said, "but it doesn't matter. Do you know why I called you the wild goose?"

"No, sire." He, too, smelled of aloeswood, and of something else, masculine and not unpleasant.

"On my recent visit to your father's home, I saw you riding with your brothers. You reminded me of a famous poem.

As they lift their wings
Against starry skies.
The moon is counting each
Of the wild geese flying
On this autumn night."

She looked at him in wonder, remembering. Her father had been entertaining visitors from the capital. Her oldest brother, proud owner of a new horse, had wanted to try him out, and so they had all got on their horses and raced through the valley.

"You were there and saw me?" she asked, her eyes wide and her voice breathless at the memory of that perfect night of galloping hooves, of flying free on the wind that lifted her long hair and her horse's mane and molded her clothes to her body. Yes, there had been geese that evening. They had raced the geese and each other, she and her brothers.

He smiled, nodding. "We watched the moon from the veranda. The geese passed over, flying south, and there you were, following them. You wore something white and looked like a ghostly bird skimming the earth."

She chuckled.

"I have never seen a woman ride like that," he said softly.

She heard admiration in his voice and suddenly felt warm. "It was not very ladylike," she said with a small gasp. Then she remembered where she was and why, and suddenly the fear was back and the grief. Tears welled up and she turned her head away.

He reached out to touch her cheek. Cupping her chin, he turned her face to him. "Are you unhappy about the arrangement, little one?"

She looked at him fearfully. "I . . . don't know what to think. I don't belong here . . . I . . ." and to her horror, she burst into violent weeping.

He took his hand away and said nothing for a long time. When she had calmed down a little, he pressed a paper tissue into her hand. "You are tired from your journey," he said. "Go and rest, little wild goose. We shall talk again."

Imayo

The Emperor watched her run away across the glossy surface, sleeves billowing and skirts hissing along the floor. She burst through the door to the gallery and disappeared.

He was disappointed, even a little angry. Her flight reminded him again of the soaring geese and the white-robed girl skimming across the night-darkened fields on the back of her horse, but the gorgeously robed and painted creature who had crept in and fearfully ascended the dais to sit stiffly beside him was nothing like that memory. Except for her reluctance, she was like all the rest, those young women who had been brought to him through the years, as indistinguishable from each other as dolls or as the hundred representations of the Kannon in the Sanjusangendo temple.

He bedded many palace women, some more than once, in case he might after all discover some hidden talent, some unique trait. Most could play an instrument, or talk amusingly, or tell stories, or compose little poems. That sort of thing was common enough among noblewomen.

None of his carefully selected wives and concubines had proved to have special gifts either. And yet, from the time he had been a mere boy, he had hoped to find a soul mate—a talented musician or a poet—as his companion, a woman whose passion matched his.

It struck him that not one of the ungifted had been a very passionate lover either. Mostly, they had lain beneath him, rigid, their eyes squeezed shut, biting their painted lips—and when he had left them, he had never felt more than the mild distaste that follows a mediocre meal.

He sighed and called, "Otomae, you can come out now."

A soft rustle, and a small gray nun's figure appeared, mouse like, from behind one of the painted screens. She sat down beside him where the girl had been. He regarded her fondly. "Well?"

Her wrinkled face broke into a smile. "Bravo, Your Majesty."

Otomae's voice was still the most beautiful of voices to him and filled his heart with pleasure. Her narrow face, framed by short white hair, was almost equally dear. He shook his head. "Ah, Otomae, how can you say that? I have been grossly duped. She knows nothing of *imayo*."

His beloved Otomae was no nun. Far from it. In her younger days she had been a street entertainer, one of the singing and dancing *shirabyoshi*, and at times a prostitute. When her fame had reached his ears, he had still been a young man and she already middle-aged. She never became his lover, but she was his teacher and the closest thing to a soul mate he had ever found.

"She is very young and frightened," said Otomae. "I think you shocked her when you asked if she knew *imayo.*"

He sighed. "It is far more likely that Kiyomori and her father lied."

Reaching for a narrow box made of black lacquer painted with golden reeds, he took out a flute - an ordinary bamboo flute, old but with an incomparable sound. It was the only one of the imperial treasures he had kept after his abdication.

He fingered the flute. They had meant to try out a new melody, but he had lost his desire. "There must be women who satisfy a man's desire. The poet Narihira poured out his passion in matchless verse. Prince Genji loved many women deeply, including his imperial father's favorite. My own father was so besotted with one of his wives that he allowed her to decide the succession."

The Fujiwaras used to train their girl children to seduce and bewitch young emperors so they could produce imperial heirs. And now, Taira Kiyomori was following the pattern. He had already matched him with a Taira consort.

Otomae broke into his glum musings: "Shall we continue our work?"

"No."

Their work was the collection of the songs performed by *shirabyoshi* in markets and on streets, those haunting words and melodies that would otherwise cease to exist.

This passion for imayo had almost cost him the throne when his august father, urged on by his Consort, refused to make him crown prince, saying that his obsession made him unfit to rule.

Still upset, the Emperor put away the flute. "Kiyomori is behind this," he said. "He hopes to distract me from the nation's business with this girl. He called her an artist of uncommon talent. Like a fool, I believed him."

He did not mention his tantalizing glimpse of the girl astride her horse, flying along the moon-lit valley with a flock of geese, her long hair streaming behind. His utter enchantment and sudden physical desire had shaken him to the point of dizziness. Light-headed with wine, moon light, and the thought of a girl on horseback, he had burst out with the offer.

Otomae said softly, "There is something about her. Don't judge her too quickly."

"She is a child, the daughter of a minor noble. What could she know of the art?"

Otomae chuckled. "You mean she is not a streetwalker?"

He was not amused, though the image was fitting. "I mean that I bought the girl because of extravagant promises made by her seller, and the merchandise is not as represented. I have been cheated. The girl's father is richer by ten *shoen* of good rice fields and his son by a lucrative post in the outer palace guards."

The door at the end of the room opened and Lady Sanjo peered in.

Otomae hissed softly, then said, "Please excuse me now, sire." She bowed, murmuring, "You may yet find some use for your purchase," and rose to leave.

The Emperor watched the frail gray figure disappear through another door before turning his attention to Lady Sanjo, who tiptoed in and knelt.

"What?" he demanded impatiently, eyeing her with distaste. She looked worn in this light. What possessed some women to paint their faces and drag their thinning hair behind them like young girls? Women ought to become nuns when they lost their beauty.

"I wondered if the young woman had offended Your Majesty," Lady Sanjo lisped in the girlish voice she reserved for him alone. Her expression was hopeful.

He knew that this woman felt some perverse lust for him. Her efforts at seduction amused him in the way that grotesque scroll paintings of diseased people or of hungry ghosts amused him.

Now he saw the hunger in her eyes as she simpered, fluttering a bony hand before her thin lips, and he suppressed a laugh. He considered her question. There had been offense, yes, but one could not quite blame the girl. She had obeyed her father, that was all. In this deception, she alone had been honest, making it clear that she had no wish to be near him.

"Not at all," he said, and added spitefully, "She is quite charming and only needs some time to feel at home."

He watched Lady Sanjo's face fall. She touched her forehead to the floor and prepared to withdraw.

"You will take charge of her and report to me when she is ready," he said. "And I particularly wish to know if she has any talents."

"Talents?" Lady Sanjo was so crushed she could barely speak.

"Yes. She is said to have a charming voice. As you know, I have a great desire to hear charming voices about me."

"I have been told I have an attractive voice," Lady Sanjo cried and flushed unattractively. "I would not wish to sound boastful but—"

He interrupted quickly, "Ah, you are a woman of many talents." He laughed, but when she crept a little closer, he said quite coldly, "Thank you. That is all."

She bowed again and backed out on her knees.

He watched her creep away, pushing her full skirts out of the way. The girl in her graceful flight had forgotten that you do not turn your back on an emperor, not even a retired one.

Alone again, the Emperor contemplated his retirement.

His father had been only twenty-one when he had turned over the throne to the five-year-old Sutoko. At that age, a man had his life before him and enjoys all the benefits of wealth and power without any of the chores and restrictions of actually occupying the throne.

His own fate had been a darker one. Poor, foolish Prince Masahito, a poet and a dreamer, had had a short and troubled reign. Bloodshed and rebellion had marked it. And since then, he had rarely been at peace from those near him. Sometimes he found it convenient to play the fool around Kiyomori. There was safety in foolishness. People rarely regarded you as a serious obstacle in their path to power.

No, there was little pleasure in his life. His consorts wanted his embraces only to conceive. They were brief and loveless couplings. Sometimes he doubted his children's paternity. The galleries of the palace teemed with male attendants, and even a consort's curtained dais might be invaded stealthily at night while her ladies-in-waiting slept with their robes thrown over their faces.

He had done it himself in his younger days. Perhaps, like the cuckoo, he left his sons and daughters in other men's nests. The thought cheered him a little. He hummed:

"None rests her head on my arm anymore
Where long ago my sweetheart's lay;
We two made love hungrily,
Knowing that happiness is short."

Too bad the girl did not know *imayo*. They could have spent such pleasant evenings together, he and the girl and Otomae. Under those layers of shimmering silk gauze had been a young body. Why not forget for the span of a few moments of hot lust that he was no longer Prince Masahito, no longer an Emperor, and soon perhaps a priest? Why not teach someone so young the ways of the bedchamber?

With a smile he opened a document box and took out a sheet of fine paper. Reaching for his ink stone and the water bottle carved from a piece of translucent jade, he rubbed fresh ink, dipped his brush, and wrote quickly:

My head grows white as snow,
But my heart still follows the white goose in flight,
Across the mountains to the distant sea.
Wherever it roams, wherever it nests,
In time it will return to me.

From Lady Sanjo's Pillow Book

Today the new girl arrived—a rustic from a military family. Need one say more? We worked for hours to make her presentable, and throughout the fool had not a word to say for herself. I was secretly pleased.

I suppose if His Majesty had not graciously sent a palm leaf carriage for her, she would have arrived in a sedan chair. Or worse: on a horse! Apparently provincial warriors bring up their daughters much the same as their sons. I overheard His Majesty telling the imperial adviser of the third rank - amazing how military men rise in this world - that He was charmed when He saw her ride a horse. I thought He was joking. But alas - He sent for her.

They had her togged out in silk, but the colors were all wrong and the silk so wrinkled from travel that I let one of the maids have everything she wore. There was no time to unpack her single trunk (!), but fortunately His Majesty had sent some gowns for her. I had instructions that I was to make a selection. This proves how highly He regards me, but I must confess it put me in a quandary. I meant to have her appear as uncouth as possible to open His eyes to her unsuitability. As it was, I was forced to demonstrate my good taste instead. Her youth and the season required the colors of blossoming: a three-layered dress of varying shades of plum-red beaten silk and a pale green over robe. Her costume, in any case, was charming.

As for the girl herself: a heavy application of lead-white on her face, neck, and those rough red hands—honestly, they must have had her cutting reeds—pretty well hid those dark features more commonly seen in peasant women. Her hair is thick and long enough, but crimped around her temples. We had to apply hot oil and stretch it. No doubt that hurt - a true warrior's daughter, she did not flinch once. With a great deal of effort and some discreet pinning of the more unmanageable portions, her hair looked passable.

It is very strange that His Majesty should have chosen so poorly. He is in every other way a man of such exquisite taste. One can only assume that he did not get a good look at her.

The other ladies laughed. Very improper, of course, but the young fool was too stupid to know. I held the mirror for her when we were done, but she barely looked in it.

Reminder: My own mirror must be replaced. It has warped so badly that my cheeks look sunken, which adds a very unattractive sharpness to my features. When I first noticed it, I became so concerned that I placed a pickled plum in each cheek before presenting myself before His Majesty. To my surprise this gave my speech a rather attractive, youthful lilt. He looked at me very attentively and smiled. The dear man. I am convinced he is secretly captivated and only maintains his reserve out of respect for my husband. Perhaps in time he will come to see that a woman whose husband has been stationed in distant provinces for more than a decade is free to take a lover. To paraphrase a poetic line: "Though my pain is cruel, I cannot put him from my mind."

There was that night two months ago when I thought he had decided to visit me under cover of darkness. I was lying awake, wishing for just such a thing to happen when I recognized his step approaching my door. My heart beat so I thought he must hear it through the shutters. But Lady Dainagon's miserable cat had taken to sleeping there and he must have stepped on the creature's tail. There was a great deal of noise, which woke up the other ladies and, when I opened the door to pull him inside, He had fled.

The next morning I paid one of the groundskeepers to take care of the cat, but His Majesty did not come back, though I often wonder if he is waiting somewhere in the corridor, wishing he could hold me in his arms.

Sadly I have been "waiting in vain night after night."

Lady Dainagon wailed for weeks for her lost pet, and we all went on rather amusing searches, crying,

"Here, kitty. Here, kitty," to the great entertainment of the young gentlemen, until Her Majesty forbade it.

And I, after "waiting in vain" for a whole month, went to see His Majesty. Plums in place, I presented him with a poem and whispered, "I am entirely at your Majesty's service."

He looked surprised and very moved at my fervor. I thought I saw tears of gratitude in his eyes, but matters of state interfered with our happiness once again – as in those terrible days when both Their Majesties, father and son were attacked. The sacrilege of that! I was never so frightened. Soldiers everywhere. Ladies screaming. No doubt they were being raped, though none would admit to it later. And His Majesty kidnapped from our midst, along with his son, who was only seventeen then. Of course, they did this while our protector Kiyomori was on a pilgrimage. I'll give him this: he rushed back and rescued their majesties.

And now, just when we are settling down after Her Majesty's departure, His Majesty has brought this young girl into the palace and instructed me to keep an eye on her and report to him. I must think what to do.

Tooth Blackening

Toshiko was shown a place to sleep. At home she had her own room and privacy. Here was surrounded by other women. When she returned from her interview with the emperor, they looked at her, then turned away.

Lady Sanjo, who had taken her to His Majesty, pointed vaguely toward a dark corner, and Toshiko went there. She found several neck rests, took one, and lay down as she was, placing her head on the unfamiliar support and pulling her outer gown over her for warmth. She was so tired that the humming voices of the others lulled her to sleep.

The sounds of steady, thrumming rain on the roof and the splashing on the stones outside woke her. For a moment, the darkness was puzzling, then she remembered where she was, and desolation swallowed her again. At home this would have been a delicious sort of waking, that moment of fusion of dream and reality when she hovered between both, half tempted to slip back into sleep, half curious about the new day. But now reality brought only despair. She opened her eyes to the grey obscurity of the hall and, like a frightened mouse, listened for human sounds. When she heard none, she sat up.

Here and there on the dark glossy planks lay silken figures. Their long hair writhed like black snakes across gowns whose colors looked faded in the faint light leaking through the shutters. They seemed like dead people, as if she alone had been spared by some demon who had come in the night and killed the others.

Spared for what? To be at the ogre's mercy, captive and tormented until she died?

She thought of flight, of leaving this dark world of death and returning to her home – to life, to a world of sunshine and swaying grasses, of horses and falcons, and the freedom to ride with her brothers.

But she could not leave, not ever. She, too, was dead–dead to her family, as they were dead to her.

Gradually distant sounds of palace life penetrated the thrumming of the rain: a guard's shout, quick footsteps passing on the covered veranda outside the shutters, subdued voices, a crash as something fell.

And slowly in the room, the dead women began to stir, to sit up, stretch, and talk to each other. A shutter opened and a maid looked in. Their day had begun.

Bemused, Toshiko watched from her corner as each of the ladies was greeted by her own maid who tended to her morning toilet while exchanging soft chatter. Everywhere there were elaborate preparations with much running and fetching. Someone called for more light, for food, and the shutters were raised, revealing an unrelenting gray sky and a slanting rain which made the world outside appear as if seen through silver gauze. Maids rushed about with bowls and water pitchers or small trays with the morning rice gruel. Here and there large round mirrors appeared, and candles were lit as the ladies applied cosmetics to their faces or fresh blackening to their teeth.

Lady Sanjo arrived suddenly at Toshiko's side. She cried, "Heavens, has no one seen to the new girl? She must be made presentable."

Toshiko, aware of her sleep-rumpled condition, got to her feet and looked about for her cosmetics box, her mirror, her combs.

Lady Sanjo glared at her. "You have brought no maid," she said accusingly.

Toshiko bowed her head. "No. I was told—"

"How stupid!" The other woman snapped her fingers irritably, looked around, and fixed on a young lady nearby who was almost ready. "Shojo-ben, do you mind sharing your maid until someone can be assigned?"

Lady Shojo-ben smiled and bowed, and Toshiko blushed with embarrassment and bowed back, murmuring her thanks. A rather plain woman in a dark silk gown joined them and was told to get Toshiko's boxes and hot water.

Lady Shojo-ben was small and very pretty. Her hands were like fluttering butterflies as she asked if Toshiko had slept well.

"Yes, thank you. I was tired. It was a long journey and then to be called into the August Presence . . . it was exhausting," bubbled Toshiko, grateful for the other's friendliness.

Lady Sanjo made a hissing sound. "Guard your tongue, girl," she murmured, and Lady Shojo-ben blushed and lowered her eyes.

It became very quiet in the large room. Toshiko felt confused and then realized that they must think – oh, no – they must think that she and he –. She began to tremble with shame. "It was nothing," she cried, looking around at the listening women and their maids. The room seemed to be full of ears, all avidly waiting for her next word. "He didn't . . . nothing happened." Lady Sanjo now looked as fierce as a demon and hissed again. "We only talked," Toshiko finished lamely.

Someone giggled, then immediately suppressed the sound.

Lady Sanjo gripped Toshiko's arm painfully and nearly jerked her off her feet, pulling her out of the room and onto the veranda where the rainwater rushed from the overhanging eaves and drowned out most sounds, away from the open door and the room full of ears.

Pushing Toshiko hard against the wall, she brought her face close and said through gritted teeth, "You rude, disgusting girl! You will never – do you hear me, you stupid thing? – never mention His Majesty again. You will never discuss what passes between you, or tell what was said. If you cannot do this, you will be sent home in disgrace this very day. Do you understand me?" And she gave Toshiko a shake.

Toshiko nodded. She tried not to breathe – the other woman's breath stank – and felt hot tears springing from her eyes, and then she felt the sharp pain of a slap.

"Stop that! No tears, do you hear?"

Toshiko swallowed her tears and nodded again.

"Well?"

"I shall obey, Lady Sanjo."

"Remember it. You are in my charge, and I shall have my eye on you every moment. At the least impropriety . . ."

And now Toshiko understood that this woman hated her and that she must submit to anything she demanded or dishonor her parents. She sank to her knees. "I swear," she whispered. "I'll be obedient. Please do not send me home, Lady Sanjo. Please." And that act of submission took more courage than the defiance that tore at her heart.

But the rest of the day was not altogether bad. She dressed, and Shojo-ben's maid helped her with her toilet and praised the thickness and length of her hair. Toshiko bent over her mirror in the half-light of the cloudy day, determined that Lady Sanjo should find nothing to criticize. She located her jar of tooth-blackening and applied another coat to be sure that not the least spot of white showed.

White teeth are like the uncouth fangs of wild animals.

Long ago, when she had still been alive, her mother had said this to her, explaining the need for tooth-blackening. Toshiko was thirteen then and had become a woman. "It is time to put away the wild and childish things and prepare to become a lady," her mother had said. Applying the evil-smelling paste of metal filings and soured wine to her teeth marked her new status as much as did plucking her eyebrows and her hairline. She learned to cover her face with the paste of ground rice flour and to use burned oil of sesame to paint new eyebrows high up on her forehead and to outline her eyes. She reddened her lips with safflower juice. And she learned to wear her hair loose. It was all very unpleasant. Being a lady made it nearly impossible to engage in the things she loved so much. Ladies spent their day sitting or lying down, whereas men rode horses, hunted with falcons, played football, shot arrows at targets, and practiced sword-fighting.

She had complained, but her mother had been firm. "You are a woman," she had said. "It is your karma." And then she had begun to comb her daughter's long hair.

That was the only pleasant part of the daily toilet. Both her mother and sister had combed her long thick hair and rubbed almond oil into it to make it glossy and smooth, and she had done the same for them. To have her hair handled produced an inordinately lovely sensation. It made her whole body feel warm and languid, and delightful little shivers of intense pleasure ran through her. She grew proud of her hair and begged to have it combed.

But she had still found moments to slip away to the stable to saddle her horse and ride with the wind. That, too, was a deeply physical pleasure, though of a different, more intensely alive kind. She had felt in control then, filled with power. When her hair was being combed, she seemed to turn to liquid.

Lady Shojo-ben's maid combed her hair now, but Toshiko could not enjoy it because some of the others came to speak to her. They were curious. They asked about her family and about her skills, but their eyes remained cold and when she had answered they turned away, as if she were of little interest.

Only Lady Shojo-ben was truly kind. She showed her around her new home. Their quarters were in the Hojuji palace, which was very large, to judge from the building they were in, and from the many roofs and galleries Toshiko could see through the open doors. These were the women's quarters, but His Majesty's official wives were elsewhere at the moment, in their own palaces in the city or in nunneries. The retired Emperor had seven sons by several wives, and the succession was assured. The high-born mothers of these sons no longer felt it a duty to be on call, but because the reigning sovereign was a mere infant, some of the other ladies still hoped that His eye would fall on one of them, that they would bear Him another prince, and that this would raise them and their families in the world. That was why Toshiko was here and why the others were wary of her.

When they reached the long gallery that led to the imperial apartments, Toshiko stopped. She recognized the mirror-bright flooring and the ornate double doors at the end, and shivered with sudden dread.

Lady Shojo-ben looked at her, blushed a little, then took her hand and said, "Are you afraid?"

Serving a "son of the gods" was like a religious duty, like praying to the Buddha, or copying the lotus sutra hundreds of times. But Toshiko was only fourteen and had not bargained with the gods for this. Her prayers had always been for her loved ones or for a new horse, or bow, or a sword like her younger brother's. But it had been her parents' prayers that were answered when she was called to court.

Remembering Lady Sanjo's warning, Toshiko said nothing, and after a moment Lady Shojo-ben said, "You must not worry. He is very kind. Mostly he is devout and very busy with matters of state. And when he does not work or pray, he makes a collection of the songs called *imayo*."

Toshiko's eyes widened. "*Imayo* songs?" She recalled his question and felt ashamed and a little frightened. Had she already ruined her parents' hopes by that small, well-intended fib?

"Yes. Sometimes he sings them for us. They are quite pretty. Only, you know, *imayo* is usually performed by certain . . . women. They are called *shirabyoshi*." Lady Shojo-ben paused, then leaned closer and whispered, "They say some of these women have visited His Majesty to perform for him."

"Really? Here?" Toshiko brightened. She knew all about *shirabyoshi*. Two of these magical creatures had come to her home. But since Shojo-ben seemed to find them somehow shocking, she did not want to say so.

In the country, there was little entertainment, and the Obe family was close-knit. When the two female entertainers had stopped on their travels to offer their services, Toshiko's father had let the whole family as well as the servants watch their performance. It was a holiday for all of them. To Toshiko, the two women had been enchanting. They had worn vaguely masculine outfits in pure white with red sashes and red trousers and had sung and danced like celestial beings. Later, Toshiko had borrowed her younger brother's riding costume and secretly practiced their songs and dance steps. Her father had caught her at this, been amused, and had one of the performers teach her some of the movements and songs. Many of the songs were folksongs she had already known.

On the night of the performance, the women of the household had withdrawn early, but the men had stayed. Toshiko found out the next morning that everyone had composed love poems. In fact, the younger *shirabyoshi* had exchanged more than poetry with Toshiko's handsome older brother. He had gone about in a dreamlike state for days and had followed them when they departed. Toshiko's father had brought him back several days later. As a country girl, Toshiko had a fair notion what passed between men and women, but she had been shocked to hear that her own brother had done such things.

All of that now seemed ages ago and made her sad again. She was here, far from home, and His Majesty had asked if she could sing *imayo.* Surely, if he invited *shirabyoshi* to perform for Him, He would find her untrained voice and pitiful dance steps ridiculous. She was glad that she had denied any talents along that line but worried that her parents wished her to please Him.

Lady Shojo-ben talked a little about the other ladies. There were ten of them here at the moment. The number fluctuated. About forty ladies were in service at the retired Emperor's court, but his wives had taken the others with them into the city on the other side of the Kamo River. The Taira consort, the retired Emperor's most recent favorite, liked to be in the capital and closer to the palace. Since the little Emperor was still an infant, the retired Emperor and Chancellor Kiyomori ruled the nation.

The ten ladies were the remnants of the Taira Consort's court, and most were no longer in their first youth or they were married. Lady Sanjo was a principal handmaid and in charge. In the absence of the Consort, she reported to the Emperor. Ladies Chujo and Kosaisho had grown children and husbands serving at court. Lady Dainagon was a widow and Lady Saibara was so plain that she had never had a husband. Of the younger women, Lady Harima was skilled with the zither and lute, and the Ladies Ukon and Kunaikyo composed poetry. Until Toshiko's arrival, Lady Shojo-ben had been the youngest. As daughters of the first families in the nation, all of them outranked Toshiko Except for Lady Shojo-ben, they behaved with barely hidden disdain toward the newcomer.

Yet of all of them, only Toshiko had been brought here by special invitation by the Retired Emperor.

Later that day, she was given an assignment, to be in charge of fans, writing boxes, games, and musical instruments. Lady Sanjo showed her where these were kept and how they must be stored. It seemed a simple enough chore - the sort of job given to someone with no special talent or intelligence.

Lower-class serving women came to clean and serve meals. Toshiko found the food bland and of mediocre quality. She was used to the varied fare at home where the men regularly hunted and the manor was well supplied with delicious fresh fowl and fish. But she had been warned not to mention this. The taking of life, whether fowl or fish, was strictly forbidden at court. Most of the meals here seemed to consist of rice and vegetables, along with a few fruits and nuts. But Lady Shojo-ben shared some sweet cakes with her. She kept them in a small box that was regularly replenished by one of her family's servants.

In the afternoon, she and Shojo-ben played board games, while Lady Harima practiced her zither. The music and the soft sound of the rain soothed Toshiko into tranquility. But the light faded quickly on this overcast day, and as darkness fell, panic returned. Would she be called again into His presence? Should she tell Him the truth this time? What would he do, if she did? Her heart beat fast with fear and excitement, but nothing happened, and she retired to sleep peacefully.

From Lady Sanjo's Pillow Book

A dreadful day!

Lady Dainagon's cat returned today. I was on the rear veranda at the time, when the creature, looking half dead and disgustingly dirty, walked up the steps and laid a half-eaten rat at my feet. The rat was mangled, its pale intestines poking out of the slimy brown belly. The cat looked up at me with the most malevolent expression.

I screamed.

That brought the others. They were as horrified as I. Lady Harima fainted and Lady Ukon was sick all over the floor. I pulled myself together and shouted for servants when the new girl pushed past me, picked up the rat by its long tail and flung it over the balustrade into the shrubbery. The cat bounded after it, found it, and proceeded to devour its prey—head, tail, and pink feet—before our horrified eyes. With more shrieks, we rushed back inside. Only the new girl, uncouth creature that she is, remained on the veranda, leaning on the balustrade and watching the cat.

After we had calmed down a little, Lady Dainagon thought she had recognized the cat.

"Was it my darling Mikan?" she asked. She had named the kitten that because its color used to resemble that of an orange. I had a sneaking suspicion that it might indeed be the nasty creature - come back to haunt me. Of course, in its present condition it looked more like a dirty rag.

I said firmly, "It is not. There is no resemblance whatsoever. This is a very ugly wild cat with an ear missing. No doubt it is diseased. I had better send for servants and have it destroy—, er, taken out of the palace." I almost made the mistake of shocking Lady Dainagon into another fit of tears but caught myself in time.

"Oh," said Lady Dainagon sadly. "It would have been such a lovely miracle if it had found its way back to me. Imagine, a poor lost kitten, roaming all over the land, facing untold dangers, nearly starving, but persisting until it is reunited with its mistress. Animals are capable of amazing loyalty."

Really, the woman is demented when it comes to cats. I pointed out, "This creature came to me, not to you."

Lady Dainagon sighed and said, "I am sure you are right, Lady Sanjo. I was only dreaming a little."

Just then the new girl came back inside, carrying the nasty animal in her arm. "Poor kitty," she said to no one in particular. "Just look at it. It has had a rough time lately. It's covered with wounds and pitifully thin."

"Out!" I cried, rising and pointing to the door. "That filthy thing is repulsive."

The stubborn girl did not obey me. She looked at the others and pleaded for the cat. "We could clean it up. Once it was a very handsome kitty. It only needs a home and regular meals."

"No," I cried, but in vain. Lady Dainagon got up and ran over.

"Oh," she quavered. Then she extended a hand and touched the nasty fur. "Mikan?" she asked with a little sob, and the miserable cat started to purr.

"Why, it knows you." The new girl laughed with delight and passed the cat to Lady Dainagon. "How wonderful! Is it yours?"

Lady Dainagon held the cat and wept with joy and grief over its condition. "Oh, what happened to you, my little love?" she crooned. "Please, someone, fetch a physician."

A physician! The scene turned my stomach. The disgusting thing still slavered bloody bits of rat from its mouth, and its orange fur was matted with dirt and dried blood. One eye was closed completely under a crust of yellow pus, but Lady Dainagon and the new girl made it a nest from a pair of silk *hakama* and called for water to wash its wounds.

All morning, they kept the servants running back and forth. They consulted a physician about its condition, and a soothsayer cast the miserable animal's future. There was so much commotion that the story came to His Majesty's ears and he arrived Himself, unannounced, in our midst to ask what had happened.

Ah, what were my feelings to see Him, who had "grown distant as a cloud in the sky." I was all aflutter, having had no time to arrange my costume or comb my hair or put the plums in my cheeks. No doubt He was shocked at my appearance. Of course, I went immediately to kneel and explain the incident, but He hardly glanced at me and brushed past as if I were no more than a servant. Instead He went to where Lady Dainagon and the new girl were still fussing with the miserable cat.

"And is this the faithful cat who returned after amazing adventures?" He asked with a smile.

Lady Dainagon quite properly bowed to the floor, but the new girl picked up the horrible creature and held it out to His Majesty as if He were just anybody. Showing Him the cat's wounds, she said quite brazenly, "Indeed, sire. Just see how many battles he must have fought. A most heroic cat."

"He?" He asked, smiling more broadly at the silly girl.

To my horror, the girl raised the cat's hind leg and said without a blush, "Oh, yes. As you can see: A veritable tiger of a he-cat."

I could tell His Majesty was shocked by such country manners, because He turned to Lady Dainagon to ask, "And is he truly your lost cat?"

Lady Dainagon said softly, "Yes, sire."

The new girl, not about to be prevented from making a complete fool of herself, said, "He purred as loud as thunder when Lady Dainagon came up to him. But before that happened, when he first arrived, he approached Lady Sanjo and presented her with a gift."

I gasped. His Majesty turned to look at me. Surely she would not go on.

She did.

"He brought Lady Sanjo the largest rat you may imagine, sire, no doubt to buy himself back into her good graces," she announced in ringing tones, finishing up with an unmannerly peal of laughter.

For a moment we all held our breaths in horror. Then His Majesty, always kind and gracious, deigned to join in the laughter. He said to me, "Why, Lady Sanjo, what have you done to the poor cat to make him pay such a heavy fee to be readmitted to your presence?"

I did not know what to say. His question came so unpleasantly close to the truth that I thought the groundskeeper must have talked and His Majesty had somehow found out that I had paid the man to drown the cat.

His Majesty left after saying a few pleasant words to the other ladies, and I slipped into my corner to calm my beating heart. Oh, "to find shelter in some mountain village where I can sink from sight," I thought.

The girl must go! She is a demon, sent to torment me, yet I cannot get rid of her as long as His Majesty approves of her. I must think what to do. It will take time. Patience, patience!

I spent the rest of the night "wringing my tear-drenched sleeves." I stared into the darkness, thinking of ways by which I might make His Majesty feel such disgust toward her that he would send her away. Considering her crudeness of speaking openly about her visit to His Majesty's apartment with the other ladies, she could be made to overstep the boundaries of decency quite easily and irretrievably. But He has made me responsible for her. If she offends, I too will be punished.

Oh, I must be cursed.

The Physician

Yamada Sadahira was raised in the South, the only son of a provincial lord who owed allegiance to the Taira clan. During the Hogen rebellion, he became an unlikely hero at fifteen and broke with his family.

The abdicated Emperor Sutoku had taken up arms against the new emperor, and young Sadahira answered Taira Kiyomori's call to arms because his father was too ill to come.

The war tragically pitted brother against brother and father against son, as the four most powerful families in the nation, the imperial family, the Fujiwara court nobles, and the Taira and Minamoto warrior clans chose sides.

At fifteen, Sadahira thought of battle as an adventure. He donned his armor and rode off to the capital at the head of a contingent of Yamada soldiers.

Filled with a wild joy at the idea of winning fame, his excitement was fed by much older and more experienced warriors who treated him with respect because he commanded a hundred mounted fighters and another hundred foot soldiers. Never mind that he was a mere boy who had never fought, never killed a man, never handled a sword with any kind of expertise. It did not matter. He was a Yamada and represented his house.

Sadahira's moment of glory came unexpectedly and with unexpected results.

The abdicated emperor and his supporters were holed up in the Shirakawa palace across the Kamo River from the imperial palace. During a night of frantic meetings, the reigning emperor and his Taira and Minamoto generals decided that they must attack quickly and force a decision. In the pre-dawn hours, Sadahira set out with the rest of their army. He wore his father's fine armor, carried his best bow (he was quite a good archer), and rode his father's big black stallion.

When they were within shouting distance of the west gate of the Shirakawa Palace, they delivered a series of challenges to the enemy. Each of the commanders rode up, stopped a small distance from the gate, and called out his offer to fight any man who thought himself good enough. For a while these challenges went unanswered. The enemy refused to engage. Eventually, Sadahira took his turn. He spurred the great black horse and charged toward the gate. Reining in in a cloud of dust, his heart pounding with pride, he announced his name and descent and delivered his challenge.

At fifteen, Sadahira's voice had not quite changed, and when he demanded that one of rebel warriors meet him in single combat, the answer from within the walls was a burst of laughter. Shaking with humiliation at this insult, Sadahira galloped closer and called out his challenge again. This brought more laughter, as well as shouts that Lord Kiyomori must be a coward if he sent babies to fight his battle.

Sadahira wept with fury and shame as he turned his horse to ride back.

But behind him the laughter stopped and the gates creaked open. Through the gate rode a single warrior. He wore armor braided with grass green silk over a blue-patterned robe and gripped a black-lacquered bow. Walking his bay horse forward, he watched the boy through the slits in his helmet. Then he stopped.

Half-blinded by tears, Sadahira turned back and placed an arrow into the groove of his bow. "Please, Lord Hachiman," he prayed. "Please let me be steady, so I can show them. Please make my horse hold still and make my arrow find its target."

The distance between them was not great.

Looking past Sadahira at the gathered troops, the warrior demanded in a deep voice, "What sort of men would send a child to do a man's work?" Then he told the boy, "Go home, Sadahira. This is no place for you."

Sadahira saw red. He raised his bow, strained hard to pull it, and released the arrow. It whirred away.

At the last moment, the warrior raised his bow and tried to take evasive action, but he was too late. Sadahira's arrow struck the front pommel of his saddle, passed through it and then through his belly and into the back of the saddle. The horse capered as its rider slumped over with a cry, his nerveless hand dropping the bow. Behind him, foot soldiers rushed through the gate, followed by shouting horsemen. The wounded warrior on his horse galloped away. He died pinned to his saddle. His corpse was still sagging sideways on the running horse when battle was joined. The Hogen rebellion was over.

And Sadahira was a hero.

But the man who had died that agonizing first death was Toshima no Jiro, a close family friend who had once saved Sadahira's life. His second effort to save Sadahira cost him his own life.

When Sadahira realized whom he had killed, he returned home and told his father that he would never fight again. He would become a monk.

Because he was the only son in a military family, his father stormed, argued, begged, and finally compromised. Sadahira would enter the university and become an official. His reasonable hope was that in time his son would change his mind or that another war would break out and he would be forced to take up arms.

And so Sadahira had attended the university and studied medicine.

Now, ten years later, he was a junior doctor of medicine. He was highly trained and eager but sadly lacking in paying patients when a call summoned him to the sickbed of the Retired Emperor's favorite cook and gave him hope that this would soon change.

Being unfamiliar with the palace layout, he took a wrong turn among the warren of buildings, courtyards, and galleries. He opened a small door in one of the walls, expecting a shortcut to the next courtyard. Instead, he stepped into an enclosed garden adjoining the wing of a larger building.

It was only a small area, nicely planted with a stand of golden bamboo, a few clipped shrubs, and some ferns. The plants clustered around three large rocks surrounded by patches of moss and large round pebbles. The rest of the ground was covered with the same fine pale gravel that formed the surface of the palace courtyards. It looked like a very private, almost forgotten, corner of the palace, enclosed by high walls on three sides and the veranda of the building on the fourth.

On this veranda knelt a young girl, singing softly as she bent over some furry creature. She made a charming picture.

But the animal suddenly gave a loud yowl, leaped from the girl's hands, and flew off the veranda and into the garden.

"Oh, you bad cat," cried the girl, putting a bloody hand to her mouth. "Come back here, stupid. I'm just trying to help." She got up to look for the cat and caught sight of Sadahira. "Oh."

Sadahira wanted to withdraw quickly, afraid that he had intruded into a restricted area, but she was very young and she smiled at him. That smile twisted his heart. Just so his little sister used to smile at him, long ago when he still lived at home.

"Forgive me," he said with a bow – she wore rather rich robes for a mere child – "I'm afraid I am lost."

She laughed. Her laughter sounded like bells to Sadahira. "I'm Toshiko," she said, "and being a stranger here myself, I cannot direct you. Since you are here, could you help me catch a cat? He has a very bad ear and refuses treatment."

"Really?" Enchanted, he walked to the veranda and looked up at her. "It so happens I'm a physician."

She clapped her hands. "Wonderful." And without further ado, she jumped off the veranda in her billowing gowns and full trousers and pounced on a shrub. "Quick," she cried, "I have him, but he's strong."

Sadahira set down his bamboo case and went to her aid. Together they pulled the fighting, hissing, scratching animal forth. He carried it back to the veranda. "Heavens," he said, looking at the cat more closely, "he's not very attractive, is he?"

"Shh. He's a very vain cat. I tell him that he looks heroic with all those scars from his battles."

They smiled at each other.

"It's his right ear," she said helpfully after a moment, and he took his eyes from her face—a very pretty face—and examined the cat.

"I see what you mean. Will you hold him for a moment while I get my case?"

When he returned, she had the cat in her lap and was stroking him until he purred and closed his eyes. "He belongs to Lady Dainagon," she confided as he rummaged in his case, looking for a salve. "He ran away and when he came back he was like this. Only the ear got worse."

Lady Dainagon? Perhaps she was a young relative or companion of one of the Emperor's women. He cast an anxious glance around. They were alone, and the shades of the room beyond were down. He hoped no one was inside.

"The cut is inflamed and festers," he said, "I am going to apply a soothing salve made of ground sesame seeds, but it should be cleansed frequently with vinegar or some wine in which ginger root has been boiled. I don't have any with me. Perhaps you can do this yourself?"

She nodded. "Easily. I have treated animals at home."

"Good. In that case, a tea made from figwort and cloves and allowed to cool will also clean his eyes nicely. Wash them and the ear once a day. I shall leave the salve for you. If you apply it to the ear, it will heal quickly. " He found the little jar of salve and showed her what to do. The animal twitched once or twice but then settled down to let him check the other wounds.

"You have gentle hands," she said approvingly.

"Thank you." He was done but saw the oozing scratch on her hand. "In that case," he said lightly, "please let me treat the scratch while I'm here."

"Oh, it's nothing." She blushed and hid the hand in her skirt.

"The cat has dirty claws. Why not let me at least have a look at it?"

She brought forth her hand as if she were ashamed of it – a small hand, still childishly soft but capable and strong, he thought, with tapering fingers and lovely nails. He held it reverently. The scratch had bled but did not look deep. He took a soft paper tissue from his case and another jar of ointment and carefully and gently cleansed the wound. Her hand was warm and trembled a little in his. It feels, he thought, like holding a small, trusting animal. When he was finished, they looked at each other. He felt warm and quickly laid her hand in her lap.

"Thank you." She pulled the purring cat a little closer as he repacked his case.

"It was my pleasure." He stood to make her a bow. "My name is Yamada Sadahira. My family is from Kii province. I am delighted to have met you . . . and Lady Dainagon's cat."

Her eyes widened. "Kii Province?" she cried. "My mother is from there. My father is Oba no Hiramoto. We live in Iga Province."

He bowed again. "You are far from home, Lady Toshiko."

To his dismay, her tears spilled over. She put the cat aside and got to her feet. As they stood side by side, he realized that she was quite tall. She smiled a little, brushing her tears away with both hands like a child.

"Yes," she said. "But it cannot be helped. Only I have not heard from home in such a long time and I'm worried about my mother." She paused and then confided in a rush, "I had a dream, you see. A dreadful dream. I'm afraid that she is dying."

He saw the panic in her eyes and his heart melted. "If you like, I could take a letter to her and report back to you."

Her face lit up. "Oh, how kind you are! But it is too much trouble."

"No trouble at all. I'm going home shortly anyway. It will be on my way," he lied.

"Oh . . . in that case . . ."

"Shall I return tomorrow for your letter?"

"Yes. If you are sure. Nobody comes here as a rule. The first half of the hour of the hare? It's the time of the morning rice, and I can slip away then."

He bowed again and left.

Later in the day, he asked someone about the Oba family and was told that Oba's daughter was the Retired Emperor's newest acquisition. Shock and pain struck with equal fierceness: shock that he had mistaken one of the imperial women for a mere child and conversed freely with her, even touched her – and pain that she was not for him. She was fourteen, it appeared, old enough to be bedded and bear an imperial heir. The thought sickened him, and he wished they had not met.

But he had given his word, and the next day, dressed in his best silk robe and court hat, he returned. The courtyard was empty. He waited a little, nervous about being seen, and was just turning to leave, when the green shade moved a little and a small hand gestured. Climbing quickly to the veranda, he asked softly, "Lady Toshiko?"

"Yes," she whispered. "I don't have much time. You are so kind to do this. I have thought about it all night." The hand reappeared and pushed a pale blue folded letter his way. Then, before he could respond, she gave a little gasp and whispered, "I must go. Thank you."

He took the letter and left quickly.

Lady Oba

Toshiko's mother was startled when the visitor was announced. With her husband and oldest son away, she had expected a quiet day.

The visitor's name was Yamada. She once knew someone by that name, but this visitor had come from the capital. Perhaps, she thought hopefully, he was bringing good news about Toshiko.

Her husband was getting impatient and angry because no invitations had come from His Majesty. Their oldest son, Takehira, was looking sullen. He had expected to join the imperial guard long before now. When his younger brother, Yasuhira, brushed off Takehira's complaints with the comment that only a fool would want to live in the capital among the perfumed dandies, Takehira had punched his face.

But Lady Oba worried mostly about Toshiko. Her daughter was alone at court, without her family's support or even her own maid, and Toshiko's father refused to allow her a visit home or her mother to go to her. Only this morning, he had made his feelings clear to his wife. He wished no contact with Toshiko until she achieved success. Lady Oba had tried to argue but that only made matters worse. He and Takehira had stormed off to drown their frustration in pleasure.

She knew where they went because this was not the first time. They were with women in the nearby town, and she was glad to have them gone.

But now this Yamada had come, and she felt hopeful. She put on a gown of crimson brocade over pale violet silk and prepared to receive him. The formal reception hall was an old, dark room. Its heavy timbers rose from black, polished floors and thick shutters protected it from winter storms and the rain torrents of summer. It was rough and plain — like the men of the Oba family — but it was the most formal room they had, and she did her best to give it a touch of elegance.

The southern sets of shutters stood open to the veranda, where her husband had entertained the Emperor and his nobles. The view from there was famous, because the Oba manor overlooked a wide valley of moving grasses, a winding river, and blue hills beyond. The sun was bright, and the greens and blues outside were as intense as the colors on the painted screen she had her maid place behind her.

She was seated on a thick grass mat bound in black and white brocade, and the layers of her many gowns spread handsomely around her.

When the tall young man came in, her first reaction was disappointment. He was too soberly dressed —

in dark grey silk brocade with a small white pattern – and he wore an ordinary cap. Surely, she thought, a message from the Emperor would be brought by an official in court costume or a senior officer of the guard.

The young man approached, bowed, then seated himself on the cushion she gestured to. She guessed his age to be about twenty-five. He had a nice face, clean-shaven and a little too long and thin, but his eyes were large and gentle, and stirred a memory. She was still searching his features, when he addressed her.

"My name is Yamada Sadahira, Lady Oba," he said. "My people are by way of being former neighbors of yours. And since I planned to pay them a visit, the Lady Toshiko asked me to stop here on my way to make sure that you are well. She has suffered from bad dreams and was worried about your health."

Lady Oba's heart began to beat so she barely heard the end of his speech. Of course. This must be <u>his</u> son. Her eyes searched the young face again and found there, after so many years, the faint image of the man who had courted her, who had sought in vain to marry her – and she tasted again the bitter despair of her youth.

There were differences, of course. Sadamori had looked fiercer than his son. When she had been scarcely older than Toshiko, she had loved this fierceness and his protectiveness of her. But her family had promised her to Oba Hiramoto. A woman's duty is obedience, and she had obeyed and become an obedient wife to a man she cared little about.

Her visitor was puzzled by her silence. He repeated, "I bring a letter from your daughter, Lady Oba."

She took a quick breath and said, "Yes. Thank you. How kind of you. You must forgive my rude staring. You are a great deal like your father, you know."

He looked astonished and then smiled very sweetly, and her heart nearly burst. Just so had his father smiled at her and made her knees turn to water.

"Ah," he said. "You knew my father. That is good. I could not be sure you would remember."

That brought color to her face. She changed the subject. "Toshiko should not have worried. I am quite well, as you can see. I think of her often." She wanted to ask about his father, if he still thought of her, but that would be improper. So she waited.

He nodded, still smiling. "When I met your daughter, she was tending to an injured kitten."

"You saw Toshiko?" She could not keep the astonishment out of her voice. Customs were more casual in the country, but Lady Oba knew that at court a young woman must not be seen by men who are not close blood relations.

Or lovers.

Fear seized her, and she looked at him with new eyes. Had her daughter's heart been touched by him – as her own so many years ago by his father – and had this young man, who might have been her son, already seduced Toshiko?

"I am a physician, Lady Oba," he said, meeting her eyes earnestly, "and was called upon to treat the kitten."

"Oh, I see." The relief felt like a cooling breeze on her hot face. Perhaps he thought Toshiko a mere child - no wonder when he must be nearly twice her age. Tending to a kitten! Toshiko's playful manner evidently had not yet left her. She hoped there was no trouble over the kitten incident.

But this particular young man was much too personable to have ready access to her daughter. Lady Oba decided to speak bluntly. "It was very kind of you to offer your assistance and to come and bring me news of her. As her mother, I am worried. Toshiko is only fourteen and has spent all her life at home. She must find it very difficult to adjust to her new duties and to behave with circumspection. I am sure you are aware she serves in His Majesty's household?"

Young Yamada's smile faded abruptly. He straightened his back and bowed. "Yes, of course. To be sure, I was not aware of it when I treated her cat, but I have since been informed of the great honor His Majesty has done your family. My felicitations."

He did not look at all as if he thought it a fortunate thing. Lady Oba inclined her head. "Thank you. I fear that my daughter may suffer criticism if it should become known that . . . she has received your visits."

He flushed to the roots of his hair. Perhaps it was only his pride she had hurt but with two young sons she had a sharp eye for the signs of infatuation. He reached into his robe and brought out a folded letter. This, too, Lady Oba thought ominous. Why not carry the letter in his sash or sleeve? Why so close to his body? Extending it to her with both hands, he said very stiffly, "Your daughter sent this. I was going to offer to take your reply, but perhaps you will wish to employ another messenger."

Ah, so he had taken offense. She should have been more circumspect in her reproof. Regretting her bluntness, she turned the letter over in her hands and sighed. "That was ungrateful of me. Please forgive my poor manners. I am terribly worried about her because she has neither friends nor family to protect her."

He opened his mouth, closed it again, then said merely, "I understand, Lady Oba," and prepared to rise.

"No, wait," she cried. "I am sure you will honor a mother's concern for her child's future. If you will accept our hospitality, I would be grateful if you would carry my answer back to her." She bit her lip. Her husband would be in another fury if he found out about this. "It will be best if we don't mention the matter to anyone else," she added, blushing with embarrassment.

If he was surprised, he did not show it. He said, "Thank you, Lady Oba. I am completely at your service."

It was a vague reply, but she did not have the heart to press him further. "My husband is absent, but my son Yasuhira will see to your comfort. And my letter will be ready before you take your leave in the morning."

As he left, she looked after him, thinking how much she would have liked him if things had been different. If he had been her son, hers and Sadamori's.

Then she unfolded Toshiko's letter and read. It was a loving and dutiful letter but one that left too many things unsaid. Her daughter did not mention His Majesty. Did that mean that he had taken no interest in her, or that he had and she was too ashamed to mention their intimacy? Instead, she wrote of insignificant events: the cat, her assignments, the oil they used on their hair, her lovely new clothes, and her friend, Lady Shojo-ben. Not a word either about Doctor Yamada. Lady Oba put the letter in her sash and frowned.

Young Yamada's manners were good, as were his clothes. He was of good birth, yet only a physician. Like the Obas, the Yamadas were military men and held provincial offices. Why was such a very strong and healthy male a mere doctor, a profession not much better than that of a pharmacist or soothsayer? How could Sadamori have allowed it?

She knew her own sons and their ambitions and felt a small pang of envy. Warriors often died young and violently – unlike courtiers, bureaucrats, or doctors – but neither Takehira nor Yasuhira were studious types. Their lives were predetermined: They learned how to fight and how to die.

Women learned how to obey. Her daughters were raised to serve men who could advance Oba family interests.

Lady Oba knew that her husband had other women, but she was fortunate. She was the only official wife. He bedded his other women elsewhere. In the early years of their marriage he used to come to her bed regularly because he wanted heirs. She miscarried five times before giving him four healthy children. And then she bore a son so sickly and malformed that he died a day after the long and painful birth. Her husband stopped coming to her after that, and she was grateful, as she was grateful for the consideration he showed her by keeping his women in distant towns and villages.

She looked out over the sea of swaying grasses, the silver band of river, the blue hills, toward the south where she had grown up. The distance of time and space had turned the memories of her childhood home into a land of lost happiness, a place not to be regained until after death.

The priests taught that women could not attain paradise, but she preferred to believe them wrong.

The door slid open, and her youngest daughter slipped in. Nariko was, like her name, a gentle, agreeable child. Two years younger than Toshiko, she had none of her sister's obstinacy. Her eyes were wide with curiosity as knelt beside her mother.

"Yasuhiro is taking a guest around," she announced. "Who is he, Mother? He is very handsome.

Is he a teacher? Yasuhira says he came from the capital. Does he know Toshiko?"

Lady Oba suppressed a smile. "Nariko," she said, "calm yourself. You must learn restraint. Young women need to control their emotions. Men dislike them."

Nariko instantly folded her hands in her lap and bowed. "Yes, Mother."

"The visitor is a doctor . . ."

Nariko's eyes flew to her face. "Is someone ill?"

"You see how much you need to practice self-control? I was about to explain that he is on his way to his own family and stopped to bring greetings from your sister."

Nariko's face fell. "Oh, is that all? Just greetings? No news?"

"No news." Lady Oba had decided that there must be no mention of Toshiko's letter, nor of the one she would write to her daughter later that night.

"Then may I go with Yasuhira? I'm sure Doctor Yamada has stories to tell about the capital."

Lady Oba shook her head. "Remember your age. You have put on your train this year. It is no longer suitable that you run after your brothers and male guests."

Nariko looked astonished. "Why not? Toshiko was allowed to."

Lady Oba compressed her lips. Yes, she thought, and see where it got us. "Enough," she said. "Go practice your zither."

Grass Shades

Grass shades hang in doorways and hide the person inside while allowing her to look out. It is always the women who are inside, hidden from sight. Men remain outside, on the veranda. Inside lives and outside lives have little in common.

A woman may welcome the visit and converse, or she may hide herself away in the darkness. There are no other choices for her. The pair may exchange poems by pushing them under the shade. If so, the gentleman, if he feels inclined and his imagination has painted a seductive image of the hidden lady, may return at night to breach the thin barrier between them. But that is always his choice, not hers.

The day Sadahira returned to the hidden garden, Toshiko felt shy and stayed behind the grass shades.

She was shy because she had spent the intervening days and nights thinking of him and hoping fervently that he would come again. She reminded herself repeatedly that he would not trouble and that it was even unlikely that he would deliver her letter. A busy young gentleman did not waste his time on a mere country girl. Yet he had such a very kind face, and he had been so gentle with the cat. That surely meant that he was a good and kind man. But still, a handsome man like that no doubt already had a wife and children to occupy his leisure. Several wives even, for someone so very handsome.

Thinking so much about him during the day caused her to dream at night, and she would wake up hot with shame and half-understood desire. But sometimes dreams did come true, and in the privacy of the darkness around her, she put her lips to the small scar on her hand where he had touched her.

Every morning and every night, she returned to that small eave chamber and peered through the grass shades at the empty veranda and garden beyond. After a while, when it seemed reasonable to think that he might have completed his journey, she carried her sewing or a romance novel with her and spent the time dreaming of impossible things.

Toshiko knew all about flirtations through grass shades and about secret visits by lovers in the dark. The breaching of the grass-shade barrier signified their union. She knew these things from reading courtly tales, and she wished more than anything in the world that it would happen to her. But it could not be. It must not be – even if he thought of it, as he would not, for why should he? He was simply a kind man who had taken pity on her loneliness in the same way he had pitied the cat.

And so it was that she was shy and a little dizzy with emotion when she found him seated on the veranda outside the grass shades.

Ah, she thought, he was keeping his promise by delivering a message from home. And afterward he would leave, and she would never see him again. This filled her with such grief that, when she spoke to him, her voice brimmed with unshed tears, even though she only said, "Good morning, Doctor Yamada."

He bowed from the waist, and she wished the shade gone so she could see him better because already her memory of his features was vague. She wondered if his eyes were smiling at her as they had before. Eyes, she thought, could caress as well as hands.

Should she dare to raise the shade? Or step outside? No. Lady Sanjo was always watching—watching and waiting.

In his warm voice he said, "I hope I find you well, Lady Toshiko."

She murmured, "Yes, thank you. And you? Are you well?"

"Quite well. And your cat? How is his ear?"

"Almost well. Thank you."

It was a clumsy exchange, but she could not find the right words. She had no talent for sparkling repartee or even cheerful chatter—especially not with him. The emotion of the moment made her eyes brim again, and she was grateful for the shade between them.

"I delivered your letter," he said. She could hear his smile in his words. "Your lady mother is well and has sent an answer."

Oh, dear, she had forgotten her mother. Guilt made her voice a little stronger. "How very kind of you," she said. "I regret that I have given you so much trouble, but your news brings great joy." She stopped. It was too stiff and cold when she wanted him to know how very much his kindness meant to her.

He said nothing but seemed to look very searchingly at the grass shade between them. Then, reaching into his sash, he took out a letter and pushed it under the shade. She took it, felt the warmth of his body on it and pressed it to her cheek before slipping it inside her gown between her breasts.

And now, she thought, he will make his good-byes and walk away forever. She braced herself, considered lifting the shade a little when his back was turned so she could see him clearly one more time, to hold his image in her heart.

But he said instead, "The countryside near your home is very lovely. Your younger brother showed me around. I saw the places where you used to walk and ride your horse."

The thought of what Yasuhira might have said caused her to gasp audibly. She put her hand over her mouth.

He misunderstood. "I have distressed you," he said quickly. "Forgive me. I thought perhaps you would like to talk about your home."

She lowered her hand. "Oh, yes," she begged. "Please tell me."

"Well, then, I did not speak to your father. He was away with your brother Takehira. But your mother was very kind and saw to it that I was given lodging and a fine meal. There was fresh fish and even some wild duck. I haven't tasted food like that since I left home."

"My family still keeps to the old ways of hunting," she said apologetically, remembering the rich taste of roasted pheasant and dove, and of rabbit stew.

"Your younger brother, I think, shot the duck. He showed me the horses. They were very fine."

She wanted to ask about her own mare, Fierce Storm, but was afraid to. They had probably sold her by now. Grief overwhelmed her again. "I cannot go home," she said in a forlorn voice. "I can never return home again."

He was silent for a moment, then said, "Surely you may visit your parents sometimes?"

"I don't think so."

He moved a little closer. "It pains me that you are so unhappy."

She said nothing because speaking her true feelings would be disloyal to her family.

"Perhaps you will make friends here," he offered.

"Yes," she said sadly, and both were silent. She thought of Lady Shojo-ben and knew that even the kindest friend would not take the place of what she had lost.

Through the grass shade she looked at his wide shoulders and his shapely head. His hands rested on his knees, and he inclined his face a little toward her. She inhaled deeply to breathe in his scent and nearly swooned. Perhaps, she thought, what I am about to lose is much worse, for there is no hope for us.

He sighed as if he agreed. "I should not be here," he said, "but I'll return if you would like me to." He paused, then added, "As a friend."

"Oh, yes," she said quickly. "Please. But . . . I'm not sure . . . it is not permitted, I think."

"I see. Not here, at any rate. And not like this." He stood, then said quite fervently, "I am your friend, Lady Toshiko. Call on me whenever you need me and I shall come wherever you direct me."

Visitors

Toshiko had been lost in the perfumed darkness for four months when her father and brother arrived in the capital. It was nearly autumn by now, and the roads were dusty and crowded with soldiers and pilgrims.

Oba no Hiramoto and his nineteen-year-old son, Takehira, belonged to the warrior class, masters in their own domains but despised by the court nobility. On the highway, they met with respect, even fear. Foot travelers stepped politely out of their way and bowed. Peasants knelt. But when they reached the capital, they encountered the court nobility who showed their disdain by raising their chins and staring right through them. The Obas responded to this by making gross jokes about perfumed fops in their carriages.

The provincial warriors were fiercely proud of their lands and loyalties but had not been welcome at court until recently when the fops had come to realize that they needed the warriors to protect their ancient wealth and power.

Father and son wore full armor and were attended by ten armed foot soldiers. Hiramoto was tall and broad-shouldered but had a pock-marked face and grizzled beard. His son drew the eyes of young women because he was handsome and had a dashing narrow mustache.

The Obas were not wealthy but proud. At the moment, they were dusty, hot, and tired. City life was strange to them and that, along with what lay ahead, made them tense. The father worried about the outcome of his journey, and Takehira was filled with nervous energy. His eyes went everywhere, taking in the teeming humanity all around him, gazing at willows and canals, squinting toward the distant imperial palace and the green foothills beyond. He noted that earthen walls enclosed whole city quarters of tenements and houses, each like a village in the larger city, each, no doubt, filled with shops and amusements for his delight as a member of the imperial guard.

"Too many beggars," his father complained, and Takehira tore his eyes away from his golden hopes and looked at the people around him.

They made little headway. Large carriages drawn by slow oxen impeded them. Servants on their master's errands ducked in and out of the throng. Half naked porters bore their goods in enormous baskets on their backs. Traveling monks strode along as if they owned the street, the small rings on their staffs jingling at every step. And everybody was shouting. The ragged children with limbs like sticks and distended bellies were everywhere, crying for coppers with their shrill voices. They dashed into the street to reach for their bridles, touched their stirrups, hung onto their saddle blankets, pleaded with sunken eyes and hungry mouths. And yet the smell of cooking foods was all around them.

Takehira tossed the children some coins, and a fight broke out between the hooves of their shying and rearing horses.

"Stop that," snapped his father.

They caught up with a fine ox-drawn carriage. Its driver and runner used their whips on the crowd and cursed at people. Now and then, the reed curtain in the back twitched, revealing glimpses of colored silks inside.

Takehira stared. "Who do you think she is?" he asked his father. "A princess? Maybe it's Toshiko? What if it's Toshiko, and here we are, right behind her?"

"Nonsense," grunted his father.

Takehira dismissed the thought of shouting a greeting at the lady, and looked instead at some palace guards riding the other way with their bows and quivers of arrows slung over their shoulders. "Fine horses, those," he remarked, "and look at that armor."

This time his father did not hear him, for there was too much noise, a grand cacophony of shouts, creaking wheels, hoof beats, cracking whips, barking dogs, bells, and laughter.

They took Third Avenue to the river, passing more walls and fences of every kind, tall plastered ones with massive gateways, wooden ones, modest ones of woven bamboo, and poor ones made from twigs and brushwood. Everywhere, as far as the eye could see were homes, temples, shrines, palaces, markets, and villas.

At one corner, two pretty young women in red silk skirts and colored jackets laughed and waved to them.

"Can they be shrine maidens?" Takehira asked his father. "They seem very immodest."

Hiramoto looked and gave a snort. "Whores."

Takehira grinned. "Really?" He whistled to the women as he passed.

Both immediately plunged into the street and ran alongside their horses. One put her hands familiarly on Takehira's knee. "Welcome," she cried in a high voice. "We know first-class lodgings where your lordships will be treated like princes. Please follow us."

Hiramoto reached for his sword. "Away, scum!" he roared.

The women shrieked and scattered.

Takehira looked after them regretfully. "What's your rush? We should stop and find lodging before we make our bow to His Majesty."

But his father only grunted again. A long bridge spanning the Kamo River took them out of the old city and into the green eastern hills where new temples and palaces with shining blue-tiled roofs and gilded pagodas beckoned from the trees.

They had been told that the Retired Emperor resided in His current residence until the Hojuji Palace was being built next to the temple by the same name.

Like His predecessors and any number of princes of the blood, He planned take the tonsure. That time, Oba no Hiramoto feared, was near. He had been praying that his daughter would find imperial favor before it was too late.

Takehira hoped that she had already succeeded and that fortune would fall on his family like summer rain, fortune beyond the wildest expectations of provincial gentry, fortune which would increase their power and influence in Settsu province for generations.

The perfumed fops needed the military power of the warrior families, and the warriors needed the political power that lay in the hands of emperors, ex-emperors, and chancellors of the realm.

But most specifically and immediately, Takehira expected an appointment with officer's rank in the imperial guard. That would bring with it a nice income, friends among the nobles, an endless series of entertainments, and all the women he could wish for.

At the enormous covered gate to the cloister palace, they identified themselves and their errand to guards, and passed into an equally enormous courtyard surrounded by many galleries and halls. The midday sun shining on glossy tiles, red painted columns and balustrades, and the white gravel underfoot blinded them.

"Amida!" breathed Takehira.

They reined in and blinked at the scene. Carriages, as many as thirty of them, waited along both sides of the rectangle, their oxen unharnessed and their drivers and escorts sitting cross-legged in the shade of the ornate two-wheeled vehicles. Soldiers walked about, their bows in hand, to keep an eye on things. Black-capped and silk-robed officials held up their trains as they stepped gingerly in their full trousers. Palace servants, in tall black caps and white clothing under brown cloaks, ran with messages and documents, and Buddhist priests stood in small groups.

"What happens now?" Takehira asked eagerly.

His father bit his lip, then called one of his men to his side. "Go announce us!"

The soldier saluted, then looked around at the many halls. "Where?" he asked.

Hiramoto muttered a curse. "Idiot. Over there." He pointed to the largest hall.

The man trotted off and returned quickly. "Master, they say they don't know us. They say to go away."

Hiramoto cursed again and hit the man on the head with his wooden baton. "You and the others go wait over there." He gestured toward the carriages. "Come, Takehira." He spurred his horse and galloped to the stairs leading up to the building, coming to a halt in a shower of gravel. Swinging down from the saddle, he took the stairs two steps at a time. A court official wearing a pale green silk robe and small lacquered court cap took a step back.

"You there," Hiramoto roared at him.

Takehira grinned. His father had attracted the attention of the entire courtyard. He decided to follow suit. More galloping and another rearing, splattering, whinnying halt later, he joined his father on the veranda. The official, who had sent their man away only moments ago, glared at them.

Hiramoto advanced on him. His heavy boots made the boards of the veranda tremble. His large sword swung and his heavy armor flapped and clinked as he moved. Takehira followed gleefully.

The official retreated farther. "Stop! You cannot come here like this," he squeaked.

Towering over him, Hiramoto put his hand on the hilt of his sword and raised his voice. "I am Oba no Hiramoto, son of Oba no Kageshita and nephew of Oba no Kageyoshi, descendants of Oba no Kagemasa, the hero of the five-years' war, and I am here to see the cloistered Emperor and my daughter who is in his service. Announce me instantly or I'll find the way myself."

The official paled. "Your pardon, sir," he stammered with a bow. "Your soldier, er, servant, did not mention your errand."

"He's an idiot," growled Hiramoto. "And so are you to offend strangers without knowing their business."

The official bit his lip and stared in despair at their dusty clothes. Takehira put a frown on his face and a hand on his sword. The courtier gave up his resistance. "You will have to remove your weapons and boots."

Disarmed and in their stockings, they were passed on to another official.

Inside the great hall, more men were waiting, but these were nobles, high-ranking clergymen, and senior officers of the guard. Takehira eyed their uniforms and court dress with admiration and interest, but his father still glowered.

"I have written," he grumbled. "Why this delay?"

Officials came and went. They wore black slippers and moved along in stiff, softly hissing silk robes. Their faces were powdered, and a faint scent of perfume accompanied them. Hiramoto wrinkled his nose in distaste. They both stood stiffly, in their dusty clothes, their helmets under their arms. Finally another official, more polite than the first, asked their business and departed. When he returned, he told them that he regretted but His Majesty was in a meeting of national importance. If the gentlemen would wait in another room, his Excellency, Counselor Tameyazu would come to speak with them.

Hiramoto's face relaxed. He said, "A great man, Counselor Tameyazu. I know him well. He came to my house with His Majesty."

The official bowed more deeply, then led them to a small room under the eaves.

Here Takehira eyed the thick, springy grass mats under foot and the fine green shades that kept the sun out. "A comfortable place," he observed. "Wonder where our Toshiko sleeps." He lifted the shade and peered out at another courtyard and more large buildings. "I haven't seen any women, have you?"

His father grunted and sat down on a cushion, crossing his legs.

"I expect she looks as beautiful as an angel these days," Takehira continued. "Can you imagine our Toshiko behaving like a real lady?" He laughed. "A grand lady, with other ladies waiting on her hand and foot. I bet this palace is full of beauties."

"Quiet," growled his father.

Takehira sat down and fell into happy musings about graceful maidens in many-colored silk gowns. In his mind, they flocked around him and looked admiringly at his armor. From this delectable image, his mind wandered to the delights of being a guard officer, participating in drills and performing on horseback with bow and arrow. He was a fine rider and an excellent marksman and pictured himself the center of applause, stripping off his sleeve to reveal his fine arm and shoulder muscles as he stretched the bow and placed the arrow in its groove. Ahead would be the ringed target, and his arrow would hit its center. Perhaps even the Emperor would see him, and all his women . . .

The door opened abruptly, and Counselor Tameyazu came in. Tameyazu was a middle-aged courtier, clearly of high rank. Takehira stood and saluted. Hiramoto simply stood and nodded. Tameyazu inclined his head with a thin smile but he did not sit down nor invite them to do so.

"Ah, Oba," he said in an affable tone. "Good of you to come. All is well in Iga, I hope?"

"All is well, sir," said Hiramoto stolidly.

"Good, good." Tameyazu waited.

Hiramoto cleared his throat. "My son and I have come to return His Majesty's visit and to see how my daughter fares."

Tameyazu nodded. "I see. Very kind of you to wish to repay His Majesty's favor, but not at all necessary. I shall inform Him of your courtesy, of course."

Hiramoto reddened. "My daughter Toshiko? She is well?"

Tameyazu frowned. "Your daughter? I'm not sure . . ."

Hiramoto tried once more, a little desperately. "It pleased His Majesty to invite her to serve him. I . . . we wondered if her service has been satisfactory."

"Dear me," Tameyazu said blandly. "I wouldn't know. She is probably in the women's quarters. You must inquire there. I shall send someone to take you. Now, you must excuse me, it is a very busy time. Enjoy your visit to the capital." He inclined his head again and was gone.

"What the devil is this?" snarled Hiramoto, after a moment's stunned silence.

"What was that all about?" Takehira was confused. "When will we see His Majesty?"

"We won't. But I shall want to know the reason why before we ride home from here like beaten dogs. This must be your sister's fault. I shall get to the bottom of it."

A servant arrived. They put on their boots again and walked to another building. Here they were asked to wait again.

This time, they were in an inner chamber. Takehira had no opportunity to see any females, but he could hear women's voices and the rustling of long gowns across the floors of the corridors outside. Now and then someone giggled. Somewhere a door slid open, and lute music sounded faintly from the distance.

When their door opened, he expected to see his sister. But it was another lady. She was his mother's age but not nearly as handsome. When she lowered her fan to adjust her train, he saw that she had a narrow face with a sharp nose. She bowed to his father in a perfunctory manner, then knelt, announcing in a prim nasal voice, "My name is Lady Sanjo. I am mistress of His Majesty's women's quarters. They tell me that you are the father and brother of Oba no Toshiko?"

Hiramoto glowered at her. "That is so. And I wish to speak to my daughter. Please bring her."

Lady Sanjo drew herself up in disapproval. "That is not usually permitted. But as I may take this opportunity to warn you that your daughter has proved less than satisfactory in her manner and appearance, I shall make an exception. You may wish to discuss arrangements with her, as I assume she will shortly accompany you home." She rose and, with another meager nod, swept out of the room.

From Lady Sanjo's Pillow Book:

I knew it would happen. The arrival of the new girl did not remain a secret long. It has attracted curious males. Any new female at one of the courts is like a dish of honey to the young officers and the sons of court nobles.

I recall when I was an object of interest and, if I do say so myself, they kept coming even after the novelty wore off. I suppose they could not "drink their fill from water sweeter than another well." Of course, I was always careful to hide, or at least raise my fan when in public view during the brief times when we entered or left our carriages or attended Her Majesty. But one cannot always know when one is being spied on, and perhaps one's fan does not open when it should. These young gallants are very daring and persistent when they hear of a particular beauty, and it would be rude not to answer their admiring poems. These days my position with His Majesty protects me from unwanted attentions, I am glad to say. Nowadays, they gaze at the moon, "and fondly think of the vanished past."

But to return to that brazen Oba hussy. It has been stiflingly hot lately, and we have kept all the doors open and the lattices raised. All the ladies wear their thinnest gowns and few layers of them. In this undress, the girl managed to show herself off to the Captain of the Right Guards, who had just left His Majesty. He told all his friends that there was a new lady in His Majesty's women's quarters and heaven knows what else. I was unaware of her shameless behavior until it was too late and we were plagued by constant visitors asking about her. What an irritating girl! She is truly like "the ceaseless cry of the cicadas."

Of course, I should have suspected it would not end there. Far too many young men lost their way and had to be chased from the women's quarters like pesky gnats. Far too often did I find one of them seated outside the shades conversing with someone and lingering with the moon until dawn. As a rule, one assumes that a lady has received a visit from a brother or that the visitor carried a message from her parents or husband, but alas, people tell lies.

One day, I caught her. She was in one of the eave rooms, kneeling just inside the lowered shade and pushing something under it to the outside. And there on the veranda, clearly outlined by his shadow, sat a man. Their hands must have touched. No, worse. The exchange of poems speaks of intimacy, of shocking night time visits, of bodies touching and hands caressing, of burning flesh.

It had to be stopped. Heaven forbid His Majesty should discover her betrayal. Or one of the other ladies should find out. Such affairs cannot be kept secret for long. And what if there were results? In either case, the blame would fall on me. The thought of His Majesty's disappointment was an agony and I prayed for deliverance.

Thank heaven, my prayer was heard: Her father and brother arrived, and instantly I saw the path to salvation. They must be made to take her away with them. The "tears she sheds in parting" will turn to dew and refresh me in the days to come.

They were country boors, both of them, just as I expected. Crude, gross men with dark faces. They even wore armor - inside an imperial residence! After all the horrors that soldiers have committed in this city, and even to the person of His Majesty, these two wore their armor! Not even the Taira and Minamoto generals dare to do that.

To be fair, the brother, being young, was not without a certain attractiveness. He had a handsome set of shoulders and very good legs. I was reminded that it will soon be time for the Sumo matches. His muscles would make an excellent showing there. For all his roughness, my poor woman's heart beat a little faster at the thought. There is something most pleasing about masculine strength when tamed by a woman's gentle touch. I must try for a verse on the subject. The pine and the wisteria? A rocky promontory jutting into a softly lapping sea? A hawk, diving for a dove?

But I digress.

The father was the usual type. He addressed me rudely, demanding to see his daughter. Demanding! It made me angry to see such country scum behave as if they owned us all. I countered his bad manners by becoming very ladylike and reminding him that his daughter came here only by His Majesty's excessively generous invitation.

Then the idea came to me in a flash, a moment of true enlightenment. I added that by now she had outstayed her welcome—a crooked branch in His Majesty's flower garden.

It was only a little lie, really. The girl would have been sent home sooner or later. Making her leave now will spare His Majesty embarrassment.

I saw that my small stratagem was working when the father's face filled with shame and righteous anger at his offspring.

So I sent her in, certain that her mortified relatives would instantly pack her up and remove her to whatever rough hovel they inhabit in their wilderness. Once she was back in her rustic dwelling, His Majesty would hardly send for her again. No doubt he has already awakened from that "brief dream."

I planned to inform him that she had begged most urgently to visit her ailing mother. Women her mother's age are always ailing with something. As His Majesty is a most understanding man and respects proper filial behavior, he would leave well enough alone, I thought.

But alas, they did not take her. She came back and crept into her corner like a beaten dog.

A Daughter's Duty

When Lady Sanjo informed Toshiko of her visitors, she was so happy that she forgot the woman hated her. She mistook the satisfied smirk for kindness, the glittering eyes for empathy, the rapid steps for eagerness to see Toshiko's pleasure.

All she could think of was that her father and brother had come. As yet she dared not hope they that had come to take her home with them. No, that would be a joy too great to bear. But they had come to see her. It was enough. In her grief and homesickness, she had grown afraid that she would never see them again, that in time she would even come to forget what they looked like and the sound of their voices. She had felt abandoned and as if she were dead to them. Now life stirred again in her veins.

As she hurried after Lady Sanjo to the distant room where visitors were taken, she thought of the letter to her mother. She had broken a rule that one time only, because of her great fear that her mother was ill and dying. That nightmare had been so dreadful that she had moaned in her sleep. When Lady Shojoben touched her shoulder, she had woken drenched in perspiration and with tears running down her face.

She still saw every dreadful detail: her mother's emaciated form, the feverish eyes, the horrifying spots on her skin - spots of decomposition as in those frightening pictures of the dead that the local temple would put up at year's end—spots that suppurated and grew larger until her beloved mother was no longer recognizable.

She stopped in sudden fear and cried to Lady Sanjo's back, "My mother? Oh, please don't tell me my mother is dead."

Lady Sanjo turned her head. Some of the anger was back in her face. "Nonsense. Nobody is dead. Come along."

Instantly joy returned—and with the joy, gratitude to the young man who had taken her letter and thus perhaps reminded them of her. How kind he had been with his warm voice and those beautiful gentle hands. Oh, he was even more handsome than her brother Takehira.

And dear Takehira had come with her father. Oh, what happiness!

Lady Sanjo pushed back the door to the visitors' room and said, "Your daughter."

Toshiko brushed past her with a small cry and fell to her knees, touching her forehead to the boards. "Father, dear Father, I am so glad to see you." As she bowed, she was astonished that they were wearing armor. To be sure, at home her father wore his armor on official occasions, but here? No one wore armor here except perhaps the guards on duty at the gates.

She followed the deep bow to her father with a smaller one toward her brother and sat up. They looked well but neither spoke nor smiled at her. She realized that something was wrong, that her father was fiercely angry. His eyes blazed and his brows and beard seemed to bristle. Takehira's face softened a little as his eyes rested on her beautiful gowns, her painted face, her glossy hair.

But her father's face was implacable, every muscle taut and his lips compressed.

"Father?" she whispered, feeling tears rise. "Is something wrong?"

"You have shamed me."

Just that. Clipped and as fierce as his eyes. She bowed again, keeping her head down so he would not see her tears. Tears were weak. As was a show of happiness. She had offended by expressing her joy at seeing them. She had lost her self-control.

After a long time, during which she tried very hard to restrain her tears, her father said, "The female in whose charge you are says that you are unsuitable and that we must take you home."

Home? For a moment she allowed herself another weakness. The desire to leave this dark and stifling place and to see her mother again was so great that even her father's disappointment seemed small when measured against it. But then she knew it could not be because that would mean failure and failure was unacceptable. Anger against Lady Sanjo stirred.

Without raising her head, she murmured, "She does not like me, Father. Perhaps her words were not as truthful as they should have been."

"Silence!"

Toshiko tensed.

"It is of no concern," her father growled, "what a mere female thinks. We came here to make our bows to His Majesty and were refused an audience. How is this?"

Oh, heaven. "He sees very few people. He is the Emperor, Father."

"He sees my daughter. For that He owes me courtesy."

"Father, you do not understand–"

"How dare you?"

Toshiko could not control her trembling any longer. "Forgive me, Father," she whispered. "I only meant that customs are different here than at home."

"How so?"

"I don't wish to offend again."

"Speak."

"Your armor. Nobody addresses Their Majesties in armor."

There was brief silence, then her Father said, "The courtiers are glad enough of us in our armor when they need help. But let it go. I would have thought that by now you had found his ear. Was he not pleased with your singing?"

Oh dear! The *imayo*. Toshiko had to make a clean breast of it. "I have only spoken to His Majesty once. He asked if I knew *imayo*, but I was afraid that he would think me very improper if I admitted it."

"What?" A roar, followed instantly by another: "You fool! That is why he sent for you."

"Yes, Father. I know that now, but I did not at first."

A heavy silence settled over all of them. Toshiko wondered again if her father would take her home now that all was lost. Perhaps he would forgive her in time. Surely he would. He was just.

After a long time, Oba no Hiramoto said, "Sit up and look at me."

She obeyed, hoping that the traces of her tears had dried. Her father studied her appearance. The anger was gone, replaced by resignation. With a sigh, he said, "I had high hopes of you, daughter."

She looked at him without blinking. "I know, Father. If I have truly shamed you, I shall gladly die."

He compressed his lips. "The fault is perhaps not altogether with you. You are young. But you have been taught that, as long as her father lives, a daughter must study his wishes."

"Yes, Father. And after he dies, she must study his life so that she may be worthy of her own."

"You must never bring shame or dishonor on your name."

"I know, Father."

"If necessary, a son must die in battle for his family and his lord, but a daughter need only give obedient service. It is a small thing."

"Yes, Father."

Another pregnant pause fell. Toshiko began to feel a great relief. She was to be forgiven and taken back into the family. Her lip trembled and tears of gratitude pricked again at her eyelids, but she held her father's gaze.

He was the first to look away. He glanced up at the ceiling and said almost casually, "The great sage himself affirms that the three hundred songs in the world are free from evil thought."

She frowned, trying to understand. "The great sage, Father?"

He glanced at her briefly. "Kung Fu Tse. Never mind. You're just a woman. It means that your songs are not improper and that you should not be ashamed of them."

"But you brought Takehira back when he followed the *shirabyoshi*. You said they were whores and low dirty women."

Her father turned red. "Hold your tongue, girl."

She put her head down again and whispered, "Forgive me, Father."

He cleared his throat.

"You must try again," he said.

"What?" She was so startled that the word slipped out before she could stop herself.

Her father snapped, "Don't be an imbecile. You must sing to His Majesty. You must dance for Him. You must win His heart. How plain do you want me to be? I thought your mother had explained the matters of the bed chamber to you."

She was still for a moment, listening to her heart pound in her ears like the waves of the sea. Then she straightened her back, the blood hot as fire in her face. “Yes, Father,” she said dully. “I understand.”

He looked away, embarrassed. “What concerns parents must be a concern to a child. I hope we can rely on your obedience in this.”

“Yes, Father.”

Her father rose with a groan. “Come, Takehira. I am sick of this city. If we make haste, we can reach Kohata by nightfall.”

Toshiko saw her brother’s face fall, but she hardened her heart to his disappointment. It bore no comparison to her despair.

Ghosts

When Secretary Tameyazu reported the visit of the Obas, the Emperor was at his desk.

The doors were open to the veranda and the private courtyard beyond. It had been an unusually dry and hot summer, and everyone hoped for rain. In the courtyard grew a cherry tree that servants watered regularly. Even with such care the tree's leaves were already turning yellow and falling to the gravel below. The Emperor's eyes frequently looked past it to the blue mountains in the distance, and at a bank of dark clouds building another, more threatening, mountain range in the sky.

He made a face at Tameyazu's words and told him he could not see them. The matter was trivial, especially at the moment. More evil omens had been reported by the Bureau of Divination. There was the fear of drought and a poor harvest. Bad harvests brought starvation and disease to the people. He had been thinking about making another pilgrimage to the gods of Kumano to ask for rain.

The problem with Tameyazu's news was that it reminded him of an embarrassing private matter. He had sent for the girl on a whim. It had been a momentary weakness, like the one that had caused him to bed the *shirabyoshi* Kane years ago. This case was worse, because a more unsuitable background for an imperial concubine could hardly be imagined. His passion for gathering every last one of the songs of his people for his collection had piqued his curiosity, and her appearance on horseback had blinded him to her father's greed. It had all been lies, of course, and certain to be found out, but her mercenary family hoped that by then his lust for her young body would outweigh any disappointment in her lack of talent. He should have sent her home months ago.

Women had always caused him regrets.

His own mother had only summoned him to make certain that his education progressed adequately. Whenever he faltered in his answers, she would leave with a worried frown on her face. Like any child, he had wished to please her because he thought it would gain him affection. To no avail. His mother had remained distant.

He had become very fond of his father's other, much younger, consort. She, in turn, had made much of him in the way young girls do with children, being carelessly affectionate while enjoying his childish games as she made her own painful adjustment to her new position.

He had known nothing of the imperial bedchamber in those days and barely discerned that men and women lived in worlds as different as day and night. Men forged their destinies by the light of day. Women pursued theirs under cover of darkness. He had spent much of his childhood in the feminine darkness of the women's quarters and emerged only slowly and partially into the light. During his days in the inner apartments of various palaces, he had seen the sun only rarely. He and his female guardians were protected from the eyes of the world by innumerable barriers of shutters, doors, curtains, shades, screens, and human attendants. Their inner world was dimly lit by candles, oil lamps, and torches. In the winter time, the wooden doors were closed against the icy wind, and in the summer only thin golden bars of sunlight pierced the horizontal shutters and squeezed past curtain stands.

He mused on that past, recalling the intense sensation of lying curled up in the arms of one of the women, nearly dizzy with her warmth and softness and the scent of her hair and clothing, watching the dust motes dancing on rays of light, tiny creatures transformed into specks of golden radiance as they ascended toward a distant sun. He had learned to desire women then in this darkness dense with perfume and the smell of female flesh and cosmetics. Even when there was silence, the palace hissed and whispered with silks and silk-shod feet gliding across polished wooden floors, but the women were rarely silent. They talked in high, gentle voices; they sang, they played their instruments, they laughed and wept, and sometimes they quarreled. It had seemed to him as if the very air of the inner apartments throbbed with the pent-up emotions of the women.

It was much later that he learned he did not belong there.

Tameyazu returned, breaking into his master's reminiscences. The emperor frowned at him. "What?"

"I told them you were busy and referred them to Lady Sanjo. I hope I did right?"

The Emperor remembered the Obas. "Yes. Quite right." He did not want to discuss this private matter with Tameyazu.

Tameyazu bowed and retreated to his own, smaller desk, and the Emperor returned to his brooding.

The image of that young girl flying along the valley on the back of her coal-black horse moved his heart even now.

He had envied men like Oba because they were free to make choices an emperor could not make, and Oba's children had seemed free as birds. In that mood, passion had struck him like a blow. The sight of her, astride her horse like a young male, her long hair flying behind her, had stirred something in him that he still did not fully understand. It was not mere lust. He had wanted her, but had wanted to possess her only so that she could stir his heart again and again.

Alas, if he had fallen in love it was with an illusion. The real girl was no different from all the others—perhaps more timid and, being a child, less designing, but for all that she was like one of the hollow dolls he had played with as a child.

Outside the room, a gust of wind drove small bits of gravel and leaves across the boards of the veranda. The storm was coming. The soft pattering sounds reminded him a little of rats scampering across a zither. He smiled at the image of tiny pink feet plucking taut strings.

Tameyazu rose from behind his desk and went on soft feet to close the shutters. The Emperor regretted the silencing of the sound but welcomed the absence of light for his private thoughts.

Not for long. Tameyazu officiously lit candles and lamps before sitting down again.

The Emperor made another effort to read the documents in front of him.

Rats.

There had been that amusing incident of Lady Dainagon's cat. The Oba girl surprised him that time.

She had stood there with the battered cat in her arms, her eyes shining with mischief. At that moment, she was not like the dolls around her. She had made him laugh out loud, and he rarely laughed these days.

He became aware that Tameyazu was watching him and moved irritably. What was the man staring at? He frowned, and his secretary quickly lowered his head.

Things had been different when Shinzei had been his secretary. There had been no secrets from him. But they had killed Shinzei after the Heiji plot. The Emperor raised his shoulders in the stiff brocade and shivered in spite of the brooding heat. These days most things reminded him of death.

The Taira and Minamoto were always poised to spring at each other's throats like mad dogs. He thought he could hear them growling again. It was a miracle that they had not slaughtered him and his children yet.

In all the bloody affairs of the recent past, he had learned that his imperial blood would not save his life. Too many of his family had died too young and too conveniently. His half-brother, the Emperor Konoe, had been only thirteen when he became blind and died. His brother Sutoku died in exile after being manipulated into a foolish rebellion. And who was to say that Sutoku had not been helped into the other world? Now his own son was dead at twenty-three, leaving behind a puny babe to rule the nation, and already Chancellor Kiyomori was pressuring him to appoint his cousin Shigeko's son crown prince.

He frequently carried on silent conversations with the dead Shinzei when he felt threatened by Kiyomori. Now he stared into a dark corner where he imagined the ghost of Shinzei to hover, and asked, *What should I do about the girl, old friend?*

And Shinzei answered, *Why, send her home, of course, Sire.*

The Emperor frowned. Shinzei was gray-haired even before he shaved his head and became a monk. He was an old man when they killed him, a monk past the age of indiscretions with females. The pleasures of the body no longer stirred him, and he was equally immune to the pleasures of the mind. What could he know of this dilemma?

He expressed his doubts: *I don't know. She seems . . . innocent.*

It is a little like a fever, isn't it? Shinzei suggested.

The Emperor sensed Shinzei's amusement and started to shake his head.

Oh, said Shinzei, *I remember it well enough – even after I put away the things of the world. With you, Sire, it is different. You are still a young man.*

A young man? At thirty-six? With a grown son already dead and his grandson on the throne? He protested. *I have never felt this fever, as you call it. My father had it, I_believe. Not for my mother, but for Tokuko.* He chuckled. *Have I ever told you that I desired my father's concubine when I was only seven?*

Across the room, Tameyazu raised his head to look at him. The Emperor glared and cleared his throat, and the man quickly bent to his work again.

I have no privacy, he grumbled to Shinzei. *They watch me to see if they can read their future in my behavior. Where were we?*

Your father's wife was very beautiful and entirely charming. Shinzei's voice carried a smile. *It is no wonder you should have felt that way. And, yes, your*

August Father had the fever very badly, I think. For many years. He was afraid of you.

The Emperor said complacently, *I thought so. He would not allow us to be together after the time he found us lying in each other's arms.*

Shinzei asked, *You were lying together?*

Oh, nothing happened. But only because I was too young. And I never felt that way again.

Shinzei sounded intrigued. *Until now?*

It is not like that, Shinzei. She is a child. I do not want to hurt the child by rejecting her. Her parents will punish her.

Shinzei pondered. *True, the father is not the sensitive type, but surely you do not wish to reward such a man?*

No. And I am angry at his deception. Never mind. Something will come to me.

But Sire, surely the answer is obvious.

It is?

Indeed. Sleep with the girl. She will feel flattered and loved, and you will get over your fever. Then you can send her home with a small token of your affection or pass her on to one of your wives as a lady-in-waiting.

The Emperor stared fixedly at the wall where he imagined Shinzei's comforting figure. A slow smile formed on his lips. *Of course. And it will irritate Lady Sanjo immeasurably. Her irritation amuses me.* He started to laugh.

"Sire?" Across the room, Tameyazu half rose.

"Nothing. You may check these lists and report any problems." The Emperor got up and walked out of the room. Tameyazu prostrated himself on the cold floor.

From Lady Sanjo's Pillow Book

My disappointment was great when her father did not take the Oba girl away with him. But all is not lost. For a time, she stayed out of my way. This makes it harder to catch her with a man, but I was so angry for a while that I could not look at her.

Happily, the other ladies are taking their cue from my cold disdain. All but Shojo-ben avoid her. She does not seem to mind this. In fact, she does little but hum tunes to herself and spend time in the eaves chamber where I caught her passing notes to her lover. I leave her to it, thinking that she will surely carry her immodest behavior too far, and someone else will catch her at it and make an outcry. It will come much better from one of the other ladies, or even from a servant, than from me. Everyone knows my dislike for the girl.

But the weeks have passed without anyone noticing anything - other than her singing — and, considering it my duty, I decided to make my report to His Majesty who is to me "like the moon and stars above."

I found Him with that ancient nun at work on His collection. She sings while He plays His flute. The nun is a most peculiar woman. The situation would be highly improper, if it were not for her age. Rumor has it that she once was a common streetwalker until Lord Kiyomori found her and set her up as his mistress, having her perform for his guests. If so, the matter is scandalous enough: a harlot in the presence of His Majesty? I cannot believe it myself.

I have noticed that His Majesty is very familiar with her but He treats her with the utmost respect, once even calling her *sensei,* as if she were His teacher. People say that His Majesty has a regrettable tendency to associate with low persons when He judges it a question of art. One day, before He resigned the throne, He is said to have stopped His palanquin in a street of artisans because He recognized the name of a painter on a sign. He got out and walked down a filthy alleyway and into the man's house. Sitting down on a dirty trunk in His imperial robes, He watched the painter for an hour or more, then thanked Him very politely and asked for a memento of the visit. Alas, the man had nothing to give Him. (Would that I could make up for all His disappointments. "Ah, I know not the destination of my love.")

It is this sort of thing that made His Majesty's father think Him unsuitable for the succession.

But I digress.

Having taken pains with my appearance, not forgetting the plums in my cheeks to make my face look fuller, I knelt before His Majesty and announced that I had a report of a private nature for Him.

The nun–Otomae, I think, she is called–gave me the most peculiar stare. It was almost as if she were trying not to laugh. I was so disconcerted that I nearly swallowed one of the plums.

To my disgust and embarrassment, His Majesty said, "Please speak freely, Lady Sanjo. The reverend sister is completely in our confidence."

Speaking freely was not as easy as He thought. The plums slow my tongue and make me lisp. "I beg Your Majesty's pardon," I ventured, "but this matter concerns one of Your Majesty's ladies."

"I expected it would," he said, "since that is your duty."

Well, I had no choice. "The young Oba woman," I told him, "has corresponded with someone." I rather liked the word "corresponded." It implied the most intimate relationship without actually naming such a dirty thing.

He laid down His brush and raised His eyebrows at that. "Did you say 'corresponded'? Try to speak more clearly. Do you mean she has written a letter? Or received one? Or both?"

I could not very well say more than what I had seen. "I caught her s-slipping a note to a male visitor, Your Majesty," I said. "My assumption is that it answered one of his."

There. It was the truth, but it would make Him think that they had spent the night together and the man had sent her a next-morning poem to which she had then replied.

His Majesty looked astonished. "Do I assume that you are concerned because of the identity of this male visitor?" he asked.

"Oh, I don't know that," I cried. One of the plums shifted and I had to swallow it whole.

"Well then, why *are* you concerned?"

I gulped and stuttered, "But Your Majesty . . . I thought . . . you asked me to report on her."

He frowned. "Hmm. And is that all you have to report?"

"Well, she is also humming to herself," I offered, thinking that would make it clear that she was far too happy to be innocent.

He sat up and looked at me more sharply. "What is wrong with your face? It looks lopsided."

Oh, dear. I flushed under my make-up. "A bad tooth, Sire."

"Hmm. What was she humming?"

"I could not hear the words, Your Majesty. Little songs. Common little songs, from the sound of them. She looked happy." People sing when they are happy, so that was a sensible deduction.

His Majesty exchanged a glance with the nun, then said, "Ask her about the songs she sings and report back to me."

I touched my forehead to the boards and crept away. Really, I thought to myself, He has some very peculiar interests for such an august person. And He is far too young to have lost all memory of romance. It crossed my mind to pretend an avid interest in songs myself to make him more approachable. Why should He spend all his time with an elderly nun when He could be with me? After all, given daily close proximity, who knew what might not happen? As the poet said, "The strength of our love may yet prolong our unfinished dream forever." This made me so happy that I forgot all about the awkwardness with the swallowed plum.

I was still turning the idea over in my mind when I reached the door. His Majesty and the nun had returned to their conversation, and I was about to open the door to leave, when His Majesty called out after me, "On second thought, Lady Sanjo, bring her back with you. I will ask her myself."

Ah, I thought, that should prove interesting. I obeyed with alacrity.

In the first place, I knew that the Oba girl had just washed her hair. Nothing looks more slovenly than a female with wet hair and disordered gowns. Perhaps He would be sufficiently disgusted to ask her about the letter. Secondly, if she really knew something about those silly songs He was forever gathering and singing, then I might make use of her to teach me.

She was undressed, sitting near a brazier filled with glowing coals to dry her hair. I was glad to see that none of the others had offered to help her by brushing and fanning the long strands and that her hair was still heavy with water and tangled.

She blanched and balked when I brought her the message. "I cannot go like this," she cried. No wonder. She had also washed her face and looked positively naked without paint, just like the peasant she was. No man could possibly find her attractive.

"Nonsense, you look fine," I snapped. "Besides, you cannot refuse an imperial command. Heavens, don't they teach you anything in the country?"

"Oh, please, Lady Sanjo," she pleaded, "couldn't you explain? If I might just have a little time, I could change my clothes, paint my face, and dry my hair a little more."

"No," I said firmly. "You will report to His Majesty now."

I could see from her face that I would have no more trouble from her. She bowed her head, tied her wet hair with a ribbon and threw a red jacket over the thin white undergarment. I would have forbidden that also, but water had soaked the gauze and it clung most indecently to her figure.

We returned to His Majesty.

I saw immediately that He was startled by her appearance and smiled to myself. She fell to her knees and murmured an apology about having been caught unprepared.

His Majesty shot me a glance, but said that it did not matter, that He only had one little question and then she might go back. This pleased me, since it showed His lack of interest in her as a female.

The girl sat up and looked at him expectantly. Very improper, of course. I myself kept my face down and only stole a glance now and then.

His Majesty said, "Lady Sanjo tells me that you sing sometimes, and I recalled your father mentioning that you had a knowledge of local songs."

"Yes, Your Majesty," said she, still staring brazenly at His face. "I was ashamed to say so before."

He smiled at that. "Would you favor us with one of your songs?"

"Now? Like this?"

His Majesty smiled more broadly and nodded.

She bowed. "With Your Majesty's permission, may I rise? The songs are performed with movement."

To my amazement, His Majesty clapped His hands. "*Imayo*," he cried. "Do you hear that, Otomae? It was true what they said. Yes, yes, of course. Rise, Lady Toshiko, and let us see and hear you."

I was appalled, but the strange nun looked as pleased as His Majesty and nodded encouragement. The girl rose, took up a pose, and began.

"They're in love," she sang, raising her arms and looking up at the ceiling, "the weaver maid and the herdsman in the sky." Lowering her arms slowly, she turned, and dipped. "The pheasants in the field, the deer in autumn." She twisted her body, waving her arms from side to side. "The women who sell their charms in the street." I cannot possibly describe the gestures that accompanied that scandalous line. "And in winter, so are the mandarin ducks." She pressed her hands together, then she bowed deeply to His Majesty.

It was an exceedingly vulgar performance. Most of the images in her song were ordinary enough – that old legend of the star-crossed lovers in the sky, deer and pheasants, ducks – I daresay I could have done better, but no lady should be aware of street women. Her voice was also quite crude and strong. The song was uncouth enough, but when she danced, all semblance of decency departed. She behaved like a harlot would – or as I imagine she would, for I am, of course, not familiar with such creatures. Whenever she flung out her arms, her jacket parted and nothing was left hidden from our eyes. I still shudder with shame and disgust.

To my surprise, His Majesty and the nun listened and watched with the greatest interest. Of course, even an emperor is merely a male beneath his silk robes. Some people have said that His Majesty has put all thoughts of sexual matters from His mind to prepare himself for a religious life. If true, it would be a great pity. He is still a most handsome man. But I saw with my own eyes how He flushed with pleasure as He watched the slut.

I thought the nun would surely object, but she smiled widely - her teeth were not blackened and at her age very unattractive. Given her silence, I thought it must be true that she once was a harlot. How abominable to pretend holiness when one's mind dwells in the gutter of writhing bodies.

Since the proper deportment of the young ladies falls within my responsibilities, I was forced to interfere. As soon as the girl was done, I hissed to her, "Cover yourself! Are you totally shameless?"

She turned quite red and instantly fell to her knees, bending her head to the floor. Apparently the fool had been so flattered by His Majesty's interest that she had forgotten her state of undress.

"I do beg Your Majesty's pardon," I said quickly. "This young woman is still very new, and Your Majesty's summons found her unprepared."

He looked angry, as well He might, and snapped, "I said it did not matter," adding, "You may leave us now."

I bowed and started to back away. To my dismay, the girl did not move. "Toshiko," I whispered, angry that she was making things even more difficult than they already were.

"Only you, Lady Sanjo," said he. "Lady Toshiko will stay."

Well, I was furious. I had to return alone to our quarters where I was instantly surrounded by the others who wanted to know why the girl had been called so urgently and in undress. If it had been night, they would have assumed that she had found favor, but it was still an hour until sunset and they were puzzled what His Majesty could want with her at that time.

"His Majesty is working on His song collection with an assistant," I said, "and had a question about the music of her homeland."

It was probably the truth, but I had seen His eyes widen when Her jacket fell open. Oh," the anguish of my heart!"

I was not surprised when she did not return until the middle of the night. Only a few ladies were still awake and watched as she went to her bedding and lay down as she was, pulling the covers over herself.

We live in a degenerate age.

A Degenerate Age

Even a man who feels his life slipping through his fingers may have a moment of pure delight. In the midst of his disillusionment, mourning all the things that could never be, the retired Emperor had found enchantment.

It left him deeply troubled and confused.

For one thing, the girl who had been pawned off on him was not quite a child after all. This he saw the moment she began to dance. It was not just that the thin gauze of her white undergarment revealed that she had a woman's body, hitherto hidden by voluminous layers of silk, but even his jaded eyes recognized in her movements the studied seduction practiced by the most adept performers of *imayo*, by women who sell their bodies to the men they entertain.

For a moment, he had stared in disbelief. The girl's face, bare of make-up, was as innocent as a child's, the face of a young girl before she puts on the train of womanhood and applies the paints that hide her features and give her the appearance of a doll. But this girl's gestures were those of a practiced harlot.

In his first astonishment, he had almost thanked Lady Sanjo— not only because she informed him of the girl's singing talents, but because she brought her to him in a state of undress that awakened fires he had thought long since dead. His blood warmed —no, boiled—as he watched that young body gyrate, those small hands inviting him to touch, to take, to ravish. He felt such a surge of lust that he hardly heard her song. Instead his eyes searched those smooth limbs, tantalizingly revealed and hidden as she swayed and bent. Her hair, heavy with moisture, clung to her white neck but swung free below and scented the air with perfume. Alas, he thought, it was a wise man who said that even a mighty elephant may be tethered with the twist of a woman's hair.

But Lady Sanjo had not planned this at all and broke the spell by hissing a reproof that caused the girl to collapse with a cry—like an empty doll that has been dropped.

Instantly, the dream dissolved. Toshiko sobbed on the floor before him as only a young child sobs, inconsolably. Lady Sanjo seemed like a serpent to him then, poisonous and always underfoot, ready to strike at his joy.

And he was again himself, a man well past his youth and weary of the world. A father with daughters older than this girl. A man who had done his duty, played the bedchamber games with wives and concubines, fathered his children, and rewarded their mothers with income, rank, and titles. An evil karma had brought him war, rebellion, and the deaths of brothers, sons, and friends. He yearned for serenity now, hoped to lose himself and his memories in prayer and meditation. He wanted to shave his head and put on the stole of priesthood so that the weight of this world would fall away from him. He wanted to pray for the dead and the living and be at peace.

And this young woman was an obstacle in his path.

He was angry - mostly at himself. He pitied the girl as one pities a child who has been punished for a mistake in her calligraphy exercise.

But the flush of guilty pleasure was still on his face when he glanced at Otomae and saw that she was amused by his arousal. She had nodded to him and then gone to the weeping child, taking her in her arms, murmuring consoling words. And she had asked her where she learned the song.

The girl clutched her jacket to her body and, in her shame, would not look at him, but her halting answers explained much.

Oba noToshiko had been taught both song and dance, those lewd gestures and alluring poses, by a trained *kugutsu,* one of the traveling women of pleasure who perform for men of wealth and power in hopes of seducing the master or heir into a torrid affair or one-night stand. And that woman had been Akomaro, one of the greatest artists of *imayo* and a famous harlot.

He wondered at first why the young daughter of a noble house had been allowed to watch and imitate such performances but decided that it had all been part of Oba's plot to seduce him. It was well-known that he invited talented *shirabyoshi* to perform for him, and so Oba had turned his daughter into one. The thought was sickening – all the more so because, the longer he listened and watched Otomae and the girl, the more convinced he became that the child had little or no idea of what her words and gestures meant.

What had the world come to?

He remembered that tear-stained face with its downcast eyes, those small, childish hands clutched in her lap. Was she still a virgin or had her training included instruction in sexual matters?

What would Shinzei say now? But Shinzei did not appear. Otomae was chatting lightly about *imayo* songs and about the girl's home, and the Emperor withdrew into himself. Only when the guard called out the hour of the boar, did he stir again. He dismissed the girl with a peremptory word.

"What do you think?" he asked Otomae when the great doors had closed behind her.

"I think she's a rare treasure, sire," said the nun with a smile. "She probably knows all of Akomaro's songs."

He frowned. "That is not what I meant. She disturbs me."

"That, too. Is it such a bad thing?"

"How can you ask? And you a nun!"

Otomae laughed. "I was a woman once, even a very young one like your pretty little lady. She will give you pleasure, sire."

"What? You approve?"

"Of course."

He looked at her, saw the twinkle in her eyes, and traced remembered beauty in the lines of her face. There had been a time when he was very young that Otomae had set his blood on fire. Age had nothing to do with that. She always made him feel younger than his years. His mood lifted. "Are you not jealous?" he asked with a smile. "How mortifying for me."

She put a hand on his. "You are the Emperor, but also my very dear friend. I take joy in your joy."

He snatched up her hand and held it to his cheek. "You know I have no joy except when I am with you. But you are an infrequent visitor. I have been seeking peace from the affairs of the world. Now this girl is getting in the way."

She touched his face with her other hand. "Oh, my dear," she said lovingly. It took great temerity to touch a son of heaven so familiarly – and it gave him such comfort that tears rose to his eyes. "You are not old in years and body," she told him. "And both men and women may find peace in each other's arms. The Buddha does not forbid it."

"'All attachment to another is impurity of the heart, and all our difficulties spring from it,'" he quoted back.

She sighed. "Then I am a very sinful woman."

He wanted to bury his face in her shoulder and be held by her the way she had held the weeping child, but he only took her hands into both of his and said, "Oh, Otomae, she is too young for me. What does she know of the world?"

Otomae gently freed her hands. "Then teach her, sire," she said firmly. Rising to her feet, she bowed and walked away on silent feet.

"When will I see you again?" he called after her.

She did not answer. The door closed softly behind her.

The Man of Learning

Doctor Yamada lived in the Tokwa Quarter, not far from where the Rashomon gate had once stood and near To-ji temple. His house was the largest in a quarter where most homes were small, one-storied affairs, roofed with boards that were weighted down by stones. It had once been a cloth merchant's house, but the man and most of his children had died in the last smallpox epidemic, and his widow had sold the property and returned to her family.

The doctor's garden was quite large, because he had bought an adjoining property when that neighbor's house burned down. Here he grew his medicinal herbs around a small pavilion which served as his pharmacy. But the original garden behind his house was his special joy. He had planted a smaller version of the charming landscapes that surrounded the elegant villas and temples. Many-colored azaleas grew here, and cherry trees. Handsome pines twisted above picturesque rocks. Moss and rare ferns flourished in shady corners; colored koi swam in a small pond where lotus bloomed; and frogs had taken up residence on the pond margin. When the weather allowed it, all of his free time was spent in his gardens.

Otherwise, his needs were simple and taken care of by three servants: an older woman, a man who was severely disfigured by burns, and an orphaned boy. The woman, Otori, had served him since childhood and ruled the small household, including its master. She cooked, washed, cleaned the house, and dealt with peddlers and patients who came to his door. The man's name was Togoro. He did the heavy work and kept the property in good repair. The boy had no name. They called him "Boy," or sometimes, "Demon," or "Stupid." Since he was a foundling, nobody knew his age, though the doctor guessed that he must be about fourteen. Boy swept, ran errands, and stole occasionally.

For Doctor Yamada, daily life ran smoothly in Mibu street – or at least it did until his fateful meeting with Oba no Toshiko.

This morning, he got up and stepped out into his garden. The sky was clear and the early sun flung golden patches across his shrubs and trees. On the roof, the doves murmured in the warmth, and a sparrow splashed in the shallow bowl of the stone water basin beside his veranda. Catching sight of the doctor, it shook off drops like sparkling jewels and flew away.

A hollow bamboo pipe, balanced on a wooden contraption, carried water from a cistern above. The doctor tipped it down to refill the basin and washed his face and hands. Then he drank from a small bamboo dipper to rinse out his mouth and spat the water into the green cushion of moss below the basin.

He cast a glance around his property, then filled a bucket from the rain barrel and started watering. A self-sufficient man, he participated in the life of his garden, happy when a plant was thriving and unhappy when it did not. The plants were in his care and, like his human patients, they suffered the vicissitudes of fate, disease, starvation, or cold and flourished in times of plenty. It was enough – or at least he had always thought so.

Moving on to the herb garden, he harvested leaves and roots for his small pharmacy. As he hung them up to dry under the roof of the veranda, his thoughts shifted to the patient he would visit later. The Retired Emperor's cook was a man unacquainted with the principles of moderation and therefore suffered periodically from wind and a painfully distended belly because he ate too much. This last bout was particularly severe. The doctor had administered purges, and the cook had taken to his bed with a good deal of weeping and moaning at the cramping of his insides. Today the doctor hoped to find him much improved, but he checked his supply of powdered ginger, bark of cinnamon, and fermented black beans, in case the flux had not abated and a stool-firming decoction was in order.

Inevitably, a visit to the cloister palace turned his thoughts to Toshiko. She was too young for the life she was embarked on, too young to be so alone in the world, too young to bear the burdens of womanhood which would soon be hers.

His studies at the university had included sexual matters and the female anatomy. Besides, he knew the facts and dangers of childbirth first-hand. He was afraid for her because he had seen too many women die during and after giving birth. Not that he was likely to assist in the delivery of an imperial concubine—or any noblewoman, for that matter. Such births were handled by midwives, occasionally with the advice of old men. But he had helped poor women give birth in hovels where no one cared that he was young and male, and he would never forget the bleeding that no art of his could stop. The only time he had seen more blood well forth from a human body had been on the battlefield. In either case, there had been no surviving such wounds. And that child Toshiko was much less sturdily built than those poor women had been.

"Master?" Otori called him to his morning rice, and he walked back to the house. She always brought his bowl of hot gruel to his room there. He usually gulped it down while checking his medical texts or making notes about the treatment of his patients that day.

Today he had no difficult cases, and his mind was on other things. Instead of eating, he sat down and looked around his room. In his modest dwelling, he was surrounded by the things that had given him pleasure and contentment for the past five years.

His medical books and scrolls of illustrations were neatly stacked on shelves, interspersed with the tools of his profession: sets of silver needles used in acupuncture, silver spatulas in many sizes for probing the body's orifices, an ivory doll with which he explained the seat of the disease to the patient and his family, and on which the patient could point out the location of the pain.

But in his mind was more than medical knowledge. His studies at the university had opened a world to him unlike any the warriors in his family would ever have understood: poetry, music - he played the flute and was passably adept on the zither - painting, and the pursuit of those unseen forces of fate, the incredible intricacies of horoscopes which lead to the making and reading of calendars, the language of dreams and omens, and most of all the behavior of his fellow humans.

To this he had since added a familiarity with plants and with the small creatures he encountered in his daily life: the cats and dogs of the neighborhood, and the birds, mice, beetles, spiders, bees, and fish of his garden.

His solitary life had seemed full until now. He used to feel passion and joy in observation, experiment, and discovery. He had been happy and his life in harmony with the universe. Now nothing would satisfy him but the girl from the palace.

As a physician, he recognized his symptoms as a form of disease. It was unnatural for a man in his mid-twenties with a fulfilling profession and a rich and useful life to yearn for a fourteen-year-old girl. He had never needed women before, except for the occasional visit to a courtesan when his physical well-being required it. Physical needs could be satisfied quite easily with such women, but the very thought of lying with Toshiko made him uncomfortable. It seemed as unnatural as if she were his sister or daughter. Clearly his condition was abnormal, disharmonious, even culpable.

Otori returned for the bowl and saw that he had not touched the gruel.

"What's the matter?" she snapped with the easy familiarity of a family member. "You don't like it? Or are you ailing with something?"

"No," he said listlessly, shoving the bowl toward her. "I'm not hungry."

"Not hungry!" Her sharp eyes fixed him. "It's no life for a man," she said, wagging her finger. "Work, work, work, and never any joy. When will you take a wife and play with your own children the way you play with the neighbor's brats?"

He had heard the speech before and ignored it. "I'm seeing His Majesty's cook this morning," he said, getting up. "If someone calls, tell them I'll be back soon or take a message."

"Don't I always?" she grumbled. "Better wear your good robe if you're going to the palace. You never know who'll see you. It wouldn't hurt to get a few noble patients for a change."

That, too, was a familiar complaint. Since his income came from his family's estates, he did not have to rely on his fees as a physician and, to her mind, he treated far too many poor people for free. A steady trickle of unsavory characters frequented his house, and she was convinced that this detracted from his reputation. About this, at least, she was quite right. People think that a man who works among filthy and disease-riddled beggars and prostitutes cannot be an able physician, and worse, that he is likely to bring their diseases into the houses of his paying patients.

But one of his university professors had recommended him to someone on the retired Emperor's staff, and here he was: physician to the Emperor's cook.

Obediently, he changed into a silk robe and put on his court hat. His full trousers were dark about the bottom from the dew-covered garden, but they would dry, and the old water stains were hardly noticeable among the pattern of small blossoms. Taking up his case, he left the house.

He did not get very far. A small boy was lying in wait for him and rushed up to seize the doctor's free hand with his small, grimy one. "Come," he cried, pulling him toward a malodorous tenement.

The doctor resisted. The child barely reached his waist.

"Please, Doctor," the boy cried, "please take a look at her. Just a little look. She's not eating anything and she throws up all the time."

No use pointing out that people don't vomit what they haven't swallowed. Doctor Yamada held his breath as he ducked into the small, dark hole where a woman was lying on a straw pallet, covered with a ragged piece of cloth. She looked up at him from dull eyes in a worn, middle-aged face. But poverty and illness add years, and he was not surprised when she told him that she was only twenty years old. There was no one else except her son. Yamada did not ask, but the boy's father had probably left, if he had ever shared a roof with them. Three other children had died, she said. Now there were only the two of them. She told him these things pleadingly, with a glance at her son. Yamada thought: only twenty, and four children already? The poor started young and burned out quickly. The "vomiting" was not from food. She was bringing up blood and would die soon. But he left her medicine and some money for nourishing soup and wine to give her strength. And he told the child where to find him.

Their smiles were full of hope and relief. He bit his lip, tousled the boy's hair, and left.

The sunny autumn morning seemed dimmed when he emerged from the tenement. He took the bridge over the Kamo River and walked into the leafy eastern suburbs without taking the customary pleasure in the lush trees and the gilded roofs and spires of pagodas and palaces.

The Retired Emperor's palace was large. His cook lived in better quarters than many an impoverished nobleman who huddled with family and servants in some ruined mansion in the old part of the city. Doctor Yamada was shown to the ailing man's room which overlooked a garden full of thriving cabbages and onions. The fat cook was sitting up in his comfortable bedding, his shaven head polished to a shine, and his huge belly decorously covered by a flowered robe. A tray with a number of empty dishes stood beside him. He was clearly feeling better and had a visitor who sat on a cushion beside him.

Doctor Yamada glanced at the stranger, who was older than he and not particularly handsome with his square face and incipient jowls. He wore silk but no hat, which meant that he had walked here from his private quarters in the palace. No doubt he was some minor functionary in one of the Retired Emperor's bureaus. Since the visitor regarded him with a cheerful smile, Yamada made him a small bow, then turned to his patient. "And how much food have you consumed this morning, Kosugi?" he asked, frowning at the tray. "Are you bound and determined to disobey my instructions?"

Kosugi gulped and rubbed his shiny scalp. "I'm much better, Doctor. An empty belly undermines a man's strength, and I must get back to work today." He shot a glance at his visitor.

Yamada snorted his disbelief. Kosugi, like most fat men, enjoyed his rest, and this time he had been sick enough to claim at least two more days of leisure. The doctor lifted one of the empty dishes and smelled it. "What is this? Surely not fried fish? Are you mad? What else did you devour, you great gobble-guts?"

The visitor chuckled at this.

The cook blushed. "Just a little rice, that's all. And a very small egg. A few vegetables. And a pickle or two."

"A pickle or two? I told you to stay away from raw things and from salt and vinegar, and you eat pickles?" Yamada looked at him in disgust. "I trust at least you avoided mental activity and sexual intercourse."

Kosugi brightened. "Of course, Doctor. I was most particular about those."

The visitor laughed softly.

Yamada set down his case and bent to prod Kosugi's fat belly. "Does this hurt?" he asked when his patient grimaced.

"No, but . . ." muttered the cook, ". . . can't it wait till later?"

"Why? I'm a busy man. People are dying while you waste my time."

Kosugi rolled his eyes toward the visitor who said, "You should have introduced us, Kosugi. Your manners are abominable."

Kosugi flushed. "It's only Doctor Yamada, Sire."

Sire? Yamada swung around, shocked. The stranger looked delighted by his confusion. Panicked by his mistake, the doctor knelt, touching his head to the boards. "I beg your pardon, Your Majesty."

A soft laugh. "Of course, of course. How could you know, Doctor? Please get up and continue. Your examination is most instructive."

Yamada sat up. So this was the retired emperor? This unassuming man in the gray silk robe, sitting on the floor beside his cook? He looked at him nervously. The Emperor smiled. He has bad teeth, Yamada thought and felt a little better.

"I suffer occasionally from an excess of wind," the emperor told him affably. "Naturally I blame it on Kosugi's terrible cooking, but I don't have the heart to throw out the fat slug. What do you recommend, Doctor?"

Before he could stop himself, Yamada said, "Throwing out the fat slug would solve two problems, Sire, yours and his. He eats too much of his own rich cooking."

The emperor laughed heartily. "You hear him, Kosugi? He is a learned man. Who are we to question his wisdom?"

Kosugi looked shaken. He scrambled to his knees and clasped his hands beseechingly. "Sire, please don't listen to him. He's only a quack. What does he know about fine cooking? Lord Kiyomori praises my dishes, and Her Majesty always asks for my sweet dumplings when she visits."

The Emperor waved a hand. "Don't worry. I like your dumplings, too. But the doctor is quite right.

Rich food does not agree with a man's constitution. A beggar's life is hard, but at least he will not die from overeating. Is that not so, Doctor?"

Yamada was angry with both of them. He was normally mild-mannered and did not stand on his dignity, but when a mere cook, who only yesterday had been weeping and begging for relief, called him a quack, he drew the line. And having just visited a young woman who was dying, not from excess but from abject poverty, he said harshly, "Men die as easily from hunger, sire. But since Kosugi thinks so little of my skills, I shall leave him to his fate. I have more deserving patients waiting." He bowed very deeply to the emperor, then snatched up his case and left the room.

No doubt, they were too astonished to stop him.

Yamada strode off, still fuming, past the elegant halls and out through the palace gates. Halfway home, it occurred to him that he had just lost his only respectable patient and that Otori would blame him. And next he realized that he no longer had any excuse to see Toshiko again.

That he might also have offended the emperor did not bother him at all.

The Dragon King

The Retired Emperor sat on his dais, his feet crossed at the ankles, and his stiff black silk robe spread neatly around him. A step below him kneeled the men who ruled the nation under his direction. Though the meeting was formal and of great significance, most of them had just realized it was a token affair.

The Fujiwara regent was in attendance, along with the three great ministers, and three high-ranking councilors. They were all middle-aged men. The regent represented the reigning Emperor—who was the Retired Emperor's little grandson—and looked unhappy but resigned.

Except for Chancellor Kiyomori, they were all senior Fujiwara nobles who had survived two turbulent purges and had earned their high ranks and positions because of their loyalty. The Retired Emperor knew that they respected him and feared Kiyomori. He was, as always, intensely aware that, but for Kiyomori, none of them would be sitting here today. Kiyomori had saved all their lives and the throne.

Twice.

Listening with half an ear to the regent's recital of the laws of succession, the emperor watched Kiyomori.

The Taira clan chief and the nation's chancellor was nearly fifty, a large man who dominated any crowd and had been a fine warrior like his father before him. But these days, Kiyomori was a courtier-official, someone who wore fine silks and brocades and who perfumed his robes with rare incense and carried painted fans. Yet he was as deadly in the political arena of the council chamber as on the battlefield.

At the moment Kiyomori was staring at the floor, tapping his fingers, impatient with the painstaking way in which Kanezane was citing every last precedent for choosing a crown prince. He had brought a fan when he arrived, an exceptionally fine one made of cedar wood and covered with painting and calligraphy, but when the Retired Emperor had admired it, Kiyomori had pressed him to accept it as a gift. So now Kiyomori tapped his fingers instead of fanning himself.

The Emperor looked at the fan and pursed his lips. The painting was a scene from the tale of the dragon king's daughter in the Lotus Sutra. A religious theme. Or was it? The colors were very rich, especially the figure of the dragon king, who was covered with jewels and pearls. The landscape was lovely also. It showed Kiyomori's family shrine at Itsukushima on the shores of the Inland Sea – the Inland Sea which was the legendary home of the dragon king who was also the clan deity of the Taira family.

The Lotus Sutra told the story of the dragon king's eight-year-old daughter who won salvation because she was both devout and clever. She changed herself into a male in order to fulfill qualifications that can be met by men only. Women liked this tale and spent much time copying the passage and presenting it to their favorite temples to remind Buddha that even a woman may have a chance at eternal life.

The Retired Emperor did not think that religious significance had been in Kiyomori's mind when he had commissioned the fan. He, too, was the father of a girl, and Noriko was about eight by now, like the dragon king's daughter.

He raised his eyes from the fan to glance at Kiyomori. Their eyes met, and Kiyomori smiled and nodded. At that moment the Retired Emperor caught a glimpse of the future envisioned by Kiyomori and understood why Kiyomori had brought this particular fan today, knowing full well that he would ask to see it.

He disliked being manipulated, especially by Kiyomori.

It was tempting to judge a man by his actions. In some ways, Kiyomori's character was transparent: he was motivated in all his actions by the relentless pursuit of power. Such men should be feared. They were dangerous and, when successful, easily hated. Kiyomori had been very successful and had gained for himself the hatred of many men.

But the bonds between them were very old, and very strong and close. They were alike in many ways: in their faith, in their love for all the arts, and in their single-minded desire to rule the nation. But there was more: Kiyomori was said to be a son of Emperor Shirakawa. If the story was true, they had the same blood, and they shared a past and the bitterness of being a rejected by their fathers. Emperor Shirakawa had seen fit to bestow his pregnant concubine on Taira Tadamori, his favorite general, as a token of his gratitude.

Had Tadamori been appreciative? And how had she felt? Did Kiyomori know the truth of the matter? Had his parents explained it to him?

When Kiyomori had been a boisterous young warrior, he had taken potshots at the armed monks of Enryakuji, and when the Retired Emperor had been a very young Prince Masahito, he had idolized him for it. Kiyomori had been his hero. He had wanted to be like him. He had wanted him for his brother instead of the cold and arrogant Emperor Sutoku.

But Kiyomori had played the role of a favored subject – politely and with due respect for the young prince and humble acceptance of his own inferior place.

Now the Retired Emperor sat on his dais and wondered how a man like Kiyomori dealt with such disappointment. He had risen to unimaginable power since those days. The young Taira warrior from the western provinces had quickly become a general, a governor, a court noble of the third rank, and now the chancellor. He was his brother-in-law, because Kiyomori's wife's younger sister was his Consort and the mother of Prince Norihito who was the subject of this meeting.

Kiyomori's hair was thinner and gray now, and his skin was pale from spending most of his time inside. He was a warrior no longer, and he never acted on impulse these days.

All this fuss about naming a crown prince. The Retired Emperor himself had been passed over for the sickly Konoe, and would have been passed over again if his father had not finally felt embarrassed. But he had been made to abdicate after only three years.

It was his turn now to name a crown prince. That was why they were meeting.

Kiyomori, who had dominated the discussion from the beginning, now forced the decision. The others nodded. Kiyomori glanced at the Retired Emperor, who also nodded, thinking that perhaps he had let Kiyomori have his way in too many things.

The meeting broke up. Motofusa, the regent, still looked unhappy. He would have preferred to keep the succession in Nijo's family. Motofusa prostrated himself and departed. Kanezane and Tsunemune, ministers of the right and left, and the three councilors followed suit. The Retired Emperor muttered his thanks.

Only Kiyomori remained behind. The Retired Emperor was mildly irritated. It was done on purpose, of course, to impress the others with the fact that

Kiyomori was closer to him than they were. As if there had been any doubt in their minds.

Yes, Kiyomori's ambition had borne fruit. His obsession with power was natural if he knew of his imperial blood – if he knew that he might have been emperor but for the thoughtless way in which his natural father had passed his pregnant mother to a Taira general. On a whim. When the same whimsical disposition might have had the boy adopted by Shirakawa's empress, or Toba's, and named crown prince.

There had been a time when the Retired Emperor had believed that Kiyomori loved him unselfishly. Kiyomori had always been loyal and supportive. He had come to his aid against Sutoku. He had taken up arms again and rescued him when the Minamoto had made him and Nijo their prisoners. For that alone, Kiyomori deserved his rewards.

Kiyomori cleared his throat and startled him out of his distraction. "Yes, Kiyomori," he said. "What is on your mind?"

"Now that the succession is settled, sire, we should consider that the Emperor is only two, a delicate age. It will be years before he can father an heir, and many things may happen in the meantime. The nation is in unrest."

Ah, yes. Here it was. And he had no reason to oppose it. He wanted another son on the throne as soon as possible. But Kiyomori did not want Mochihito to succeed, though he was the oldest and the obvious choice. Kiyomori wanted Norihito, the fourth prince, because he had Taira blood. And so it was to be Norihito. Only, Kiyomori wanted more. He wanted a Taira emperor on the throne so that he could rule through him.

For form's sake, he muttered, "Emperor Nijo intended his own line to continue, and my father, Emperor Toba, and his consort, Bifukumon-in, had the same wish. Surely all is well now that we have named a crown prince in case of an unforeseen tragedy."

"Neither your father nor his consort could have predicted what would happen, sire. The security of the nation requires that we have an able ruler and a secure succession as soon as possible."

We? The Retired Emperor sighed. It was all fixed, of course. Now that Norihito had been named crown prince, the little Emperor would abdicate, and Kiyomori's nephew would ascend the throne. And Kiyomori would be made regent. The Retired Emperor opened the fan and looked at the image again.

Kiyomori, the Dragon King.

And the "Dragon King's" daughter would be the next empress. It had all worked out perfectly for Kiyomori, and he saw no reason to object.

"Another abdication?" he asked, fanning himself.

Kiyomori bowed. "An excellent idea, sire. The prince is in every respect worthy."

The Retired Emperor sighed again. "I am getting old," he said peevishly. "Norihito is only five. I have lost one son and seen my grandson become emperor.

And now another son will take over. Where will it end? I am weary of ruling for children."

Kiyomori made a strange noise. It almost sounded like suppressed laughter. The Retired Emperor frowned at him.

"Forgive me, sire," said Kiyomori, looking abashed. "Something caught in my throat. As for Your Majesty's age, why, you are in the prime of your life." He paused, then added, "I hear there is a new lady in your household."

The Retired Emperor's brows contracted. "What?"

"Again, your pardon, sire. Oba Hiramoto, one of my vassals, approached me on behalf of his daughter. It seems the young woman is very unhappy. She pines for your favor." Kiyomori smiled a little and made a dismissive gesture. They were both men of the world.

The Emperor flushed. "Since when is it your custom to enquire about my household arrangements?" he demanded.

Kiyomori bowed very deeply, keeping his head down. "I have offended again. It was only my intention to prove that Your Majesty is very far from being old."

The Emperor cleared his throat. He knew he was being flattered. With his nephew in line for the throne, Kiyomori engaged in a little pandering. No doubt, he thought that a new affair would preoccupy him and leave Kiyomori a free hand to arrange the government as he wished.

But winter was coming, and he felt old. His mind drifted to the Oba girl. She was fourteen, at the beginning of life.

"I am tired," he said and dismissed Kiyomori.

The Letter

At first, Toshiko's shame and grief knew no bounds. She wept all night, silently so that the others would not hear, and at daybreak, she did not emerge from under her covers until they had gone about their own business.

By then, she had had time to come to terms with her ruined life and stiffened her resolution. All might be lost, but no Oba surrendered meekly. She knew now that she was surrounded and outnumbered by her enemies. Children of warriors, both male and female, were raised to fight to the death, and if the battle was lost and death did not come to them, they knew how to end their lives rather than live in shame.

Toshiko had thought of using the sharp dagger that rested, wrapped in a fine piece of figured silk, among her possessions in her trunk. It had been her father's gift to her when she was born and had marked his acceptance of her as his daughter. Her brothers had received swords, but she and her sister got daggers. She knew its purpose. Both her father and her mother had explained it and shown her the place on her neck where the sharp point of the dagger must enter with a quick push. They had explained the need for force and speed and warned against hesitation or half-hearted attempts, for these only prolonged the pain and revealed her cowardice. Toshiko was not afraid, but toward morning she decided that the battle had barely begun and she had lost only the first skirmish. To be sure, her defeat had been shameful because she had exposed her nakedness to a man, and that man the emperor, but with courage she might still regain some honor, and that would be better than to die now. She had this small hope because the nun had been kind to her and had praised her song.

So she rose, determined not to let her enemies see her beaten. A sort of sacred fervor seized her. Gone was the Toshiko who played with kittens and even the one who yearned hotly for the touch of the man she loved. All that was over. Indeed, her love had been doomed before it had begun. Her father's words and her mother's letter had made that very clear.

She also accepted that she was no longer the carefree girl who rode with her brothers along the river, though she would always owe obedience to her family. She was an Oba, and no Oba was afraid to face what life demanded of her.

As she dressed, she swore to herself that she would never be caught off guard again. A woman's preparations were not unlike those of a warrior going into battle, though her "armor" was altogether more insubstantial: gauzy silks in many layers, paints for the face, scented oils for her hair, and a cloud of incense to surround her. In her silver mirror, she saw that her face was blotchy and swollen from crying and applied the white paste thickly. Her eyes, she outlined in kohl and she brushed in the moth eyebrows above her real ones. Then she painted small crimson lips over her own. When she was done, the false face hid the real one as well as any visor. She brushed her tangled hair, working in the oils to straighten the kinks left behind from lying on it while it was still moist, making it shine with a bluish, metallic gloss. Finally, she dressed in one of her most flattering costumes, layering the colored gauzes carefully, tying a sash firmly around her small waist, and covering all with a finely embroidered jacket. The colors were bright and cheerful, as if she were celebrating a special day.

The others glanced her way and whispered but they did not speak to her. She was glad. She was no longer of them. She was Oba no Toshiko who fought her own battles.

Only Shojo-ben approached her a little later when they were served their morning rice.

"May I join you?" she asked a little shyly, bringing her tray with her.

This was not Shojo-ben's usual manner. They had become good friends and normally chatted easily. But all was different now, and the new Toshiko welcomed the distance.

"Of course," she said, moving aside politely to make room for Shojo-ben's full skirts.

Shojo-ben knelt daintily and took a little sip from her bowl. She did not seem to know how to start. Finally she said, "Lady Sanjo told us that His Majesty sent for you to ask about songs."

"Yes. I know some *imayo*."

Shojo-ben leaned forward to peer at Toshiko's face. "Is that what you have been humming?"

"Yes." Toshiko volunteered nothing.

Shojo-ben sighed and ate a little more. Then she said sadly, "I envy you. I wish I had a talent that might please Him."

These artless words undid Toshiko's resistance. She put down her food. "Oh, Shojo-ben," she said, "you are very charming and much more elegant than I am. Surely He takes notice of you."

But Shojo-ben shook her head. "You are the only one He has sent for in years. Except, of course, Lady Sanjo, and her only because she makes her reports." She giggled behind her hand. "She tries harder than any of us. I have never been near him. Sometimes at night I wonder what it would be like." She covered her face, and cried, "Oh, please forget I said that."

Toshiko had also lain awake dreaming at night, but not of the emperor. She said firmly, "It wasn't like that, Shojo-ben. There was an old nun there. They talked about *imayo* and *shirabyoshi*."

Shojo-ben brightened a little. "He is so handsome," she murmured, adding wistfully, "and you are so pretty. He will soon send for you again and then you will be alone together."

Toshiko felt the blush under her stiff make-up. She said quickly, "His Majesty is nearly as old as my father."

Her friend choked on some gruel and started coughing. When Toshiko looked up, she saw that several of the others were watching them avidly. The thought struck her that they had sent Shojo-ben to question her. This suspicion stiffened her resolve. She raised her chin defiantly and said, "Well, perhaps not quite so old . . . and perhaps . . ." She let her voice trail off.

Shojo-ben dabbed at her lips. "What does age matter? Of course He will like you," she said enviously. "How could He not?"

Toshiko smiled and got up to take back her tray. "We shall see," she said lightly.

At this point, Lady Sanjo arrived for her morning inspection. She stared hard at Toshiko's elaborate costume and asked in an acerbic tone, "Do you consider those colors suitable?"

Toshiko bowed. "I think so, Lady Sanjo. I believe His Majesty is fond of this shade."

Lady Sanjo flushed and moved on to someone else. But later, when Toshiko was reading quietly in her corner, she returned and sat down beside her.

"What happened last night after I left?" she asked bluntly.

Toshiko gave her a startled look, then lowered her head. "I had rather not say."

"Nonsense," Lady Sanjo said firmly. "I am in charge of His Majesty's ladies. They have no secrets from me."

Toshiko remained silent.

Lady Sanjo cleared her throat and tried again in a softer voice. "My dear girl," she said, "please realize that I am your friend. Put your trust in me. I stand in your own dear mother's place now. Surely you would wish to discuss certain matters with your mother."

Still Toshiko did not speak.

"A young woman at court encounters many difficulties," Lady Sanjo said after a moment. "You saw what happened last night. If you had confided in me that His Majesty wished you to sing for him, I could so easily have spared you that shameful exposure."

Toshiko bowed her head a little more and thought of the deceitful ways of fox spirits who tempted humans only to devour them later.

Lady Sanjo sighed. "Well, no harm was done, I think. In fact, His Majesty seemed to enjoy your song. Am I right?"

Toshiko murmured, "His Majesty was very kind."

Lady Sanjo's eyes widened a little. She studied the slight figure before her. "He is a very kind man. What exactly did He say . . . or do?"

"I . . . don't remember much."

"I am sure you were quite overwhelmed by the honor. His Majesty's visitor left, I assume?"

Something that the nun had said suddenly came back to Toshiko, and she looked up into the avid eyes. "Her name is Otomae. She told me that His Majesty particularly likes *imayo* and that I dance very well. She said many years ago she herself used to dance for His Majesty but that she is too old now."

Lady Sanjo was not interested in the old nun. She smiled a little and nodded. "And then?" she asked. "She left you alone with Him?"

Toshiko knew what the woman wanted to hear. She dropped her eyes. "His Majesty honored me greatly," she whispered so softly that Lady Sanjo had to ask her to repeat it.

"His Majesty honored me greatly," said Toshiko a little louder, and not entirely truthfully.

Lady Sanjo gave a gasp. "You mean . . .?" She stopped and tried again, "My dear Toshiko, I wish to be of assistance in every way. Only ask, I pray."

"Thank you, Lady Sanjo. You are very good, but I have no questions."

"Surely if a very young woman, and you are barely past your childhood, were to receive the attentions, I mean the very particular attentions, of His Majesty, she might find the experience overwhelming at first. I think you may have found last night confusing. As a married woman, I can help you understand and guide you so that you will prove worthy of the distinction. Do you understand?"

Turning her face away, her embarrassment now quite real, Toshiko nodded her head. Lady Sanjo moved closer and put an arm around her shoulders. "Come, my dear," she said, "was it so very frightening? Did His Majesty hurt you?"

Toshiko turned her head and looked at Lady Sanjo in surprise. "Oh, no, Lady Sanjo. His Majesty was very gentle."

They were so close now that she could see the hot color under Lady Sanjo's make-up. The other woman moistened her lips. "He was?" she asked, looking at her hungrily.

Toshiko nodded.

"I'm glad," Lady Sanjo gasped—her breathing was becoming quite rapid. "In the case of His Majesty you may feel awkward speaking of such things but . . ." She faltered and looked almost faint.

"Are you ill, Lady Sanjo?" Toshiko asked solicitously. "Please do not upset yourself so. You are very kind, but my mother has explained. And as you say, it is not proper to speak of such things."

"Yes. That is very true," said Lady Sanjo, gulping for air. "I only offer advice if it should be needed." She took another breath. "Those pretty songs of yours. Perhaps you could teach me a few? People say I have a pleasant voice."

Toshiko made a vague promise, then claimed that she had to write to her family – an excuse which Lady Sanjo received with no surprise – and departed for her eave chamber.

When she was finally alone, in the room which would always be that of her love, she started to tremble. That she could have said or implied the things she had now struck her as incredible and most reprehensible. They were lies, all lies, to make them think that she had found favor when He had looked at her in disgust, and had not spoken to her until He sent her away. Her shame and the knowledge that they would gloat at her ruin had made her pretend what was not true.

After a while, she calmed down and went to sit near the shutter, opening it a little, to peer out. The veranda was, as always, empty. A light dusting of snow had dulled everything, and gray clouds covered the sky. It was a sad day, and Toshiko took out her mother's letter again.

"Dear daughter," Lady Oba had written. "It is good that you are well. I pray every day for your success. As you know, both your father and Lord Kiyomori wish this. We believe that it is your fate to bring greatness to your family for generations to come.

"As for your future: a woman's life is in the hands of the gods. If your path brings you suffering, then it is your karma that it be thus. You must accept it, as I have done, and as your sister will in due time. Pray to find the strength to forget yourself and serve the future generations. And may the gods then bless you with the joy of having prevailed in adversity."

Toshiko had hidden this letter next to her skin for weeks now. Every time she took it out she remembered him who had brought it – carrying it next to his heart as she did now – and she was again filled with a wild longing. But as soon as she unfolded it to read her mother's words, she knew that this was the suffering her mother was speaking of. She must bear it and strive to forget.

Today she thought about her parents' wish and how she had failed them even when she was trying to obey. She did not believe that there could be joy in prevailing in this particular adversity but she knew that she must have the courage to try again. She needed the daring of a warrior about to go into a battle to the death. In families like hers, the women grew up absorbing the lessons taught to the men. Toshiko used to be angry with fate for making her a mere girl. In all of her brothers' undertakings – except for Takehira's pursuit of bed partners – she had attempted to equal or perhaps even outdo them, much to their father's amusement. She knew she was a better rider; she could even stand on the back of a galloping horse. In archery, she equaled Takehira, though she could not manage to draw a large bow the way he could. She had learned to wield both a sword and a halberd. But none of those things mattered now because she was a woman. It seemed to her that men had the easier part. In her battle, the woman must die in order to prevail.

She felt like weeping for the Toshiko who would be no more but put away such childishness along with the letter.

Every Day is a Good Day

Otori was not immediately aware of the loss of another promising patient. The cook had sent a whole sea bream to the doctor's house – which was only as it should be in her opinion – and nothing else happened. Her master tended to the poor now that the frost had killed most of the plants. He said little and looked unhappy.

"So," she asked one day when she came to take away his morning gruel bowl, "when will you go back to the palace?"

He did not raise his head. "Kosugi is well again. There is no need for me to go back."

She gave him a sharp look. He sounded melancholy. This, along with the half-eaten gruel, meant something was still wrong. "He sent the bream," she said. "It was excellent, but you ate only a little. Why is that?"

He looked at her then in that distracted way he had lately. "What bream?" he asked.

She gave a disgusted snort and left the room.

That afternoon, a ragged child came to the door. He was no more than five or six years old, shivered with cold, and looked half starved. Otori muttered something, dove back into her kitchen, and returned with a bowl of warm rice. The boy hesitated a moment, then took it, and ran away.

"Wait, you thieving little rascal," she shouted after him. "Bring back my bowl." Too late. The child was gone.

To her surprise, the little thief returned the next morning, without the bowl.

"Where's my bowl?" she demanded.

The child backed away a little and looked at her with frightened eyes.

She glowered at him. "Well, you won't get anything else until you bring back the bowl. Do you hear?"

He moved away then but squatted under a tree across the road. And there he stayed all day, in the cold, his eyes on the doctor's house. Otori hardened her heart. She did not have any bowls to spare, not when the master had no more paying clients and didn't go out to find any.

The next day, the child was there again. She left a stale rice cake by the gate, but the boy made no attempt to take it, and a stray dog found it instead.

Around midday, the doctor could not bear his own company any longer and decided to leave. Stepping carefully through the ruts in the road, he did not notice the waiting child, but the boy ran after him and pulled his sleeve.

"Yes, what is it?" the doctor asked. He did not recognize him. How could he? Theirs had been a brief meeting many days ago, mostly inside a dark hovel, and Doctor Yamada's thoughts were on another matter.

The boy's teeth chattered. He said urgently, "They've taken her away, sir."

"What?" The doctor puzzled over this. "Does someone need a doctor? Did they send you for me?"

The boy shook his head.

"Come, child. It is cold. We cannot stand here all day. If you haven't come about a sick person, what do you want?"

The boy shot him an uneasy glance and hung his head. Doctor Yamada sighed. Just another small beggar, sent out by his parents. There were countless miseries in this world, and every day brought new ones. He took a few coppers off the string he carried in his sash and offered them to the boy. To his surprise he put his hands behind his back, then turned and slowly walked away.

The doctor stood dumfounded for a moment, his hand still extended, when a dim memory surfaced. *They've taken her away.* "Wait," he called, and hurried after the child.

The boy stopped but did not turn around or lift his head.

"You are the boy whose mother was ill? The woman who was spitting up . . ." – he almost said "blood," but decided against it. "How is she?" But he knew what the answer would be. The boy's demeanor told him.

"They've taken her away," the boy said again, only this time he added, "They've thrown everything out and locked the door."

Doctor Yamada crouched down so he could look into the child's face. It was blue with cold and very dirty. Small pale streaks in the dirt showed that he had cried. "Did your mother die?" he asked gently.

The child looked away. His lower lip trembled a little. "They've taken her away and they're not letting me in. The landlord said to go away."

The doctor bit his lip and rose. "I'm sorry," he said. "Your mother was very ill. But now that you have come, we'll go back to my house and see if Otori can find you something to eat." Food was the only comfort he could offer. That and warmth. "You can stay with me until we think what to do." He took the child's icy hand and started back toward his house.

The boy's feet dragged a little as they got closer. "Your wife is angry," he said shyly. "I lost her bowl."

"I have no wife," said the doctor. More was the pity.

Just then the door flew open, and Otori stood there, her hands on her hips. "So," she said, "the little thief's found someone else to rob. You'd better watch out. He steals, just like the other young rascal you brought home."

The boy crept behind the doctor and peered around him with frightened eyes.

"Nonsense," said Yamada, giving Otori a fierce look. "He's the son of a patient. I told him to come to me. And he is much too young to be a thief."

"Hah, he ran away with my bowl only two days ago," Otori snapped. But she stepped aside and let them come into the house. "Ask him where my bowl is. It was a good one."

"Get some hot food," said the doctor, "and bring it to my room." He took the child through the house and into his own room where he stirred up the brazier and added some charcoal. Then he made the boy sit next to it and took off his wet, ragged socks and rubbed some warmth back into the small feet.

The child let it happen without comment, but when he was covered with the doctor's own quilted bedding, he began to look around curiously at everything.

"What's out there?" he asked, pointing to the closed shutters.

The doctor went and cracked the shutter open a little. "My garden," he said, "and my fishpond. Only it is much prettier in the summer time when the sun dapples the shrubs and birds sing and spiders spin webs, and the daylilies nod over the fish pond. Sometimes there's a green dragonfly. He doesn't come very often, and I'm always honored by his visit." He was aware that he was talking too much, but the child's condition and his grievous loss left him feeling helpless.

The boy looked earnestly at him, then crept out of his covers and came to look at the garden. His hand curled around the doctor's fingers, and he moved a little closer to him.

"What is your name?" the doctor asked.

"Sadamu."

"Sadamu? Mine is Sadahira," said the doctor, surprised. "Imagine that! It is surely auspicious."

The boy looked up, puzzled.

"'Auspicious' means good luck," the doctor explained, smiling. "I think you are good luck for me."

Sadamu glanced back at the room, out at the garden and the fish pond, and then up at the doctor again. "Why do you need good luck?" he asked. "You have everything."

Not everything. Yamada squeezed the boy's hand. "You are welcome in my house if you would like to stay," he said, not knowing yet if the child had any relatives.

The boy nodded. Just that. His earnest expression did not change. Perhaps he was beyond grief or joy, beyond caring about the things of this world – like a disillusioned old man in a child's body.

Otori's broad feet came slapping down the corridor. She carried a tray with several bowls on it. This she set down on the doctor's desk. "Well, has he sold my bowl or does he still have it?" she asked.

The boy glanced at the tray, then at her. "The landlord took it," he said.

Yamada put his hand on the child's head. "Don't worry, Sadamu. The bowl does not matter. I have many bowls."

Otori bristled, but catching the doctor's eye, she turned and marched off, muttering under her breath, "Sadamu!"

"Come and eat," Yamada invited. "And if something is left, you can feed the fish."

There was some sort of soup, fragrant rice, and sweet dumplings. Two servings of everything. Clearly, Otori had hoped Yamada would also eat and, after offering food to the boy, he did. They sat together near the brazier and ate, the child hungrily, the man slowly, his eyes intent on the child. Before he had finished his rice, the boy got to his feet, holding the half-filled bowl.

"The fish must be hungry," he said.

The doctor carried the child out into the chilly garden and let him scatter the rice grains on the winter-black pond. The carp rushed up from the murky depths, snatching crumbs from each other and turning the surface of the pond into a swirl of brilliant orange and silver, lashing the water into spangles and flashes of refracted light.

Yamada hoped to see delight on the child's earnest face, perhaps even to hear a gurgle of laughter, but the boy merely watched. His eyes widened a little for a moment, but otherwise he was unmoved.

They returned to the warm house and finished their meal.

"Will you wait here for me," Yamada asked when all the food was gone, "or do you want to come with me?"

Sadamu wiped his hands on his wrinkled and very dirty shirt, and got up. "I'll come," he decided with a glance toward the back of the house where Otori could be heard sweeping.

They stopped in the kitchen to return the tray with the dishes, and Yamada asked Otori to wash the child's face and hands. She did so with surprising gentleness.

Then they left, hand in hand, for the tenement where the boy used to live.

The landlord, a greasy character with one eye, was leaning against the doorway, cleaning his teeth with a straw. When he saw the boy with a gentleman in a silk robe, he straightened up and bobbed bow after bow. "So glad to see you again, Sadamu." He grinned, laying a clawlike hand possessively on the boy's head and rolling his one eye in Yamada's direction. "Found your family, have you?"

Sadamu kicked his shin. "Where's my mother?" he yelled. "What have you done with her?"

The landlord hopped aside and rubbed his leg. "Poor boy." He laughed a little. "He's confused and upset because his mother died."

"He is not confused," said Yamada. "What happened here?"

"Oh, you don't know? She died two nights ago. Owing me money, too. I'm a poor man and had to rent the place again."

"Where is she now?"

"The monks came and took her away. About my money . . ."

Doctor Yamada looked at him with distaste. "That is none of my business. You must apply to her relatives."

The man's jaw sagged. "But I thought you . . ."

"What was her name and where was she from?" the doctor snapped.

"She said her name was Miyuko. And that she was a soldier's widow." The landlord snorted. "Not that I believed it. More likely she was a whore."

"Come," said the doctor to the boy. They turned to go.

"Wait!" The landlord took a few steps after them. "The kid's mine. She owed for two months."

Without releasing the boy, the doctor turned on the landlord. Taking him by the front of his filthy robe, he pushed him back against the wall of the tenement. "What do you mean, the child is yours?" he demanded.

A passing mendicant priest, elderly and unkempt, stopped to watch the altercation.

The landlord squealed, "He's got to work off the debt. He's big enough. The law's on my side."

Yamada released him abruptly. "I am Doctor Yamada. Tomorrow you may bring the warden to my house. If your bill is correct, you will be paid."

To the boy, he said, "Don't worry. It will all be settled. Now let's see about your mother's funeral and then we'll go home. Tomorrow's another day."

The priest heard him and nodded. "Every day's a good day as long as you don't think about the past or worry about the future." He smiled a toothless smile and extended his empty bowl.

The Little Snail

The call for Toshiko did not come until two days after her disastrous performance. This time she was ready. She had been ready every day and all day, her face fully made up, her costume exquisite, her hair brushed and oiled. It had been a matter of self-discipline.

Her courage was much more difficult to maintain. As she hurried down the long, polished corridor toward the Emperor's apartment, her heart beat so violently that her ears were ringing.

She entered and saw that he was again in the company of the nun and had writing utensils and papers spread out on a small desk and on the mat beside him. Her relief was almost dizzying. She approached on soft feet and prostrated herself.

"Ah, Toshiko," the emperor greeted her affably. "Please come and join us. I am trying to finish a part of my collection of songs before the pilgrimage."

He was leaving on a pilgrimage? Toshiko looked at Him in dismay. How was she to accomplish what she must do if He was about to leave – for many weeks. She had heard about His frequent visits to worship at the Kumano shrines but had somehow thought there would be time.

"Why, what is the matter?" he asked, raising his brows at her expression.

She felt the blood rise hotly under her make-up. "I . . . did not know, sire. I did not know you are leaving." Even she could hear the grief in her words.

The emperor smiled and extended a hand toward her. "Come, my dear," He said in the friendliest manner. "I am not leaving quite so soon."

Slightly dazed she went and took his hand. It was warm and soft. As she touched it, she felt a slight thrill run up her arm and warmth spread through her body. He pulled her down on a cushion beside him and said, "We shall have time together before I leave, and I shall come back a better man than I am now, I hope. And while I am gone, I shall remember to say a prayer to the gods that you will be waiting for me when I return."

She was speechless and merely looked at him gratefully. It could not be this easy, could it? But no. They were not alone. Otomae was sitting there, regarding them with a knowing little smile. And behind the daytime screens, the curtained dais where He slept, lay in darkness, its draperies drawn around it. She felt hot and breathless.

The moment passed. The emperor turned to his papers, selecting a sheet, and handed it to her. "Can you read this? Will you see if it is correct?"

His brush strokes were more elegant than any she had ever seen. She read the poem. It was the song she had performed last time, and shame flooded over her again. She dropped the sheet and covered her face with both hands.

"What? Is my calligraphy so horrid you cannot bear to look at it?" He teased.

She could smell His scent. He was so close that it almost made her dizzy. "No, sire," she murmured. "It is the song I performed. I am so ashamed."

She felt his hands on hers, pulling them from her face, and raised her eyes. He looked very kind and smiled a little. She thought that his eyes were as gentle as a doe's.

"You have no need to be ashamed, Toshiko," He said. "I am getting very impatient with that aging virago who seems to take out her own discontent on you. She meant to embarrass you and make me send you away. It did not work. I thought you enchanting, and I hope you will honor me with another dance tonight."

She forgot that they were not alone. Her hands lay in his warm ones. She could not keep them from trembling a little, but so intensely aware was she of his touch that she did not want to take them back. And so they sat for a long moment absorbed in each other, and Toshiko felt with amazement for the first time a sense of power.

He finally released her hands with a slight squeeze. "Otomae," he said, turning to the nun, "will you help Toshiko with the costume?" He gestured toward a lacquered trunk decorated with flying geese. Otomae smiled and got up. She moved somewhat painfully. The emperor said to Toshiko, "Go with her, my dear. It would give me great pleasure to see you dance just the way your teacher Akomaro did."

Toshiko was much younger than Otomae, but she found her legs strangely unsteady when she stood. Otomae was holding a white silk jacket, cut like a man's hunting cloak, and a pair of pleated red silk trousers, the traditional costume of shrine maidens and shirabyoshi. Where was she to change? The nun did not waste any time. She quickly gathered Toshiko's long, loose hair and tied it in back with a white silk ribbon. Then she removed the embroidered Chinese jacket and laid it aside. When Otomae untied her sash and let it fall to the floor, Toshiko realized that she was being undressed here, before the emperor's eyes, and murmured a protest.

Otomae paused to look at her. "It is for His Majesty," she said softly. "Do not be afraid to give him pleasure."

And so, layer after layer, the colored gauze gowns were removed and laid aside. Toshiko kept her eyes on the floor and turned obediently when Otomae tugged her this way and that. And then she wore nothing but her thin white under gown and the white trouser skirt. The cool silk moved against her hot skin, and she shivered. She remembered how it had felt when the fabric had clung wetly to her breasts and raised her hands protectively. Her eyes flew to the Emperor. He looked back, intently, and smiled a little at her gesture.

When Otomae reached for the ribbons that held Toshiko's full trousers around her waist, Toshiko shuddered away from her touch.

"I think that is enough, Otomae," the Emperor said. "Toshiko may dress in complete costume next time."

"Raise your arms, child," instructed the nun. She wound the long sash tightly around Toshiko's waist, making her turn like a top with her arms in the air, and when she was done, she attached the long, gold-embossed sword to the sash with red silk cords. Then she helped Toshiko into the full-sleeved man's jacket and tied a man's tall black hat on her head. Except for her long hair, Toshiko looked like a young courtier.

It was a strange and uncomfortable costume to dance in. Akomaro had explained that shirabyoshi dance in men's clothing to tease a male audience and make them wonder what was under the clothing, but His Majesty had just watched Toshiko's transformation. There was little left for him to wonder about.

Otomae placed an open fan into Toshiko's hand, then stepped aside. His Majesty nodded. "Charming," he said. "Now, my dear, what will you dance for us?"

Because she was still ashamed, Toshiko chose one of Akomaro's religious songs, "When I hear the Lotus Sutra."

The emperor chuckled, but Otomae gave her an approving nod and took up a hand drum to start the throbbing measure of the dance. Otomae was very skilled, and Toshiko was fond of the Buddha song and poured out all of her hopes and secret prayers. "My body shines like a brilliant mirror," she sang, "and my heart becomes the heart of Buddha." When she was done, it took her a moment to return to the present.

His Majesty was silent at first but then He applauded. "Excellent. This song is new to me, and the delivery is quite unusual. This Akomaro was a true artist."

Toshiko bowed deeply. "Akomaro was perfection itself. I am only a poor student."

"Will you write down the words of all the songs you remember?"

"Yes, sire."

He patted the pillow beside him. "Come here."

She went to kneel beside him, feeling strange with the hat on her head and the awkward sword by her side. He did not really like my performance, she thought. He was disappointed. That is why he wanted me to sit down again.

As if to prove her correct, the Emperor turned to the nun. "Otomae, will you favor us next?"

Otomae shook her head. "No, sire," she said – though no one ever says no to the emperor. "I am old and have put aside the things of this world, except for the memories you keep stirring up. Dancing is for the young." She smiled at Toshiko. "Pleasure is for those who are still in the world, sire."

There was a brief and strangely weighty silence, then the Emperor said, "You know that I make no distinction between the performance of imayo and religion. As for my being in the world, I shall follow your advice, but you must not refuse me your help in this matter."

Toshiko looked from one to the other. Something significant had just passed between them, something that affected her.

Otomae hesitated, then got to her feet. "Because I bear you great respect, sire, I will just this once, dance for you. I have a song in mind that I would have you remember in the months to come. It is called 'Dance, Little Snail.'"

"Oh, I know it," cried Toshiko. "It is charming but sad . . ."

They looked at her in surprise, and she stopped, embarrassed.

"Go on," said His Majesty.

She stammered, "Well, Akomaro said it was very sad but I never knew what she meant."

The emperor reached for a box and took out a plain flute. "I also know it. It is not sad at all. Give us your version, Otomae." He put the flute to his lips and played a few notes.

Toshiko became wide-eyed with surprise. "Oh," she cried, "how beautiful! I did not know you played so well, sire." It was a very stupid thing to say, and she immediately clasped a hand over her treacherous lips.

He lowered the flute, leaned a little closer, and whispered, "For such a charming compliment, I promise to play often for you, little one. We shall make music together all night long. Perhaps we shall even drown out the cuckoo's cry that marks the dawn."

Toshiko understood his meaning. Face flaming, she bowed. "I scarcely know if this is a dream," she murmured. "Perhaps the cuckoo will wake me." He laughed softly, and her heart pounded so that she pressed a hand to her chest to still it. But the gesture reminded her of Lady Sanjo and she quickly lowered it again and took a deep breath. He laughed again and reached for her hand.

Otomae cleared her throat, and they drew apart like children caught at a forbidden game. The emperor snatched up his flute again and began to play in earnest.

Otomae moved her fan with extraordinary grace, but Toshiko watched blindly, her breathing shallow and rapid. She knew she should pay attention but was much too conscious of Him. Otomae's voice had astonishing strength and sweetness. It was full and had a much greater range than Toshiko's, and as she sang, a powerful emotion seemed to flow from her to Toshiko.

Dance, little snail,
Dance!
Don't falter, snail,
Or my horse will kick,
My horse will stamp,

My horse will crush you.

And Otomae's foot stamped and ground the invisible snail into the soil, until the viciousness of her words and movements seemed like a knife in Toshiko's belly.

Then the nun paused, adjusted her posture, and changed her tone and melody to cheerful banter:

But if you dance well for me,

I'll let you dance in my garden.

There was a moment's silence when she stopped. Then the emperor applauded. "You have not forgotten your art," he said. "That was wonderful. Will you repeat the song with this child? I have a great desire to see you dance together."

But Otomae begged to be excused, and the emperor did not press her.

Toshiko thought that they would have made an odd pair, a young girl beside an aged nun – like something seen in a magic mirror that shows the beginning and end of life. Akomaro had been in the middle of hers, at the height of her skills of giving men pleasure. Now Toshiko's own fate had begun.

The emperor asked her, "What part of the song made you sad?"

"I'm not sure, sire, but I think it is the fear the little snail must feel."

"Ah!" Otomae said quickly. "How clever you are, little one. Yes, that fear is a terrible thing. It is much more terrible than being crushed because it is the fear that forces the snail to dance."

The emperor laughed. "Come, surely nothing can be worse than being crushed. While the snail lives, dancing is a very pleasant occupation."

Otomae raised a thin hand. "You and I know very well what the little snail signifies, but this child does not – and yet I think she has a notion already. Have pity, sire."

The emperor flushed. "Be careful, Otomae."

The nun bowed.

Biting his lip, He turned away and took up his papers. He talked about other songs, asking about different versions. Toshiko said little. She was confused and a little frightened by what had just happened.

And by what was to come.

A short while later, the guards outside twanged their bowstrings and announced the hour of the boar. His Majesty dismissed the two women abruptly and without his earlier smiles.

The Consort Pays a Visit

The day after the "Little Snail" incident, the Emperor threw himself into the planning of his pilgrimage. He had not liked Otomae's warning and did not believe that for a woman love meant terror because the man forced her into compliance.

The little snail must dance or be crushed.

Worse, she had implied that men assumed women enjoyed being taken. At first he had been angry, but the matter began to trouble him, filling him with new doubts about his intentions.

After a restless night weighing his desire for Toshiko against possibly painful regrets, he decided to seek spiritual enlightenment. He emptied his mind of lustful thoughts and spent the pre-dawn hours in prayer and meditation. After sunrise, he kept his secretaries busy with the details of the pilgrimage. He consulted them about new temples and shrines to visit and checked his budget for further generous donations and endowments to religious communities. He received a group of clerics and discussed their needs (they always had needs) and asked for spiritual advice on how to cleanse his mind of worldly matters. They offered the same old lessons: Empty your mind by meditating on the Buddha. He resolved to try harder.

Then, around midday, he got the news that his Consort had arrived.

This lady was not the mother of the late emperor Nijo – with her he maintained friendly but distant relations. No, this was Shigeko, mother of the new crown prince and sister-in-law of Chancellor Kiyomori. Shigeko had been his frequent bed partner until last year when she had moved back to the capital to be closer to life in the imperial palace. Being busy with many plans at the time, he had hardly missed her.

The news of her arrival now filled him with astonishment. She rarely came and then only for brief visits. On this occasion, she had arrived with a procession of court carriages and mounted attendants, bringing along her ladies-in-waiting, a contingent of Taira warriors, and the little crown prince.

In one respect, the visit was natural enough. He had just approved the elevation of her son to crown prince, and she wanted to express her gratitude. But he had an uneasy feeling that she was overdoing it. She had come too quickly and unannounced, and she seemed prepared for a longish stay.

Her arrival threw even a very large organization like the emperor's retirement palace into turmoil.

From the moment of the first message, people were running in and out of his private office with questions about arrangements until he gave up and went to seek out his wife.

Shigeko was in the North Hall, in apartments set aside for her. Everything was in a state of confusion with maids rushing about, carrying parcels, trunks, and folding screens. He paused in the doorway to look for his wife and saw her directing two ladies in the best placement of a painted screen.

And then his mind played a trick on him. Seeing the familiar figure of his consort, he found himself comparing it to the young girl who had stirred fires he had not felt for a long time. Shigeko was small, but she had learned to walk like an empress, slowly and upright, showing off her train and her many lined gowns to perfection.

Toshiko, for all her youth, was both taller and more strongly built, perhaps because some warrior families raised their women as if they were men. The image of her on horseback flashed again across his mind and suddenly, even as he watched his wife, he was again consumed by the same wild lust.

So much for his good resolutions.

Someone saw him then and alerted Shigeko. She turned, bowed, and went to seat herself on the curtained dais, where her ladies spread her skirts around her. She was beautifully gowned as always, and surrounded by equally beautifully dressed young women.

As he walked toward her, he thought that there had been a time when he would have looked her attendants over with an eye to an affair, but he had lost interest in the surreptitious bedding of hollow dolls.

The ladies prostrated themselves before him and then crept away to leave them alone.

He smiled at Shigeko. "Welcome, my dear. What a happy surprise." Sitting down beside her, he added, "My loneliness was infinite, and every morning my sleeves were drenched with tears."

She smiled back and tossed her head a little in disbelief. "Why, sire," she murmured, "how can this be, when I hear that you spend your nights singing songs?"

Aha. So that was it. Someone – Lady Sanjo, no doubt – had informed her about Toshiko. Pleased that Shigeko should rush to him because she felt threatened by a new girl in his household, he regarded her fondly.

His consort still looked very charming at twenty-four. In fact, her prettiness had caught his eye when she had not been much older than Toshiko and in his sister's service. In those days, shortly after he had abdicated, his gratitude to Kiyomori had still been at its height, and he had allowed Kiyomori's kinswoman to tempt him into an affair that had blossomed rapidly.

Yes, Shigeko had been young. And he had already been suffering from a fear of old age. Besides, when his father had forced him to abdicate, he had felt pushed aside once again. There had seemed to be nothing in his future except taking the tonsure and spending the rest of his years in prayer and abstinence.

In sheer rebellion, he had begun a passionate affair with Shigeko and, within a year, she had borne him a son. She was the daughter of a ranking official and related to Kiyomori, and he had acknowledged her and the child. With his self-confidence restored, they had settled into a comfortable relationship. She had made efforts to please him, and he had been receptive.

So now he told her that she was beautiful and that he had yearned for her. It was a kindness and not altogether an untruth.

But Shigeko refused to play the game. "I have brought you your son," she said in a businesslike manner.

"Oh?" He looked around. "Where is he? Is he much grown? Is he clever for his age? You know, of course, that he will be emperor?"

"Yes, sire, I know. Your son will be a great ruler."

"I hope so," he said with a nod, then added, "I certainly trust he will turn out to be more filial than Nijo."

The memory of those unpleasant battles with his oldest son was still amazingly painful. Nijo had preferred his grandfather's company and treated his father with the disdain that Toba had taught him. The whole court had been shocked by this. That betrayal had left wounds, and for a time he had become distant and cold to all his children.

"This time it will be different," Shigeko assured him. "Kiyomori will make certain of that."

Anger at Kiyomori's manipulations resurfaced. The emperor looked at his consort and saw that she was content, even triumphant. She knew that her elevation to empress was a foregone conclusion, and that Kiyomori would become regent for his nephew. Her face shone with the achievement. This was what all his women had wanted. Perhaps Kiyomori's hand had been in it from the very start and he had arranged for Shigeko to seduce him – in the same way that he had brought him Toshiko now.

Kiyomori, the pimp.

And what was he but a puppet in their hands, seduced by his lust into obeying their wishes?

He suppressed self-disgust and wondered why she had come to him with enough attendants and baggage for a long stay. Did she expect to share his bed again so she could bear him more children? In all decency and out of courtesy, he must oblige, of course. The notion dismayed him, but he had no time to analyze this feeling because they brought the new crown prince son to him.

The boy was lively and tore away from his nurse's hand to run to them. For his five years, Norihito was well grown and handsome. Like all children at this age, he looked adorable in his miniature court costume and with his thick hair tied into loops above each ear. The Emperor was fond of children but awkward in their company. He had no wish to hurt his own children the way his own father had hurt him, but he did not trust them either.

So now the Retired Emperor received the handsome, laughing child warily.

"Bow to His Majesty," reminded the boy's mother, and Norihito bowed charmingly.

"Come here," said his father. "Let me see you better."

The boy climbed up onto the raised dais and sat down between his mother and father.

"I'm very well. How are you?" he said, looking up at his father. Shigeko raised a hand to hide her smile. No doubt, the nurse would later tell everyone what a happy picture they made.

The Emperor looked at his son and saw, as always, with a sense of wonder the smooth, clear skin, the glossy hair, the bright eyes and soft red lips. Children were so perfectly made that no adult, no matter how beautiful, could equal them. It was a pity that, the older they became, the more they lost that perfection, that inner light which seemed to fill their bodies and made them resemble gods. His son was as pleasing to his eyes as the finest work done by the artists he employed.

For a while, the little prince bore the scrutiny with patience but he could not contain his excitement long. "They say I'm to be emperor," he informed his father. "Just like you. They say when that happens they will all lie down before me and nobody will dare look at my face. Is that true?"

The consort clicked her tongue, but his father chuckled. "It is true <u>if</u> you become emperor, but that may not be for some time and maybe never. The present emperor is younger than you and may rule for many years until he himself has sons to succeed him."

The boy frowned. "They say he may die because babies die quite often."

His mother gasped and cried, "Oh, do not say such things! They will bring you very bad luck. It is quite horrible and forbidden to speak of His Majesty's death."

Prince Norihito looked stunned by her outburst. "Why? All the women and also some of the men say so. Will we all have bad luck now?"

Shigeko gave the Emperor a helpless glance. While amused, he was uncomfortable with the topic. True, forecasting an emperor's death was a treasonable act and punished severely, and Norihito's naïve comment might be called a forecast, but the child, and those he listened to, spoke no more than the truth in everyone's mind. Small children were frail and subject to sudden death. In any case, the question was moot because very soon the little emperor would abdicate. He said rather vaguely, "Let us see what the future brings. You must wish His Majesty a long life and a peaceful reign. Meanwhile, you have much to learn before you can be a good emperor." He turned to Shigeko. "He must have a new tutor immediately. How is his calligraphy?"

Instead of answering, Shigeko signaled to the child's nurse. The woman came forward on her knees and extended a small scroll to the emperor.

It was tied with crimson silk and made of fine mulberry paper. When he unrolled it, he saw that someone had taught the child a series of signatures.

They were certainly not wasting any time. He suppressed a sigh and praised his son, adding, "But there are many, many other things to learn still. So run along now, and practice with your brush."

He was thoughtful as he looked after the boy, who scampered off, holding his nurse's hand. Norihito was still very young, but what did that matter? An emperor's duties were almost exclusively ceremonial. Norihito would be dressed up like a doll and he would be coached about what to do and what to recite for the many hundreds of annual devotions to the gods. He remembered those dull chores very well. The ruling emperor had the ear of the gods and must perform all the rituals assuring good harvests. Everything else lay in the hands of his ministers and the senior retired emperor. That was why emperors agreed to resign. It had been that way for many generations now.

Silk rustled. Shigeko was reminding him of her presence. He turned a smile on her. "He will do very well. And you? Will you be even more distant when your son is on the throne?"

She raised her fan as if to hide a blush. "It is you who are distant, sire," she murmured. For a moment she sounded almost flirtatious, but then she said, "Naturally, I shall remain close to Norihito until he is old enough to be on his own. I love my son and will do my duty as his mother."

It was simply said, and he liked her for it, but the moment's coyness in her manner had made him curious. He decided to test the waters. "But you are here now," he said suggestively, taking her hand.

Her eyes flew to his. "Now?"

Had that been shock, dismay, or – dared he hope – lust?

He laughed lightly and caressed her hand. "Not here and not now, my dear. We might be surprised. Though surely it is customary between a man and his wife." He noted with satisfaction the slight flush on her skin where the white paste did not cover it completely and felt a certain warmth himself.

She bowed, her eyes lowered. "Of course, sire. As you wish."

Late that night he went to his Consort's quarters. He walked so softly that he startled one of her women who sat up with a little cry, then recognized him in the light of his lantern and scurried away with a warning whisper to the others. He approached the curtained dais and set down his light. All was silent and dark inside. Behind him, the attendants left with a soft rustling of their gowns. Taking off his outer robe and slippers, he lifted the draperies and ducked inside.

Shigeko lay under a mound of silken covers. When he knelt and felt for her, she started up.

"Sssh," he said, unnecessarily. Her women would not dare to spy on their love-making.

Shigeko made room for him, and he busied himself with peeling back her gown. Apparently she had expected him; she wore only a thin gauze under gown.

The lamp outside the silk drapes cast a soft and diffuse light over her breasts. Her lips were slightly open, her eyes closed. He touched the firm curves of her body, fuller now that she had borne children and familiar to his hands in the near darkness. He murmured an endearment, and she sighed, then gasped at a caress. He was pleased with this and his own response. The duty visit would be accomplished pleasantly enough. He reminded himself that intercourse was healthy, that the woman's body was a source of the essential life force, and that he had abstained too long.

Pushing a knee between her thighs, he bent his mouth to hers. He tasted her, explored her mouth with his tongue, allowing their saliva to mingle, then cleared the way below and thrust.

Alas. In his hurry, desire failed him. Embarrassed, he withdrew and pretended that the quick attack had merely been part of a lengthier campaign. He concentrated on regaining his sexual vigor. The ancients taught that the jade stalk sought to draw the life force from the cinnabar gate, but they also claimed that after childbirth a woman had lost much of this life force. They recommended lying with a virgin to regain stamina.

An interesting theory.

After another failure, he decided that it must be his familiarity with Shigeko's body and with her responses to his lovemaking that had deflated his lust. He closed his eyes and resorted to imagining the soft flesh beneath him to be Toshiko's virginal body. This worked astonishingly well, but at the moment of penetration, reality prevailed and he failed again.

It was a disaster and an embarrassment.

He disentangled himself from the covers, murmured an apology, and left his wife's bed. Throwing on his robe and scooping up his slippers, he retreated to his own room.

The Doctor's Orphans

The day after Sadamu's mother was cremated at Toribeno – a trip that had taken them past the cloister palace and filled Doctor Yamada with intense longing – he decided that he must put the past from his mind and begin his life anew.

His first step was to inform Otori when she brought him his morning gruel.

"Otori," he said without preamble, "I have decided to adopt the boys."

She gaped at him. "What? What boys? There's only the one."

"No, there are two. You have forgotten Boy."

For a moment she looked confused. Then she cried, "You are mad, Doctor. That one? That useless scum? The one that bites the hand that feeds him? The one whose face is as crooked as a demon's because he has a demon's soul?"

"He is a boy like any other," insisted the doctor, "and like Sadamu he needs a family. I have no family myself but the means to support one. It is good fortune that has brought us together."

She forgot all about her position in the house and plopped down on the mat across from him. "Listen to me," she said fiercely, shaking a finger in his face. "I have looked after you since you were no higher than Sadamu. And what a handful you've been to me! You say you have no family? Well, you're the son I never had. As a mother, I say to you now: do not shame yourself and your family by associating with low scum. You are a Yamada. You were born to be a lord and have many servants and many children by fine ladies. But you go and become a doctor, and being a doctor, you go to live among the poor. And now you want to be like them. Have you gone mad? What of your own children? Will you have them take second best after those two guttersnipes?" She burst into tears.

Yamada saw that she was truly upset. What she had said about having raised him was true enough. The care of the youngest children in a noble household fell to a reliable maid, and she had raised him as if he were her own. She was entitled to her reaction. Servants took enormous pride in the status of their masters, and he had sadly disappointed her.

"Otori," he tried to explain, "I have no children of my own and I shall never marry. I'm lonely and shall be lonelier still when I grow old. Let me do this for the boys and for myself. You will see, it will be good to have children's laughter in this house."

She wiped away her tears and stared at him. "Why won't you take a wife?" she asked suspiciously.

"I . . . there is no one I want to live with," he said lamely. Oh, dear heaven, the lie almost strangled him.

Otori's eyes narrowed. "You prefer boys to women maybe?" she asked, pursing her lips in disapproval.

He did not understand immediately, then he laughed. "No, Otori."

"But then why not take a wife? You'll see how nice a woman can be. Your trouble is just that you haven't tried it. You're a good-looking man. Your wife will think herself lucky to warm your bed and bear your children."

"No, Otori. I will never marry. Now bring the boys in."

But Otori burst into fresh floods of tears. "I don't understand," she wailed. "Please make me understand. What is wrong?"

Her grief shamed him, and he decided to tell her the truth. "Hush," he said. "It is a secret. You must never speak of it to anyone. Promise me?"

Her tear-drenched face filled with half-fearful curiosity. She paused her sobbing and nodded.

"I met someone, but I cannot ask her to be my wife. And I will not live with any other woman. It would not be fair to this other woman, for I should always think less of her because she was not the one I want. Do you understand now?"

Otori sniffed and wiped her nose with her sleeve. Then she nodded. "Who is she? Does she already have a husband?"

"I cannot tell you. Now go bring the boys."

When Otori returned with his "sons," Yamada had a moment's misgivings. Sadamu was all very well. He was only five and showed some promise of growing into a man who was at least ordinary looking. Otori's ministrations had made enough of a change to hint even at handsomeness. But Boy was discouraging. As Otori had pointed out, his appearance matched his reputation for thievery and untrustworthiness. He was lean rather than skinny these days because he got enough to eat, but he had never lost his furtive look and manner. Boy was tall, with narrow shoulders, a long neck, a broken nose which gave his face its lopsided appearance, a long chin and a crooked grin. His eyes were deep-set and wild, and his hands and feet overly large. At the moment, his arms dangled at his sides, and he was casting quick appraising glances around the room and at Yamada's face, as if he were gauging his chances of grabbing some item of value and making a run for it.

Yamada sighed. "Boy," he said, "have you been happy here?"

Boy's eyes sharpened. His head bobbed up and down eagerly. "Yes, Master. Very happy. Thank you, Master." Boy's voice had changed. This emphasized the unpleasant tone.

"How old are you now? About sixteen?"

A lifting of the shoulders.

"I cannot go on calling you 'Boy.' You'll be a man soon. What name do you want to be called?"

That astonished the youth. His sharp eyes scanned Yamada's face. Then he grinned more widely. The effect was that of a trickster trying to ingratiate himself, but he answered readily enough, "Sadahira, Master. Like you."

Yamada was taken aback. He glanced at the smaller boy, who looked mildly puzzled. "That name is taken," the doctor said stiffly. "Pick another one."

A stubborn look came into the older boy's face. "Why can't I have that name? If he's Sadamu, I want to be Sadahira."

Here were already the first signs of jealousy between the boys. Yamada's sudden decision appeared fraught with difficulties. Otori thought so, too. She grunted and snapped, "I told you he was worthless and ungrateful. You're a fool if you go through with it."

Her words had an interesting effect on Boy. He glanced quickly from Otori to Yamada. A calculating expression replaced the stubborn look. He said, "Sorry, Master. You must pick my name. I shall be proud to bear it."

"Very well. Then you shall be Hachiro. It is an honorable name in my family, and I shall expect you not to bring shame to it."

The newly named Hachiro bowed again. "Thank you, Master. It is a fine name."

"The reason I have called you both," Yamada continued, impatient now to get it over with before he lost his nerve at the older boy's manner, "is that I have decided to adopt both of you. It means that this is now your home. You will receive an education suitable for sons of mine, and after my death you will inherit my property in the way I see fit to bestow it. In return, I expect obedience, filial behavior, earnest effort at the chores I set you, and honesty. Do you accept?"

Hachiro flushed, then said fervently, "Yes, Master, I will. Thank you."

"You may call me 'Father' from now on, Hachiro."

"Thank you, Father. May the Buddha and all his saints bless you."

"And you, Sadamu?" asked Yamada, a little disappointed that the smaller boy had said nothing and was frowning.

"My father is dead," Sadamu said flatly. "My mother is also dead. I have no home."

Otori gave a small gasp.

Yamada sighed. "Yes, I know, Sadamu. That's why you are here. I will be your father from now on."

The boy said nothing and looked away.

"Sadamu," whispered Otori. "You must thank the doctor. You're a very lucky little boy, you know. Not many orphans with no family get taken in by such a fine gentleman as Doctor Yamada. Where are your manners?"

Sadamu thought about it, then bowed and said, "Thank you."

More than anything the doctor wanted to be called 'Father' by this quiet thoughtful child, but he did not press him. Instead he sent the boys away and went into his garden.

Much later, as he was grinding dried herbs in his studio, Sadamu slipped in and stood beside him to watch.

"Would you like to help me?" Yamada asked.

The boy nodded, and the doctor showed him how to use the pestle to grind the powdered herbs together with sesame seeds so that he could mix them with honey into a thick paste and then roll small pills the size of orange seeds. He did the weighing himself and smiled to see the child put a finger into the honey and lick it. Still, Sadamu did not say much and made few replies to Yamada's chatter.

"Did you know," Yamada said, "that I can mix a medicine that will make a person become as fragrant as Prince Genji?"

The boy looked up at him. "Why?"

"Oh, there are people who wish for this. Prince Genji was much admired by beautiful ladies."

"Do *you* want to be fragrant and have many beautiful women?" asked the boy.

Yamada laughed. "Yes, but I doubt it would help me much."

Silence fell again as Sadamu pounded and Yamada measured. Then the boy asked, "Why don't you have children?"

Remembering Otori's reaction, the doctor said cautiously, "I've never had a wife."

"Were you afraid she would die?"

Yamada set down the earthenware jar he had been filling with pills. "No. What makes you say a thing like that?"

"My father died. Then my mother cried and cried until she got sick and died, too. Maybe I'll die next. And then you will die."

"No, Sadamu. You will not die," Yamada said quickly and took the child in his arms. "I'm a doctor, and I won't let you die." But as he said it, he thought that the boy would now believe he had let his mother die. Helplessly, he held the child until he felt the small arms slip around his neck and hug him.

"Thank you, Father," Sadamu whispered. "If you like, I'll help you make some fragrant pills."

At that moment the doctor felt almost replete with happiness.

His satisfaction did not last long. When they walked back to the house for their evening rice, they heard someone screaming. They ran around the corner of the house and found the servant Togoro on the ground near the veranda steps. He was clutching his groin with both hands while tears ran down his disfigured face.

"What happened, Togoro?" asked the doctor. "Did you hurt yourself?"

"Oh. Oh. Oh," moaned Togoro. "Boy kicked me."

"Boy kicked you? Why?"

"He said I must bow to him and call him Master Hachiro now. I told him to piss off, and he kicked me in the balls."

From Lady Sanjo's Pillow Book

Everything men say about women is doubly true of them. We are not the only ones who are frivolous, fickle , foolish, weak, temperamental, and easily seduced.

I must say no more, except that my disappointment causes me great suffering. I, too, can now say, "My love is one-sided like an abalone shell, pounded by waves on a rocky shore." It is too painful to think that a lady of birth and refinement, a woman of superior sensibility and the most faithful affection could so easily be cast aside for a crude provincial who flaunts her disgusting body along with her dirty songs.

For days I wept quietly into my sleeves at night and strove to put a good face on it during the day. I showed everyone that I had no hard feelings and wished to help her in every way, but the ill-natured creature did not respond to my generous and repeated offers. I could see that the others were excited by the developments and watched us. I, at least, behaved like a lady. She flaunted her triumph by dressing up every day to show that she expected another summons.

The summons did not always come, of course, but she always put on her costume. Apparently His Majesty gave it to her. I cannot say that I would wish to appear thus attired. There is something very low about the costume of a *shirabyoshi*. They dress like men! But then they are mere prostitutes of the lowest order, selling their bodies at street corners all over the capital. And now we have one of them in our midst!

After days of silent suffering, I realized that I was not the only one who was being hurt by this female. The whole imperial household is suffering from the gossip. Soon our verandas will be cluttered with young men, foolish youngsters from good families as well as rude warrior types from the palace guard. They will pass poems under our grass shades and screens, and the ladies will be occupied day and night composing poetic answers. They will whisper and giggle. Then, at night, there will be soft steps, and silks will rustle, and little cries and male murmurs will disturb my rest, and then – well, I won't go on. I will lie there, behind my screens, kept awake by such sounds, sounds that go on and on, until the furtive visitor leaves. And the next morning another lady will receive her letter and write her poem in return.

I, of course, will have to stay aloof and merely listen to men's footsteps passing on the veranda, coming and going.

It came to me finally one night, as I lay there thinking about all this, that it was my duty to report the matter before the scandal could take hold and damage the reputations of Their Majesties. So I wrote to my mistress, the Consort.

I serve Her Majesty even though She spends most of Her time in Her own palace these days. When She left, She took some of Her ladies with Her, but I imagine She could not spare me here. At least one reliable person must remain behind to keep an eye on things.

I made my letter short, but ended it with a poem of my own: "See how a gaudy blossom growing in the mud captivates the sun above the clouds." I thought the images rather appropriate.

To my immense gratification, Her Majesty arrived here the very next day, proof that I had not overestimated the danger.

I reported immediately. Her Majesty, as always, looked incredibly beautiful, making me wonder why His Majesty has permitted Her to absent Herself. It was indeed as if "Her radiance had hidden behind the clouds" all this time, and I said words to that effect. Of course, even an imperial consort may feel that Her duty is heavy at times. She must bear children and may die in childbirth. I must say, though, that I would find it easy to make such a sacrifice. Oh, why does *He* prefer that young slut? Never mind!

Her Majesty spoke to me in the strictest confidence. I told Her everything, and She sent for our ladies because She wanted to see what the girl looks like.

When they arrived to make their obeisances, I remained seated beside Her Majesty. They could see that I occupied a position of the highest confidence, and that pleased me. I felt so happy at that moment that I considered asking Her Majesty to take me with Her when She left us again. Only my deep and forgiving devotion to His Majesty caused me to desist. Ah, my foolish heart. "Once I had gazed upon the sun above the clouds I was blinded to all else."

Besides, I can serve Her Majesty better here.

The Oba girl kept to the back, as well she might under the circumstances. When her name was called, she came forward. Regrettably, she was not wearing her dancing costume. Her Majesty looked at her clothes and figure and said, "I see you have recently come from one of the provinces." We all knew what that meant. The girl was hopelessly out of place at court.

"Do you have any talents?" Her Majesty asked next.

"I sing a little, Your Majesty," she answered. When Her Majesty merely raised Her brows, she added in a small voice, "And I can dance a little."

"Hmm," said Her Majesty and raised Her fan, turning away. The girl backed off on her knees and hid behind the others.

And that was it. It had been easy after all. In Her truly elegant manner, Her Majesty has indicated what She thinks of song-and-dance girls. I have no doubt that this one will soon be dismissed from service.

The Audience

The incident between Hachiro and Togoro caused Doctor Yamada to have a talk with his new son. The meeting was painful for both. The doctor was in his pharmacy and watched the boy slink in. He had the same furtive look on his pasty face but seemed less interested in herbs and medicine than in the objects inside the house. His expression reminded the doctor of a young gang member he once saw being punished in the market, and he wondered if he had adopted a criminal. The same mix of fear and resentment flared in Hachiro's eyes when the youngster saw what lay on the counter among the doctor's pharmaceutical tools.

For a long time, the doctor looked at him silently, hoping that his wordless anger would have more effect than the bamboo rod he had cut in the snowy garden. But his new son tried to brazen it out.

"You wanted to see me, Father?" he asked blandly, putting a slight emphasis on the word "father."

This angered Doctor Yamada more and his hand crept toward the rod. "Why did you kick Togoro?" he asked coldly.

"Oh. Is that what this is about?" The pretense of surprise was not convincing. Yamada saw the flash of fury in the boy's eyes. "He was insolent, Father," he said, adding, "You know, you really should speak to the servants. They don't show any respect. Why, Otori –"

"Silence!" the doctor thundered, clutching the rod. The boy backed away a step toward the open doorway. With an effort, the doctor controlled his temper.

Hachiro had been brought to him a year ago, beaten, bloody, and unconscious. Someone had found him lying in one of the dirtier alleys near the market. Yamada had cleaned and treated his wounds, fed him, and – when the boy had told him that he was without family or a roof over his head – he had allowed him to stay, offering food and shelter in return for small chores. Since the youngster had claimed not to know his real name, they ended up calling him "Boy," mostly in anger, for he proved to be unreliable at work and took whatever food he pleased. As a result, neither Togoro nor Otori showed him much kindness.

One could not expect miracles.

"Hachiro," the doctor said more calmly, "I will not tolerate physical abuse of my servants. Otori has served my family since I was younger than you are, and Togoro has been faithful and a hard worker. He, too, has been with me longer than you. Both deserve respect from you. Meanwhile, your own behavior in the past has left much to be desired. Now, what do you have to say for yourself?"

Hachiro watched the rod nervously. A look of anger crossed his face. "They hate me and tell lies about me. Togoro makes me do his work. It's not proper, when he's the servant. Otori wants a man in her bed. She should be ashamed of herself at her age. And now that you've adopted me they're jealous."

The doctor was speechless. He knew both of his servants well. Hachiro's lies were gross and repulsive.

His silence encouraged Hachiro. "How can you take their word against me?" he demanded. "Have you not made me your son? What good is that unless you treat me as your son and make the servants respect me?"

The doctor bit his lip. "Very well," he said, taking up the rod. "You leave me no choice but to do as you ask. I shall treat you as a father treats a lying, disobedient son. Come here."

Hachiro paled. "If you beat me like a slave," he cried, "the servants will find out and spit on me."

Yamada stepped forward and seized Hachiro by the arm. "And so they shall," he growled, pulling the boy out of the studio and into the bright winter sun. His call brought both Togoro and Otori running. When they saw Hachiro in his grasp and the bamboo cane in his other hand, they stopped, open-mouthed with surprise.

"You are to witness Hachiro's punishment," the doctor informed them.

He was still angry when he used the rod on Hachiro's buttocks and thighs. The boy's single cry sickened him and he stopped rather quickly. Breathing hard, he said, "I trust your pain reminds you of the pain you inflicted on Togoro. You will taste more of it if I hear of other examples of cruelty to someone less fortunate than you. And beware of telling lies about others. Now you will apologize to Togoro and Otori."

Hachiro was very pale. He obeyed sullenly and slunk away, while the two servants gaped after him. Togoro was embarrassed. He gave the doctor a lopsided grin, scratched his head, and trotted off. Otori snapped, "The child of a devil is also a devil. Beating him just makes him worse. You watch my words."

The doctor tried to return to his work but he could not concentrate. To clear his mind and rid himself of his self-disgust, he decided to visit squatters' field.

Snow hid ugliness as a rule, but squatter's field was the exception. Here even snow looked dirty. Flimsy shelters made from salvaged boards and ragged straw mats clustered together like piles of a giant's garbage, and black acrid smoke rose from smoldering fires. Shivering creatures huddled around them, cooking whatever scraps they had been able to scrounge. Disease and festering wounds were the norm here, and the doctor was greeted eagerly and kept busy until nightfall.

When he got home, depressed again by the thought of Hachiro, he found that a messenger from the palace had come during the afternoon. The man had waited nearly an hour before leaving again.

Otori glowered. “I might have known that you’d be out the very moment good fortune finally calls.” She gave a sniff and added, “It’s a good thing the fine gentleman left. You stink. Best take a bath and change before you touch the letter he brought.”

Yamada ignored this and opened the carefully rolled and tied sheet of fine paper. It was not from Toshiko. The writing was a man’s — elegant, concise, and marked with a crimson seal. He did not recognize the signature, but the content was clear. He was to present himself in the attendants’ office of the cloister palace the next day at the start of the hour of the snake.

Frowning at the letter, Yamada asked, “Did the messenger explain what is wanted?”

“No. And don’t look like that. You should’ve been here yourself. What does it say?”

“I am to report to the attendants’ office tomorrow.”

Otori’s face broke into a wide smile. “There. You see? They finally take notice of you. I bet that cook got you another patient.”

“I doubt it. When someone is ill, they want me immediately. Besides both letter and messenger are a little too formal for a mere sick call.”

“Well, you will go, won’t you?” Otori asked belligerently.

“Oh, yes. I’ll go.”

In his heart, the he still hoped that the summons would somehow bring him to the lady Toshiko. He bathed and dressed with special care the next morning and set out with a spring in his step that not even the sight of Hachiro, lurking about with a resentful expression, could spoil.

In winter, city sounds are muffled by snow. Carriages and wagons stay home and horsemen move more slowly, huddled into their clothing. Yamada knew from experience that nothing is colder than metal armor on a winter's day. Those who are walking are luckier, even when their cold-weather garb only consists of layered rags and straw capes and boots. He was luckier still in his wadded and quilted robe and sturdy, lined leather boots.

The palace was a beautiful sight this morning. Sunlight reflected from a million places: The large roofs were of an immaculate and glittering whiteness against the shiny red columns and the gilded dragons at the eaves. By asking directions, the doctor found the attendants' bureau where he was passed from white-clad servants to black-robed officials. His hopes of seeing Toshiko evaporated. This was where the business of government took place, a world of officials. Eventually he was left to wait in a chilly passage which seemed to lead to an important office. The passage was full of waiting men, and very important-looking officials passed in and out of the distant double doors. They wore rank colors on their formal hats and did not glance at those who humbly waited, shivering and with hopeless expressions on their faces.

At some point in his long wait, it occurred to the doctor that a mistake must have been made, and he approached an attendant to ask. By now, he did not feel humble and was brusque because he thought of the time he had wasted that could have been spent looking after the sick.

But the attendant assured him that all was correct and that he would be admitted shortly.

Admitted?

Yamada began to suspect that he had been summoned by the emperor himself. Since he had been waiting past his customary midday meal, his empty stomach was growling. Besides, he remembered their previous meeting and how angry and rude he had been then, and nervousness now twisted his gut, making him queasy.

When they finally called him, he was sweating with the tension in spite of the cold. This was going to be very different from that casual encounter in the cook's room. He would see the emperor officially. Few men were allowed in his presence, and most of those held ranks far above his.

The great doors opened and closed behind him. He saw a wide expanse of shining floor and in the distance the figure of the emperor bent over his desk. An official sat at another desk. The shutters were closed against the cold, but many braziers and lights stood about the two desks. When Yamada hesitated at the door, the official waved a peremptory hand for him to come forward. The doctor walked to the center of the room where he knelt and touched his forehead to the floor.

"This is the doctor, sire," said the official.

"Doctor? Oh, yes. I remember. Come closer, come closer. And you may leave us, Tameyazu."

Yamada rose and approached the emperor's desk, wondering what he was to do next and if he was permitted to look into the emperor's face. He knelt and in his confusion he stared down at the documents that lay strewn across the desk until he saw the emperor's hand reach out to cover them. Afraid that His Majesty thought he had been reading them, he raised his eyes.

Yes, the face was that of the cook's visitor, but today the emperor was not smiling. Yamada touched the floor with his head again.

"Come, Doctor. Sit up," the emperor said. "I wish to consult you about a medical problem."

Yamada took a deep breath, sat up, and risked another glance. Perhaps the emperor was ill. He looked well enough, but many ailments remained hidden from the eye. "Yes, sire?"

The emperor studied him for a moment. "You can keep a confidence?"

The doctor blinked. "Of course, sire."

"It is nothing of great import, but gossip would be very unpleasant. You are to mention to no one what we discuss."

Yamada bowed. He was slightly offended and said stiffly, "Certainly not, sire." His nervousness faded as his curiosity grew.

"I am told," the emperor said, "that you are of good birth, that your studies at the imperial university are recent, and that you excelled at them."

The doctor bowed again. He had done well at the university, but most of what he knew about medicine had come to him later, in the slum dwellings of the capital. He was tempted to say so, but Otori would not like it, so he was quiet.

"These studies have included matters of a sexual nature?"

Well, hardly in the slums. People who were starving did not worry much about procreation. It seemed to take place all too often and too easily for the poor. He said, "Yes, sire," and became nervous again. The only time powerful men of the emperor's age consulted their physicians about sexual problems was when they worried about dysfunction or a wife's inability to conceive. The retired emperor already had a large number of children, so he was probably not desperate for more. Why the sudden concern about his sexual performance?

And then he remembered Toshiko and was filled with a sudden hatred for the other man.

The emperor pursued his subject, unaware of Yamada's clenched hands and grinding teeth. "Then you are familiar with all the methods and medicines that enhance the pleasures of the bedchamber?"

The doctor raised his eyes briefly. The emperor's face had an earnest, almost pleading expression. Yamada reminded himself that this was the emperor, but that he was also a man and a patient and apparently very worried. Private feelings must be put aside when treating a patient. He said cautiously, "Yes, sire. There are various substances and activities that are said to help the male performance. I am not myself very familiar with their efficacy but –"

The emperor smiled and said quickly, "You are too young."

Yamada blushed in spite of himself. "Yes, sire, that may be so, but many men my age have such concerns. I meant only that I could not attest to these prescriptions from my observation. A great deal of our knowledge is based on what people report, and they may not always understand their bodies or tell the truth."

The emperor considered this and nodded. "Yes, I see. Well, I cannot say I have ever experienced any problems maintaining my stamina before now."

The doctor said, "In that case, surely it may be a temporary affliction, sire."

The emperor rubbed his chin and looked uncomfortable. "Perhaps, but there are reasons why I wish to be absolutely certain. You understand?"

Yamada gulped but met the Emperor's eyes and asked, "How can I help, sire?"

"You may answer some questions, and then perhaps you may wish to ask some. When we are done, I am sure you will feel able to prescribe."

The doctor bowed. Dear heaven, he thought, I want to like this man and help him, but what if my advice loses me Toshiko forever? He twisted his hands in irresolution.

The emperor said gently, "Do not be afraid, Doctor. I shall not blame you for my weakness."

Yamada managed a pale smile at this misunderstanding of his fears and reminded himself that there had never been any hope for him and that, as a physician, he had a duty to help to the best of his ability. "Please ask, sire," he said.

"Thank you. Then my first question is this: May a sudden weakness in a man be caused by a decrease in the female's life-giving force?"

Surely that could not refer to Toshiko. Suppressing surprise, the doctor said cautiously, "Ancient medical texts state that women over thirty and those who have given birth are not beneficial to the male's stamina, but I have not seen any evidence of this and I doubt it is true." Indeed, in his practice, poor women produced children far too readily and repeatedly to suggest that their men had such problems.

"Good," said the emperor. "Then would you say that the opposite is equally untrue? That a man cannot gain stamina from lying with virgins?"

Yamada's ears started to burn again. It was warm in the room from the braziers, and the air was scented with the oil of the many lamps, but he was hot for other reasons. "I don't believe it helps, sire," he managed.

"Hmm. Then an inability experienced by a man is purely his own fault or due to age or disease?"

"I believe so, sire. But a temporary weakness is not a serious or permanent impairment. It may be caused merely by distractions or tiredness."

"Distractions." The emperor pursed his lips and nodded slowly. "Yes, I think you are quite right. That may well be so. Good. It is your turn now."

Nothing in his studies and the years of his practice of medicine had prepared the doctor for the difficulty of this particular consultation. He felt the sweat trickle down his back under his robe and was afraid. The powerful are unpredictable. He did not trust the kind and reasonable manner with which the emperor had invited him to probe.

After some thought, he ventured, "From what I have heard so far, I take it that Your Majesty has been blessed with unusual vigor until very recently?"

"Unusual? I don't know. Is it unusual?"

"Yes, indeed, sire."

So far, so good. The emperor looked quite pleased, proving that emperors were just men after all. Except, of course, when they lusted after the woman one loved. The doctor said, "A healthy man may experience temporary failure at any time, though more frequently in old age."

The emperor frowned. "I am in my thirty-ninth year, doctor. Is it old age then?"

"No. I don't think so, sire. I believe both Your Majesty's August Father and Grandfather enjoyed great vigor far beyond that age."

The emperor nodded. "Quite right. Go on."

"May I ask if there is a physical impediment? Some discomfort for example?"

"None at all."

"May we leave aside that the fault may lie with the female?"

The emperor raised his brows in astonishment. "What do you mean?"

Oh, dear. Yamada felt he was groping along an abyss in the dark. Was the emperor talking about the consort? The snowy courtyard had been full of palm leaf carriages and merchants carrying stacks of silks and boxes of cosmetics. Apparently Her Majesty was in residence. Yes, that must be the answer and it presented new dangers. He said, "Sometimes there may be an impediment, and access becomes difficult or unpleasant for the male."

The emperor stared at him, then shook his head. "No. Nothing like that. Besides, it was over too quickly. But you raise an interesting problem. I suppose greater stamina is needed for bedding a virgin than for a woman who has borne a child?"

Yamada panicked again and wiped the moisture from his forehead. The emperor noticed his discomfiture and chuckled. "Do not be embarrassed to speak your mind, Doctor. You have my confidence."

Yamada took a deep breath. "I feel, sire, that the problem may lie with you, but that it is one that may easily be overcome with careful preparation. I believe what you refer to is the first of the seven sexual impediments. It is called "stopped air." This prevents a sufficient erection because the male is exhausted from excess or lacks the desire to continue." He saw that the emperor began to frown and hurried on, "The art of the bedchamber is not a business that should be hurried. Perhaps taking counsel from one of the helpful little texts that most young men are given may suggest an approach?" He let his voice trail off.

"Dear me." The Emperor burst into laughter. "I haven't thought of those little books for years. When I was very young, I studied them with the greatest interest. They contain fascinating but often quite useless suggestions." He laughed again. "'Joined mandarin ducks' was nothing at all like what ducks do, though it was one of the easier positions, but 'the soaring seagull' was impossible to achieve and, heaven knows, I tried." He shook his head with another laugh. "Thank you, Doctor, for making me feel quite young again for a moment." Becoming serious and businesslike again, he said, "I suppose all will be well, but if you have some medicine that you have found efficacious, may I have it? Just in case?"

Yamada bowed. "Yes, sire."

"Today? And I will call you again if the problem persists."

"Of course, sire."

The audience was over. The doctor bowed and took his leave.

Outside again, he was grateful for the chill air on his perspiring skin. He blinked against the blinding light, his mind in turmoil. Suddenly, he felt a powerful urge to rescue Toshiko before it was too late, and he did a very foolish and dangerous thing. Returning into the waiting area, he asked one of the servants for a piece of paper and writing utensils. Then, kneeling on the cold flooring, he rubbed a little ink and wrote the directions to his house. Instead of a signature, he drew a cat's face with one eye closed. This note he folded into a small square.

Then he made his way to the northern precincts of the palace and found the walled garden of the women's quarters. It was deserted this time of year, lying undisturbed and featureless under the soft blanket of new snow. The rocks seemed merely larger hummocks of snow, and the bamboo drooped under its burden and rustled dryly as a sparrow flew up, sending a dusting of snow to the white ground. The heavy shutters of the building were closed. The doctor walked quickly to the veranda, and left his note under a small stone just outside the shutter where they used to meet.

A part of him hoped fervently that she was inside and, hearing him, would open the shutter a little, but in this he was disappointed. All remained silent except for the sound of melting snow dripping from the end of the eaves.

Back at the gate, he turned for a last look and saw his tracks leading to her door and away again. Too late!

The Tale of the Bamboo Cutter

Toshiko's life changed abruptly with the arrival of the consort. The news reached them when one of the maids rushed in, chattering about the long line of carriages and outriders entering the palace precincts.

Their dim and quiet days were over. The ladies hurried to unpack their best gowns. Maids brought clothes racks and set them up to air fine robes of silk gauze and brocade and to perfume them with incense. More lamps were lit, bringing out the jewel tones of deep reds and golds and purples in the rich fabrics. The air was heavy with perfume. Servants rushed into the city to purchase last minute adornments and fresh supplies of make-up. And the ladies' tongues wagged, wondering why the consort had returned so suddenly and what this might mean about news from the palace and about upcoming entertainments and who might be in her entourage. The New Year was not far away, and if Her Majesty remained a while, the palace would hum with festivities, and many old friends would visit.

Toshiko was at a loss about what was expected of her in all of this. She followed the others around, trying to find out more. Lady Sanjo was besieged with questions but only smiled mysteriously. Toshiko did not like the woman's knowing manner and the sidelong glances she cast her way from time to time.

Nothing further happened the day of Her Majesty's arrival, except that some of the ladies who traveled with the Consort stopped in for visits. Even to Toshiko's untrained eyes, they dressed more elegantly and engaged in much livelier conversation. She guessed from their tales that they led a very different life in the city and began to suspect that their entertaining ways were the reason they had been chosen by the Consort. Bits of poetry flew quickly between them, along with clever comments on this and that person or thing and laughter at silly incidents they had observed at court, and many, many references to gentlemen of their acquaintance. The ladies in the retired emperor's palace had nothing like it to offer in return and expressed wonder and a good deal of envy.

The visitors eyed Toshiko curiously at first but lost interest when informed who she was. There was bigger news. The little crown prince would be made emperor soon. This fortunate event would raise their mistress in rank and lend brilliance to her court. All the ladies, even the ones who would not be invited back to court with the newly made empress, were very happy.

Toshiko wondered what the consort was like and if His Majesty would now forget her. The next morning brought the summons for them to present themselves, and she dressed carefully, not for His Majesty this time, but for her first official duty as a lady-in-waiting to his consort.

When she finally laid eyes on Her Majesty, she was struck with admiration. The consort was much younger than she had expected, having foolishly assumed that she must be His Majesty's age. She looked in every way exquisite, being small and dainty of stature, with a charmingly round face and thick, lustrous hair. The Chinese jacket she wore was of crimson silk, embroidered with golden chrysanthemums, and her gowns of beaten silk gauze were layered in shades of autumn leaves and old rose petals. Even among her beautifully dressed ladies-in-waiting, she glowed like the rarest flower in a stunning painting.

Toshiko, who had dressed in the darker hues of the wintry season, was amazed at the color and spectacle before her. Since the previous spring, her days had been spent in the semi-darkness of the women's quarters among other ladies who had been forgotten by the great world.

Until now.

Her Majesty's arrival had brought a number of high-ranking young men to the cloister palace, and music and laughter sounded in the corridors and from the pavilions.

When Toshiko, as the newest member of Her Majesty's ladies, was called forward to make her obeisance, Lady Sanjo, seated behind the consort, leaned forward to murmur something to her mistress. Toshiko's heart beat fearfully as she bowed, but the Consort was very courteous, asking about her home and what amused her. She found her voice and talked about singing and dancing *imayo*. To her relief, the moment was over quickly, and she could slip back behind the last row of ladies where nobody noticed her.

In the days that followed she was gradually drawn into the merry-making around Her Majesty. Many of the ladies played the zither and lute, and others could respond to poems with clever twists on words. She was too ignorant to participate in such activities. Her education in such skills had been sadly neglected. To her relief, nobody asked her to sing or dance, but she listened to others and took pleasure in their skills. It suited her to be thus left in peace. Sometimes she played board games with the others and enjoyed herself with the pure delight of a child, and she read avidly all the new romances that were passed around.

One day, His Majesty appeared suddenly in their midst. Toshiko immediately hid behind a screen. He had not called for her since his consort's arrival, and she was embarrassed to be seen by him.

His Majesty directed a servant to unpack several elegant boxes of books, his gift to his consort and her ladies. The books were filled with illustrated tales, and when he showed them around, the ladies gathered, crying out in admiration at the pictures of dainty, colorful figures who moved fairylike among clouds of gold dust through landscapes filled with lakes, waterfalls, mountains, and elegant pavilions.

Unable to restrain her curiosity, Toshiko crept out to catch a glimpse. His Majesty saw her immediately.

"Ah, I see Lady Toshiko is here," he said to the consort. "I am glad you have made her welcome. She arrived only recently and from outside the capital. As you know, we are very quiet here in your absence, and I am sure she has been leading a sadly dull life until now."

Her Majesty's eyes searched the room for Toshiko, who had frozen in her place, wishing she could disappear like a drop of dew in the sun. "She is still very young," the consort said without enthusiasm. "Something out of the ordinary, would you say?"

"Oh, yes." The emperor's mouth twitched with secret amusement as he looked at Toshiko. "Quite out of the ordinary. Has she sung and danced for you yet? Lady Toshiko is adept at *imayo*. As a matter of fact, she has been a great help to me with my collection."

There was a small noise, something like a snort. All eyes turned to Lady Sanjo who coughed delicately into her sleeve, and bowed to His Majesty. "Please forgive my rude cough, sire. The season has not been kind to me." Bowing to Her Majesty next, she added, "Indeed, Your Majesty, this young lady has been most accommodating and industrious in her attendance on His Majesty."

An embarrassed silence followed these words, then the consort said dryly, "I see. In that case, perhaps she should be assigned new quarters, sire?"

The emperor flushed and waved that aside with an impatient gesture. "I trust all the ladies are comfortable. Please do not trouble yourself. It does not signify."

Her Majesty nodded. "As you wish, sire."

New quarters? Toshiko was uncomfortably aware that this exchange somehow involved her position here. She looked to Lady Sanjo for an answer and saw that she wore the expression of a purring cat.

Ashamed without knowing why, she drew away even more. But the Emperor was watching her as the books passed around.

"Lady Toshiko," he called to her, "are you familiar with the *Tale of the Bamboo Cutter?"*

"I think so, sire," Toshiko said, wishing she had stayed behind the screen.

"The story is about a man who finds a great jewel hidden in a hollow bamboo. It reminds me of you." He smiled at her, then searched among the books. "Here it is. Come, you must see how fine these illustrations are." He patted a pillow beside him, and the ladies pulled aside their wide skirts to let Toshiko pass. She came forward, her face burning with embarrassment.

The tale belonged to her childhood. It was the story of an elderly childless couple whose fervent prayers for children were answered when the husband, a humble bamboo cutter, found a shining child inside a hollow bamboo. In their care, this child grew into a luminous beauty known as Princess Moon. She was courted by many great men, even by the emperor himself, but in the end she refused them all because she was immortal and had to leave the world for her celestial abode.

Toshiko had never seen the tale illustrated. As the emperor slowly unrolled the scroll, she saw that it had sections of written text alternating with charming scenes in bright colors. The only paintings in her parents' house had been her mother's screens of mountains and a scroll painting of a falcon in her father's room. Here there was a whole world in miniature, with mansions and gardens filled with people who moved about and who laughed or cried just as you would expect them to do in real life.

"Oh," she sighed, peering over her fan, "how very beautiful! And how lucky the poor bamboo cutter and his wife were. The princess brought such pleasure into their lonely lives."

"And to all the gentlemen who saw her," chuckled the emperor. "Poor gentlemen. She wanted none of them. Not even the emperor. How do you explain that?"

Toshiko did not know what to say. He was close to her and his scent reminded her of the last time she had sat beside him. She blushed and raised her fan.

"She was a divine creature and not of this earth," said Her Majesty, breaking the awkward silence. "Perhaps it was fair punishment to them for neglecting their own ladies."

"That had not occurred to me," said the emperor. "My interpretation has always been that the author was making fun of the inept and dishonest nobles of his day. Apparently he did not think much of his emperor either."

"Oh, surely not," cried Lady Sanjo. "He could not have been such a villain. He would have been sent into exile."

"Not at all. We are not such cruel taskmasters, I hope." The emperor smiled broadly. "But Lady Sanjo proves that I, too, have my critics. She does not think much of my explanation. Do you have a better one, Lady Sanjo?"

Lady Sanjo flushed. "Oh, no, sire. I am only a foolish woman and thought it just a fairytale." Then her face brightened and she rose to her feet. "But I am very eager to have Your Majesty explain the true meaning to me."

Toshiko drew back with an apology, and Lady Sanjo quickly took her place. The emperor bit his lip, but he pointed to the figures of the suitors, identifying each by name and linking him with passages in the text, while Lady Sanjo leaned closer and murmured her admiration. When he was done, he quickly rolled up the scroll and, pleading business, left them.

But soon, he thought, perhaps even the next night, he would send for Toshiko.

Bald Hen Powder

Leaving a note outside the palace women's quarters, along with tracks clearly made by a man, had been a very stupid thing. Anyone checking the small private courtyard would become suspicious and report the matter. But though the doctor realized his mistake right away, he could not go back and retrieve the note because someone was coming. He walked home very disturbed, praying in his heart to Buddha and all the gods that the snow would melt quickly and no harm would come to Toshiko on his account.

As soon as he got home, he consulted his medical books about suitable prescriptions for His Majesty's complaint. The books were thorough on sexual advice, dealing not only with the diagnosis and treatment of conditions in both men and women, but also with the proper and curative performance of the sexual act. Most of the prescriptions were very old, having been passed down by Chinese physicians who, he suspected, had consulted even older sources of Indian origin.

They seemed to have been gathered and compiled with the same fervor that marked the transmission of Buddhist scriptures.

He located quickly the sections dealing with medicines that improved sexual performance. The prescriptions were manifold, the amounts variable, and several of the substances so exotic that he had no access to them. Besides, as a physician he had little faith in any of them. One of the concoctions was called Bald Hen Powder. The explanation stated that, having been left accidentally outside, it was eaten by a rooster who promptly climbed on a hen's back where he stayed for several days, pecking the hen bald.

Yamada skipped over this one with a smile. The consort would object. After some thought, he settled on a combination of fairly harmless substances and went through the garden to his pharmacy to prepare the medicine.

As he passed the fishpond, he saw the small footprints in the snow and a few crumbs by the side of the pond. Sadamu had been feeding the fish again. This reminded him that he had a family now, and he felt comforted by the thought. There would be two boys to raise. Hachiro went to school with the monks every day, but Sadamu could keep him company a little longer.

He noticed that the path to the pharmacy had not been swept and made a note to speak to Togoro later. In his studio, he laid down his notes and began to assemble, grind, and weigh the ingredients of the aphrodisiac: dried Chinese yam, cinnamon bark, licorice root, hyssop, parsley seeds, all wholesome – unlike that recipe which used dried lacquer and could cause a stomach upset. After some thought, he added ground deer's horn and doubled the parsley seed. These ingredients he mixed and sifted carefully, then he added honey as a binder. The resultant thick dough, he formed into small pills which were to be dissolved in warm wine and taken on an empty stomach.

To make certain that they would not leave an unpleasant taste on His Majesty's tongue, he heated a little wine and took a dose himself. He found the taste very satisfactory. The wine had merely an agreeably sweet and herbal flavor. His Majesty, he was convinced, needed only strength of mind to succeed in his endeavors with his consort. Something mildly stimulating was all that was necessary. It would never do to experiment with stronger drugs on an emperor.

By now, Yamada felt pleasantly warm himself in spite of the chilly air in the pharmacy. He placed the pills into a fine white porcelain jar. Around its neck he tied a small piece of paper bearing the simple instructions. It looked very plain for an emperor, he decided, and after a moment's thought, he carried it into the house to look for a silk ribbon.

Otori heard him in the corridor and put her head out of the kitchen. "Togoro's gone," she announced.

"What?" The doctor paused, trying to understand. "Gone where?"

She came a few steps toward him, glowering. "How should I know? Nobody ever tells me anything."

"I expect he'll turn up," Yamada said indifferently and turned toward his room. On second thought, since she seemed to blame him, he added, "I'll have to leave again in a little. Back to the palace to deliver some medicine."

She nodded. "Good. We can use the money. That Hachiro's bought himself new clothes. It took all my household money to pay the shopkeeper for them. You might have told me."

That explained her ill humor. "He didn't tell me," he said defensively. Seeing her eyes widen at Hachiro's newest outrage, he added, "It's all right. I forgot that they need new clothes now that they are my sons. Come in and I'll give you the money."

"He's got his nerve doing such a thing without permission," she muttered, following him into his study. "Maybe it's time for another whipping."

He shuddered. "No. Let it go this time." She told him the cost – not insignificant – and he gave her the money. "What about Sadamu?" he asked.

"He could use new clothes more than that Hachiro."

"I'll see about it tomorrow."

When Otori had left, Yamada sat down and worried about Hachiro. First the business with Togoro, and now the new clothes. The boy was sullen and far too concerned with his new status. The fact that Otori did not confront him herself meant that she was afraid to, and that troubled him more than Hachiro's shopping spree. But perhaps the fault was his own. He had changed the youngster's life too abruptly. How could he expect Hachiro to be an obedient son when he had never had a father or a home? No doubt, he would settle down in time, especially now that his days were taken up with lessons.

With a sigh, the doctor searched for the ribbon, found a nice green one, and tied it around the jar.

It was time to make the delivery, but a strange lassitude had seized him, and he stretched out beside his desk, his arms behind his head, and stared up at the ceiling. In a way, the audience with His Majesty had been amusing. As long as the emperor did not have his eye on Toshiko, Yamada wished him every success in the bedchamber. Not with Toshiko, though. He flushed hotly at the thought of it and was suddenly so aroused that he jumped up. He paced for a while without finding relief, then threw wide the doors to the cold garden and gulped some winter the air. Maddening images of naked, intertwined bodies, hers and his own, crowded his mind. He ran down into the garden, looked for a broom, and swept the path to the studio with vigorous strokes.

Halfway through the job, he realized that he had just proved the amazing efficacy of His Majesty's medicine and paused to laugh. By the time all the paths around his house had been cleared, the effect of the medicine had worn off sufficiently for him to return to his room. There he rewrote the prescription for half the amount he had taken, and then he carried the emperor's pills to the palace.

Strangely, although his body behaved itself now, he could not quite rid his mind of desire for hours afterward.

Only In a Dream

When the maid woke her, Toshiko took a moment to peer into her mirror. The flame of the single candle flickered, but she was satisfied that her make-up was still in place and her hair tidy. Nearby, bedclothes rustled and pale faces materialized in the gloom. Someone whispered a question, but nobody wanted to leave the warm cocoon of bedding. It was bitterly cold this time of night.

The maid helped Toshiko with her costume and arranged her long hair, and then Toshiko snatched up her notes and tripped down the long corridor to the emperor's room. A servant opened the door for her.

Toshiko was still drowsy from sleep. It took her a moment to realize that she had not been called to assist with His Majesty's song collection. The large room was dim. Only one lamp was lit inside the curtained dais where bedding had been spread. This single light had the effect of making the gauze draperies translucent and giving the raised dais an importance that imbued it with an almost numinous quality. It reminded her of an altar table in a dark temple hall.

Confused, she stopped to look for Otomae – or anyone. But the dark room was empty except for the Emperor. Gone were the many lights, the desk, his scattered papers. The painted screens had been moved and now partially surrounded the massive curtained dais. She had stepped into another world. Behind her the door closed softly.

The emperor was in undress, wearing a loose white silk robe somewhat resembling a shrine priest's robe. He came toward her, his hands outstretched in welcome.

"Come," he said with a smile.

She felt a moment's panic – as if there were still time or choice to turn and run, to keep running, out of the palace and away from the capital, all the way home, to her family, her horses, her childhood – but there was no escape from this dream.

"Come here, Princess Moon," the Emperor said more urgently. "Do not turn down my invitation like that other shining lady." His voice and eyes caressed her.

She saw and heard only kindness and a fervent plea. Those who are very lonely respond to another's loneliness with a surge of sympathy. Toshiko gathered her skirts and ran to him.

He took her hand and led her up the steps to the curtained dais. Lifting the curtain and taking the notes from her feeble hand, he put them aside and invited her to sit. Then he poured some wine for her.

The curtained dais was like a small, cozy room, its ceiling a silken canopy embroidered with the sixteen-petaled chrysanthemum, emblem of the imperial house, its walls the heavy pale gold draperies that could be raised or lowered with wide brocade bands of a deep purple. The bedding was thick and soft and the color of ripened rice plants. An ornate lantern hung suspended from the canopy and cast its soft light on her crimson trousers. All beyond was in darkness.

The emperor took her hands, telling her that they were cold and that she looked frozen. She realized that she was shivering and tried to suppress the tremor. He pulled a brazier closer, then seated himself next to her. His hands reached for hers again and pressed them to his warm face. He kissed her palms, then leaned toward her to murmur something that she did not understand because the blood was pounding in her ears. She was afraid to speak in case her teeth would chatter and did not know what to do, so she simply smiled at him. After a moment of looking at her, he knelt and reached for her feet, removing her white silk socks and warming and stroking her naked feet with his hands. She gasped at his touch, not sure if from shame or pleasure.

In a little while, he poured more wine, for both of them. She drank and felt the warmth begin inside, felt her tension melting. He told her that she was as beautiful as that other shining girl, that Moon Princess found in a hollow reed. And when she stopped shivering, he removed her jacket and then untied her sash.

It is a powerfully symbolic gesture, this untying of a maiden's sash by a man. It signifies the ultimate invasion of her privacy, and if permitted, a surrender of her will and individuality. But his touch was gentle, and she was grateful for his concern with her comfort. She said so, simply, and then took his hands and bent her face into them in humble surrender to his love.

What followed in due course was well understood by a girl who had been raised in the country and who had received certain instructions from her mother. Nevertheless the act came as a surprise, and not an entirely pleasant one. Discomfort soon penetrated the dreamlike trance in which she had accepted him and had allowed him the most intimate exploration of her body. She felt his mouth and the moistness of his tongue on her tongue, tasting of wine and honey sweetness and herbs once smelled in a mountain meadow, but also of his all too human breath. Her body melted at his touch until he pushed her down and crushed her with his weight, and she felt his heat and sweat, and his body forced the breath out of her until she thought she would surely die. Then pain broke through the last illusions, and she came fully awake.

With that awakening arrived the knowledge that she was caught and defeated, and that he was no longer gentle and comforting, but absorbed in his victory, in his own pleasure, and uncaring of her. When he shifted his weight for a more forceful onslaught, she caught her breath and closed her eyes. It had to be borne, and surely there were many worse things to be suffered in life.

And then finally, after what seemed an eternity, he gasped, stopped moving, and rolled off her body. Feeling beaten and bruised, she curled up into as small a shape as she could.

After a moment, he laughed softly and said, "I must thank that doctor—and you, of course, my dear."

She was confused. He could not mean *her* doctor. Perhaps he had been ill. He was no longer very young. Pity returned, and she sat up, pulling her clothes around her to cover her nakedness, her wounded body. She did not look at him—not because she blamed him for what he had done to her, but because it was surely not right to look at an emperor's nakedness, even when he stared at one's own. She could feel his eyes on her like probing fingers and blushed hotly.

What had happened was meant to happen. It was what her parents wanted and what she had hoped and worked for. Back in the women's quarters, others were lying awake, wishing they were in her place. This was her triumph, but she felt used and dirty and was filled with shame.

From Lady Sanjo's Pillow Book

Since last night there is no longer any doubt of it: the Oba girl has succeeded where better women have failed. Alas, there comes a time in a man's life when he has an excessive fondness for youth and low life, and she combines both. It will not last, of course. Our lives are but bubbles in a flowing stream. I trust that soon she will be gone "like the swift waters of the Asuka river, never to return."

The New Year is drawing close, and since Her Majesty's visit has brought this quiet place to the attention of the great world, the girl's good fortune went almost unnoticed. I can see she does not like that. She mopes around and hardly eats anything. If I did not know better, I would think she was pregnant.

This reminds me that Her Majesty needs to be informed of the event before she leaves us for the splendid Sanjo Palace, where she will reside with the little

Crown Prince. Ah, I wish I could go with them, but my duty is here. I shall tell her, "May the sun shine on Your Majesty and His Highness from cloudless skies, as I grieve the parting from afar – now that another has found favor with His Majesty."

Then we shall see.

As I said, the girl keeps much to herself in a tiny room under the eaves where no one ever goes, but I watch her even more closely now. Both Their Majesties will expect to be informed at the first sign of pregnancy . . . or misbehavior.

It must be said that shockingly little effort has been made to guard against the latter. She continues to live here with the other ladies in spite of the fact that male visitors are allowed. It must mean that His Majesty does not intend to acknowledge a child by her. Her Majesty made certain of that when she asked him publicly if he intended to move her to different quarters. It was most elegantly done. He was too embarrassed to admit his lapse to his lawful spouse, the mother of the Crown Prince, not to mention to her attendants. But there is always the danger that he may change his mind after Her Majesty leaves us. I must act quickly.

Fortunately, we have attracted the attention of the young bucks, and gossip about the imperial bedchamber travels quickly. It won't be any time at all before the young men will try their luck with the new favorite. Since she has already shown a very common tendency toward flirtation, it should not be long before she will be caught in an impropriety.

With the first warm weather of spring, the shutters will be open, and young men (and old fools, too) will sit on the long veranda to try to catch glimpses of us. It is enough just to show a sleeve or a bit of our train; they dream the rest. One dark night the first brave man will lift the shade and slip inside. Then silks will rustle, voices murmur, warm breaths mingle, and the heated blood will have its way until dawn makes the visitor hurry away. This was always the way of it in the imperial palace, and my ladies know it and are all quite cheerfully looking forward to the New Year.

Truly, there is something indescribably romantic about waiting for a lover in the dark, hoping that each soft step and rustling silk will bring him to one's side. It has an element of mystery, because sometimes he is not the one expected, and sometimes a particularly attractive man may make a mistake and surprise one. A well-mannered gentleman never admits this but treats the lady with the same consideration he would have shown his beloved.

How amusing to arrange for such a mistake! (I refer, of course, to my younger years, though I am by no means past such adventures. In the dark, all bodies are soft and yielding, and the scent of cherry blossoms carries even into the farthest corners.)

This sort of behavior is, of course, not permitted to someone who attends His Majesty's bedchamber. How truly shocking, if Lady Toshiko were to have an unexpected visitor! No doubt, she would submit quietly, hoping the visitor would leave unnoticed and "silent as a grebe on a winter marsh."

The thought of it makes me quite warm.

On another note: I have finally decided to do without the plums when I see His Majesty. They interfere with my speech, and the last time he did not seem pleased with my appearance. In fact, the day he paid us that unexpected visit in Her Majesty's quarters, he saw me without them and seemed more taken with me than ever. He paid me the most flattering attention after I ventured to ask him to explain something in a book he had brought. (A reminder: Men like to be consulted). Perhaps there is no need to improve on what I am. A certain maturity can enhance a woman's natural beauty. As soon as he can be brought to see what sort of person the girl is, he will surely come to his senses.

Ah, spring! And, "Oh, to lose my way among the falling cherry blossoms!"

The Waning of the Moon

The Emperor was convinced that his sexual prowess, albeit aided by Doctor Yamada's wonderful pills, was proof of his continued youth and good health. In fact, he reassured himself repeatedly that first night – until he detected a certain listlessness in his partner and let her go.

The experience suggested also that a man may indeed draw new life force from the body of a virgin. Yet in the midst of his sense of well-being, he felt a twinge of guilt for having so ruthlessly imbibed at this fountain of youth, and he sent her several expensive silk gowns and the illustrated book of the Bamboo Cutter. The more personal next-morning letter he dispensed with in view of the women's gossip and his consort's presence in the palace.

When he analyzed the night's events over his morning rice gruel, he decided that the girl was hardly a Moon Princess after all. In fact, she had been in no way different as a bed partner from other virgins he had bedded. Her eagerness to come to him had momentarily touched his heart, but subsequent developments proved her to be as passive as the rest. Shigeko was a far more responsive partner than this girl. He decided to visit his consort that very night to prove the matter to himself.

Since a small fear yet lingered that his weakness might return when he was with the consort, he took a double dose of the doctor's pills and went to his wife's quarters flushed with desire.

Shigeko had heard the gossip and welcomed him coldly. "People are talking," she said.

Impatient to bed her, he would have none of it. "Come, my dear," he said firmly, "you know quite well that there is a great difference between you and a young serving-woman from the provinces. Never doubt that I treat you very differently."

She turned her face away. "You acted as if you did not like me the last time," she accused him. "And when you then sent for the girl the very next night and kept her with you until dawn, I felt abandoned 'like the reeds on the lonely shore when the crane flies to the southern sea.'"

Her poetic image was unwelcome because it reminded him of Toshiko racing the wild geese along the river reeds. He felt a pang of remorse about both women, but this was his official consort and the mother of the next emperor, and the situation was a first for both of them. He had never had the rudeness to bed another female practically under her nose. So he took her hand and leaned closer. "Remember," he murmured in her ear, "that a crane always returns to his mate. He is a faithful bird."

"Pah!" She lifted a shoulder and gave him a scornful look. "Faithful? When he keeps company with any low marsh bird?"

He sighed. "Truly, my dear, you need not be concerned." He took a resolute breath and added, "There was a reason. You see, not wishing to disappoint you again, I consulted my physician."

She frowned. "I do not understand."

A little embarrassed, he muttered, "We discussed, er, virgins." She still did not grasp his meaning, and he plunged into his excuse. "Purely as a cure. It is said to help the performance."

Her eyes widened with interest. "Oh. I see. And the doctor recommended it? Was he right?"

"Yes." Suddenly triumphant and, thanks to the medicine, entirely sure of himself, he reached for her sash. "That is why I came. Let us find out together."

The experiment proved a complete success. He made love to her more passionately than he had in years. She, for her part, was convinced of his love and flattered by his devotion. Disappointed by Toshiko's lack of ardor, he appreciated the warm response.

Subsequent relations between the imperial couple improved to an amazing degree. The very next day, the emperor sent a gold bar to the doctor's house. He also sent Shigeko a charming "next-morning" poem. For the duration of her visit, he remained faithful to her, visiting her rooms frequently and spending time with her during the day. In fact, he was mildly smitten with his spouse again, and even after the installation of the new crown prince took Shigeko away to the Sanjo Palace, he abstained from Toshiko.

But then a disastrous fire destroyed the Sanjo Palace for the second time in his memory. The flames lit up the night sky as if the entire capital had turned into a landscape of hell. The consort and the crown prince escaped to safety. The emperor expected Shigeko to return to him, but she ignored his invitation and moved to other quarters in the capital.

And so he was alone again and bitterly disappointed. After a few days of building up his resentment toward Shigeko, he sent for Toshiko.

Though she arrived promptly and looked charming in one of her new gowns, their night together did nothing for his wounded pride. When he took the time to observe her, he was filled with new doubts. She obeyed, she smiled, she responded pleasantly to his attempts at flirtation, but he felt a new distance between them. More importantly, he noted again the lack of passion in her love-making.

Where there is no love, it is impossible to pretend it for long, and the emperor had been disappointed too often to be duped in this case. Not only did this girl not love him, she did not even feign desire and submitted to his embraces unwillingly. This sort of thing made a man feel worthless and brutish.

The emperor never sank to brutality, but his silent anger affected his treatment of Toshiko in many subtle ways, some of them physical, others mental. To his irritation, she did not complain but only seemed to withdraw further into herself.

Togoro

A strange period of peace and contentment descended on the Yamada household during the New Year's holidays. Otori cooked for weeks, and the kitchen was filled with good smells and endless supplies of delicacies. Every meal consisted of a staggering number of courses.

Even Hachiro, who had walked around for weeks with his face averted and who had been leaving most of his food uneaten, seemed to cheer up a little. The doctor had been worried about him. The boy had taken the beating very badly, seeming listless for days afterward and had since begun leaving home frequently and for long hours. What he did during those times, the doctor did not know. Otori complained about it and reminded him of the boy's bad character, but he would not ask Hachiro for fear of finding out some other mischief.

The doctor's sons wore their new finery after having thrown themselves with great zeal into decking the house with branches, sacred ropes, and all sorts of decorations of their own design.

Yamada himself felt generous. The emperor's lavish gift of gold had filled him with uneasiness, and since he was not sure he deserved it, he spent his riches freely. Everyone received gifts. The holiday came only once a year, he reasoned, and they had all added another year to their lives, cause enough to celebrate. Hachiro was sixteen now at least that was the age he had chosen), and Sadamu six. Yamada himself was twenty-six and the head of his own small family. Otori refused to reveal her age, and Togoro – Togoro remained absent, the only nagging worry in his contentment.

This was not the first time Togoro had left suddenly. It had happened first shortly after his arrival at the doctor's house. The doctor had gone to look for him and found him at prayer in a nearby temple. Togoro had been apologetic, but had not explained. Yamada gathered that sometimes his life got too much for him and he found relief in religious meditation. It had happened a few more times, and Togoro had always returned after these absences. But this time, he had been gone longer than usual. The doctor checked the local temples. Finding no trace of him, he asked one of the priests. The priest remembered the scarred man and thought that Togoro might have gone on a pilgrimage up to the mountains because he had asked about the holy places on Mount Hiei.

The doctor wondered sometimes when Togoro would come back, but he was too preoccupied with work and the New Year and his private thoughts to worry unduly. When Otori grumbled about the extra work, he told the boys to help her or lent a hand himself. Over the New Year, he spent more time with his sons.

Hachiro, who was enrolled in the temple school a few blocks away, had a holiday from his studies. Doctor Yamada had bought him a place in the school with a generous donation to the temple fund, and the boy seemed to be applying himself well. He still spent time away every day, but he was making an effort to behave well at home. Yamada was pleased but uncomfortably aware of Hachiro seemed to be withdrawn and living in a world of his own.

Sadamu was a pure joy. He had been teaching the boy himself. Their studies were somewhat unorthodox in that much of them consisted of Yamada showing the child the wonders of the world around them. But there were also writing lessons. Sadamu was bright and eager for praise so he worked very hard to please his father. Already there was a closeness between them that was lacking with Hachiro, a fact Yamada ascribed to Hachiro's being older and out of the house most of the day. He welcomed having Sadamu to himself, for in his more truthful moments he knew that he could not like Hachiro the way he should. His dislike for the boy caused him guilt, and so he was more lenient and generous with Hachiro than with Sadamu. Sadamu never complained, and Hachiro seemed to accept this special treatment as his due as the oldest son.

And so the days passed quietly, and the holidays with good cheer, and gradually they settled down again to their routines.

This peace was broken abruptly the day one of the doctor's poor patients asked, "Say, Doctor, didn't you have a servant who was burned all over and ugly as a demon?"

"Yes. Togoro." The doctor paused in his work. "He left before the New Year. I've been wondering why he hasn't come back yet. Have you seen him?"

His patient was having an open sore on his knee treated. He said, "Haven't seen him myself, but I hear he got thrown in jail."

Yamada straightened in surprise. "In jail? Are you sure?" His conscience stirred. He should have looked harder for Togoro.

"He got drunk and raped a girl. She must've had a rare fright. Her father caught them together. Sorry, Doctor. I figured you knew."

Yamada gaped at the man. "No. Nobody told me. Rape? How long ago was that? Where did it happen?"

The man scratched his chin. "It was before the New Year. And before the fire at the Sanjo Palace, I think. Honest, Doctor, that's all I know."

The news was disturbing. Apparently Togoro's trouble had befallen him very shortly after he left. But why had he not sent a message? He must have known that the doctor would come. It was a puzzle.

Yamada finished with the man's leg and then went straight to his warden's office to ask for information about the rape case. But they knew nothing there, and that meant the incident happened elsewhere in the city. He next went to the city jails. In the Left City Jail, he finally got news. It filled him with horror.

Togoro had indeed been charged, tried, convicted, and had died soon after. He had died before the New Year.

As he stood in the prison office and heard the matter-of-fact announcement, the doctor grasped a column for support. The guard said, "He was an ugly bastard. We figured nobody wanted the body."

I wanted him, Yamada thought. Pity and guilt wracked him so sharply that tears rose to his eyes. The guard stared at him. "Surely not a relative of yours, sir?" he asked with a glance at the doctor's good silk robe.

"My servant. He was a good man. I still can't believe . . . tell me about the charge."

"Rape. I expect it nearly drove the girl mad—seeing that on top of her."

Yamada felt a surge of impotent anger and asked to see the documents in the case.

He was referred to the judge, who appeared to take his questions as an accusation of legal incompetence. It was only with great difficulty that Yamada got the name of the young woman who had brought the charge. Togoro had denied the crime but had been convicted on her word and that of her father who had come upon the two of them just as Togoro got off the daughter and ran away. He had been all too easily identified and was caught within the hour. Both the girl and her father testified at his trial. Togoro had said nothing.

The doctor did not know what to believe. The story seemed very strange and not like the Togoro he knew. But what did he know of men's urges? No young woman would willingly give herself to a man so horribly disfigured. And the young can be very cruel. Perhaps this girl had mocked him and he had finally broken under his burden.

Only why, after he had been arrested and sent to be trial, had Togoro not given them Yamada's name? There could be only one explanation: Togoro had been guilty and too ashamed to have Yamada know what he had done.

And so the doctor walked to one of the temples where Togoro had prayed, and there he bought incense and burned it before the golden Buddha statue. He stayed for a long time, praying that Togoro's suffering in this life had earned him a better one hereafter.

It was not until later that Yamada realized that Togoro had probably died from the brutal beatings because he would not confess. It had happened in the last weeks of the year when he had been preoccupied with his own affairs. The thought of Togoro's helplessness in his final desperate days shocked and grieved him immeasurably. Such a fate seemed grossly at odds with what life had owed the poor and gentle man. Yamada wept again – for Togoro, for himself, and for all the pain in this life.

Togoro had come to him when Yamada had just begun his practice of medicine. After waiting in vain for paying customers, he had turned his hand to seeking out the non-paying kind, those who lived on handouts from the wealthy in the shadows of the large mansions and those who hung about in the dirty alleys of the business quarter, scrounging for food in garbage. Among them, there was no scarcity of disease, and there he absorbed practical medical knowledge far more rapidly than ever at the university.

He had found Togoro lying among the garbage beside a poor eatery. If it had been a better place, the constables would have been called to remove him, but in this case the owner of the eatery took matters into his own hands and laid into the sick man with a broom handle while a small crowd of ragged onlookers shouted encouragement.

Togoro had not made a sound.

When the doctor saw what was going on, he was disgusted. "Stop it this instant," he shouted at the man with the broom. "I'm a doctor."

The man glowered but obeyed, and the others made room for him. The shivering creature on the ground looked barely human; it had human legs and human arms and wore the rags of a man. The head was another matter. It was a mass of suppurating flesh covered with flies. The man's features were so distorted by blackened skin, oozing wounds, and swelling that it was difficult to find a mouth and a nose. The eyes were mere slits in livid flesh. When the doctor overcame his revulsion and knelt to take a closer look at the injuries, he saw that the deformed man wept. He wept silently. Having made no effort to protect himself against the blows, he simply seemed to wait for the final, fatal one that would end his suffering.

Yamada looked up at the people around him. "Are you monsters to mock and beat a helpless suffering creature, a human being like yourselves?" he demanded angrily.

"He's the monster," the man with the broom said, pointing an accusing finger. "Look at him. He makes my stomach turn. And he's been there for days, driving my customers away. Who wants to eat after seeing that? I told him to leave. Many times I told him. I offered him money to go. He won't. He's cursing my business and my family by lying there."

"Nonsense," snapped Yamada, who was examining the wounded man by then. He had been in a fire. His hair and eyebrows had been burned off and the fire had caused the horrible disfigurement of his face. His hands were also covered with blackened oozing sores, and when Yamada lifted the rags he wore around his feet, he saw that the soles of his feet were raw flesh.

He looked at the owner of the eatery again. "This man has been burned severely. He cannot walk and he cannot help the wounds on his face. You should have helped him instead of beating him and calling him names. A stray dog would have been kinder."

The onlookers, deprived of their entertainment, muttered and drifted away. When the owner of the business also turned to go, Yamada rose angrily. "Not so fast, you!" he said. "I know you and I promise I shall lay charges against you if you don't this instant get the constables so that this man can be helped." The man nodded and slunk off.

Left alone with his shivering patient, Yamada crouched beside him and touched the man's shoulder. "Don't be afraid," he said. "I'm a doctor. We'll take you to my house where I can treat your wounds. What is your name?"

What was once a mouth moved a little, and a sound came like a breath. Yamada could not be certain. "Goro?" he asked.

No, it seemed to be Togoro. The burned man tried to say more but was hindered by his shaking and the fact that he was weeping again, more copiously than before. Yamada's heart contracted with pity, seeing those tears well from swollen, crusted eyelids and course down the raw flesh. The salty liquid must burn as much as the fire had. He said no more, hoping that help would come soon and that in the silence the man would stop crying.

After an eternity, the constables arrived with a stretcher and the patient was carried to the doctor's house. There, a white-faced and frightened Otori spread clean bedding in a storage room next to the kitchen. The doctor had thoughtlessly wanted to put him in his own room, but she refused to countenance this, claiming that the doctor was out so much that the nursing would fall to her, and she spent most of her day in the kitchen.

The constables left, and Yamada set about cleansing his patient's wounds and applying soothing ointments. Togoro was very patient throughout the painful process. The doctor gave him some medicine to soothe the pain, and Otori fed him small amounts of broth through a hollow straw. After a while, Togoro went to sleep. Seeing the extent of his injuries, which also covered parts of his body, the doctor was surprised that, in due course, his patient healed and recovered most of his functions. Only his hands and feet were so badly scarred that they had stiffened. He shuffled and was awkward at grasping things. His face was the worst. Even after the swollen, infected wounds had healed, he was left horribly scarred and of such ugliness that people looked away the moment they laid eyes on him.

Togoro had no memory of his past or of the fire that destroyed his life, but he suffered from nightmares and had periodic moods of deep sadness that sent him to the temples. Fire of any size frightened him and he gave any open flame a wide berth.

As with Hachiro, Yamada had to guess at his age and background. Togoro could neither read nor write, and his speech marked him as belonging to the laboring class. From the beginning, Yamada was humbled by his patience. He bore the painful cleansing and scraping of his wounds without complaint, merely looking up at the doctor with doglike devotion. He often wept when he thanked Yamada.

And when he got better, he stayed on. One day early on, when Yamada came to change his bandages, he had crawled from his pallet and was sweeping the kitchen floor, holding a short broom with both painful hands. Nobody had the heart to send him away after he got stronger, and in time they came to depend on his tireless labors.

And that was how, for this new year, Yamada added another guilt to the one he already bore.

The Secret Note

Spring brought sun and warmer weather, and in the palace, servants and maids threw open the wooden shutters, letting sunlight and fresh air into the dark, perfumed world of women and the dusty offices of men.

In the courtyard of the women's quarters, a potted plum tree was covered with buds showing deep red against the blue sky, and on the tiled roofs sat doves cooing in the sun. The ladies put out their heads and laughed with pleasure.

Time to put away the winter robes with their deep jewel colors and bring forth cherry- blossom silks and willow-leaf gauze and gorgeously embroidered Chinese jackets. These must be aired, scented, and have their wrinkles pressed out. In the bustle, there was new excitement.

Only Toshiko was listless. She was more of an outsider now than she had been before. Even Shojoben kept away these days; she had an admirer among the young courtiers and was in love. Lady Sanjo watched Toshiko with hot eyes, and her maids periodically searched Toshiko's clothing and reported to her. They were looking for the first sign that she was with child, and she hated them and herself.

She often went to the little room under the eaves for privacy. One day, she found that here, too, the heavy shutters had been raised. The veranda and small courtyard beyond lay in the morning sun. The snow was gone, leaving behind moisture that had darkened the wooden boards and the rocks and gravel beyond. The one small azalea bush, where they had caught the cat together, showed buds among its green leaves, and Toshiko stepped outside to see what color it would be.

At home, the wild azaleas in the woods behind their house bloomed in all shades of red. She used to go with her mother to dig up small plants for the spring garden her mother had planted outside her veranda. A white cherry also grew there. It must be quite large by now. Its blossoms used to open white as snow when the red azaleas bloomed. Cherry blossoms lasted only a short time. Before you knew it, they blushed a rosy pink and died. The azaleas went on blooming blood red, but the cherry petals fell like snow and drifted to cover them with a white blanket. Even in the beginning of life there was already death.

Looking at the budding azalea bush, Toshiko thought of her mother and sister and how much she loved them. Were they walking together in the spring garden today and thinking of the absent one? Her hand went to her breast where she still carried her mother's letter–the farewell to a child who had passed out of her life. When His Majesty had presented her with the precious gowns, she had kept only one. The rest she had sent home. She had not added a note, because the message of the gowns was enough. Her mother would know that Toshiko had done her duty.

After the long darkness, the sunlight felt harsh and almost painful. Toshiko shivered. There was nothing for her here, or in this coming of spring, and she turned sadly to go back inside. As she did, she saw a glimmer of white where the boards of the veranda met the wall of the building. She bent to pick up the scrap of paper – such cleanliness was ingrained from her upbringing – and saw that it had been folded over many times. It must have been there for a long time, for it was still moist from the melting snow and the ink had blurred through the paper. She unfolded it cautiously, found the writing had become illegible, but recognized – with a wildly beating heart – the small drawing of a one-eyed cat. It was from *him*. She turned and looked toward the gate – as if he would open it and walk in – and then at the rocks – in case he was hiding behind them and would now rise to greet her. But he was not there. He had come and left a note she could no longer read, heaven knew how long ago, and she had not known it. Perhaps there would still have been time then.

The sadness of it overwhelmed her.

No. It had always been too late. It had been too late the day the perfumed darkness first swallowed her, and now she was truly lost.

She refolded the stained slip of paper and put it next to her warm skin, along with her mother's letter, and went back to her duties.

After the brightness outside, the rooms were doubly dark. She passed through the eave chamber into the corridor and did not see Lady Sanjo until her arm was grasped at the door of the eave chamber.

"What were you doing out there?" the woman demanded.

Her words were rude and inappropriate to someone who was not a servant, and Toshiko was not only well-born but had been distinguished by His Majesty's favor. However, her listlessness extended to Lady Sanjo's bad manners and, freeing her arm, she said only, "I went to check on the azaleas. They have buds already."

It was a disingenuous explanation, and Lady Sanjo snapped, "Nonsense. You were looking for the man you used to meet here. I saw you picking up his note." She extended an imperious hand. "Give it to me."

Toshiko's heart failed her. In the dim corridor, the older woman's eyes glittered with excitement. "You are mistaken," Toshiko said, her voice trembling as her hand moved protectively to her breast. "I dropped an old letter from my mother, that is all."

"How dare you lie to me? I saw you reading it. Give it here."

Toshiko backed away and gathered her courage. Let the woman think the worm had turned into a hissing snake.

"I shall inform His Majesty that you have insulted me," she said angrily. "Surely even you must know that I am to be treated with respect."

But Lady Sanjo was not so easily intimidated. She called for witnesses. The ladies arrived in twos and threes, eyes wide with curiosity.

"You will attest to the fact," Lady Sanjo told them, "that Lady Toshiko has been receiving messages from a man. Just now I caught her with a letter that was left on the veranda. She refuses to give it to me."

They looked shocked and perhaps a little pleased. Toshiko knew that they must think her very foolish indeed to carry on a romantic affair, no matter how innocent, in her present situation. She straightened her shoulders and said, "I dropped my mother's letter and picked it up. Because I am far from home and miss her, I often come to this room to read her words. But Lady Sanjo has called me a liar, and that I will not tolerate." Pulling the letter from her gown, she extended it to the lady closest to her. "See for yourselves."

Lady Kosaisho took the letter with a glance at Lady Sanjo and unfolded it. "This is indeed from her mother, Lady Sanjo," she said when she had glanced at it. "It appears to be an old letter."

"Give me that!" Lady Sanjo snatched it from her hands. She looked at it, muttered something, and dropped it on the floor, then left with an angry twitch of her skirts.

As Toshiko bent to pick it up, Shojo-ben said, "Oh, that was too much. Not even she can treat you this way, Toshiko. We all heard her. I shall write to His Majesty and tell him what happened."

Toshiko shook her head. "No, please don't. I had rather not trouble him. And it is better not to make Lady Sanjo even angrier. Let us forget it."

And so things went back to normal – or almost so. Some of the other ladies became a little friendlier to Toshiko, and Lady Sanjo seemed preoccupied with other matters. The First Month's holidays kept them all very busy. They were on call for parties and banquets and must present themselves in elaborate costumes to attend the retired emperor when he received the congratulatory visits of his family and senior staff.

Whenever that happened, they filed into the hall, their faces hidden behind fans, and seated themselves in rows behind silk-trimmed curtain stands. But the stands were not very tall and had chinks and they could be moved apart a little to make room for the elaborate, multi-layered costumes the ladies wore. Many of the young courtiers took the opportunity to peer over, perhaps with an apology that they had hoped to see a relative among the ladies. As always, Toshiko stayed in the back, but the curious male eyes found her, and she learned to keep up her fan at all times.

The ladies received visits from relatives during these days, and one sunny day Toshiko was told her brother Takehira awaited her on the south veranda. The news stunned her because there had been no letters or messages from her family for many months now. She had almost accepted her orphaned state, and did not know whether to be happy or sad at his visit.

The south veranda was very long and at this hour and on such a balmy early spring day, several other guests were sitting outside the grass curtains. The maid servant showed Toshiko to the section where Takehira awaited her. From the dim interior, she could see quite well through the loosely woven curtain and noticed right away that Takehira was wearing a very handsome blue military uniform and carrying a bow. She seated herself with a slight rustle of her gowns.

Takehira, who had been studying the other visitors, turned his head. "Toshiko? Is that you?"

"Yes, Takehira. How handsome you look. Isn't that an imperial guard uniform?"

"Right." He grinned and stood to show it off. Narrow white trousers were tucked into knee-high black boots, his blue robe had full sleeves and was long in the back where his bow and quiver of arrows rested against his back, and on his handsome head was the formal black headgear with the fanlike ornaments above each ear. "Yes, Little Sister," he said, sitting back down, "I finally got my letter of appointment. I'd just about given up on you. Mind you, it wasn't quite what I expected, but it's better than staying home listening to Father's complaints all day long. I'm Junior Assistant Lieutenant Oba no Takehira of the Outer Palace Guards, Left Division." He pointed to the large black lion crests that decorated his sleeves, chest, and the skirt of his overrobe.

"Very handsome," Toshiko said, but her heart contracted. The emperor had paid off his debt to her family. "Congratulations. I am sure you will soon distinguish yourself and receive a promotion."

Takehira made a face. "Not likely, unless there's some fighting. All I do is inspect the conscripted soldiers when they arrive, make sure they are fully equipped by their people, and then drill them. You've never seen such oafs. If it wasn't for the nightlife, I'd resign. Listen, can you put in a word for me with the emperor? If you think about it, this is little enough for the brother of an emperor's favorite. I've got my heart set on a captaincy, and I'd rather be with the Inner Palace Guards. You should see their scarlet outfits. And Father says to tell you he wants the magistrate's post in our district. He's tired of paying rice tax when his daughter serves the emperor."

Toshiko was sickened by the message. A provincial official is released from annual taxes on his lands – a considerable figure in the case of the Oba holdings. Just what did her father expect her to do? She protested, "But Father is no magistrate. He knows nothing about the laws. How can he ask for such a position?"

Takehira laughed, a little too loudly – some of the other visitors turned to stare at him disapprovingly. "What a foolish thing to say," he cried, raising more eyebrows. Unaware of the effect of his bad manners, he ploughed on, "You're just a female and hardly grown for all that you warm the bed of –"

"Takehira!" his sister cried. "You mustn't . . . please do not say such things . . . and so loudly. It will ruin both of us."

He looked around, saw the eyes watching him, and ducked his head. "Sorry. Got carried away," he muttered. They both sat in silence for a while. Then he said in a lower voice, "What Father means to do is hire some fellow from the capital. Some poor law professor who'll do the job for a reasonable fee and a house for himself and his family."

"I see." Toshiko saw indeed. She saw that she had been sold, and that her family cared only for the benefits they would reap. She hardened her heart and wished Takehira would go away.

"You aren't by any chance with child?" her brother asked, leaning forward and peering at the grass curtain as if he could see through it and her many layers of clothes to verify for himself that her belly was getting larger. "That would really be a great thing."

"No," she snapped.

He caught her tone this time and chuckled. "Don't get upset, girl. You're young. Maybe you need a bit more time. But the moment you have a child, especially a boy, you'll make all our fortunes in the blink of an eye." He rubbed his hands and grinned more widely. "You're the lucky one all right. What could be easier for a woman? A man has to work all his life to get a bit of recognition, and all you have to do . . ."

"Sssh!"

He stopped, glanced right and left, and said, "Don't be so prickly. I wasn't going to say anything."

Toshiko was so angry that she could not speak for a moment. Then she informed him quite stiffly, "I am glad you came to tell me about your appointment, Brother. No doubt you will be quite busy at the palace and in town. Do not trouble yourself about me. I cannot receive visitors in any case, and I doubt we shall meet again very soon. Please give my respects to our parents and to our brother and sister. Good bye." Without waiting for his response, she rose and left him there.

An even greater loneliness settled over Toshiko after her brother's visit. For the others, there was still much excitement about parties and New Year's visits from family and friends. A few left to spend time at home. For Toshiko, there was not so much as a letter. She moved through the busy days like a puppet, allowing herself to be dressed, posed, and at times put into the emperor's bed.

She was one of the young women chosen to participate in the circle dancing at court. One morning a carriage backed up to the south veranda, and she was helped in and sent off with one of the maids to the imperial palace. This maid was hugely excited by the excursion and chattered away to her silent mistress. After they crossed the bridge over the Kamo River, she lifted the curtain a little and commented on the sights they passed on their way to the imperial palace. Toshiko wondered where the doctor lived and worked. She leaned forward to get a look at the shops, gates, and walled mansions. Perhaps in those milling crowds was the one person in all the world she wished to see again.

Encouraged by her interest, the maid became voluble. She talked of her own home in the southern part of the capital, of visiting the two great temples, Sai-ji and To-ji, of the bustling markets with their astonishing wares and entertainments, of the artisans in the different quarters reserved for their trade. Her father, it appeared, was a paper merchant.

"Where do the doctors live?" Toshiko asked.

"Doctors? Do you mean professors, Lady Toshiko?"

"No. Physicians. Do they have their own street?"

The maid laughed. "Of course not. Most people send for one of the monks or for a pharmacist. Only the good people have learned physicians come to them."

"Oh."

When they reached Suzaku-mon, the gate to the imperial enclosure, Toshiko lost interest. She lowered the curtain over the protest of the curious maid.

That day Toshiko received instruction in the dances. She was one of forty other young women. The movements were simple enough, and she wondered why the others seemed so nervous. The ruling emperor was, after all, a mere baby. The dancers were all very young and mostly very pretty. One girl was only ten years old and charming. All of them would be gorgeously robed in costumes provided by the wardrobe office.

Hardly one of the girls slept that night. They chatted and giggled while frowning older ladies paced the hall, reminding them that they would need their sleep for the next day's performances.

Toshiko discovered the reason for their excitement. Each girl hoped that she would make an impression the next day. On this one day's public appearance in their young lives, they all hoped to have their futures decided by finding a noble husband or by becoming a lady-in-waiting for one of the imperial households. Toshiko had already gained this latter status, but her position at the retired emperor's palace – she did not mention what it entailed – was judged to be duller than those at the imperial court or in the households of the crown prince or any of the dowager empresses or imperial princesses. The retired emperor was said to be on the point of taking the tonsure.

Both performances passed uneventfully for Toshiko. Indeed, she barely paid attention to the festive atmosphere and the formal rows of senior nobles who watched them in both palaces. When it was all over, she climbed back into her carriage and returned, accompanied by more chatter from the maid, who was fascinated with the romantic possibilities of having forty beautiful young women exposed to the curious eyes of men who normally only saw an edge of a sleeve or a hem of a gown.

"You have many admirers, Lady Toshiko," she said with great satisfaction as soon as they had left the palace. "Very great gentlemen and so handsome. I have brought all their letters." She held up a fat bundle wrapped in silk.

"Throw them away," snapped Toshiko.

The maid's eyes widened. "What? Now? Throw them out into the street?"

Toshiko clicked her tongue in frustration. "No. Of course not." What would Lady Sanjo do to her if she heard about this? "You should never have accepted them. Hide them and burn them later. No, better give them to me."

The maid smiled knowingly and passed the bundle across.

From Lady Sanjo's Pillow Book

Ah, spring!

How very appropriate are the last words I wrote into in my journal. We have been so busy. The beginning of the year is always the most exciting time. There are visitors and outings and banquets every single day. "Oh, cherry blossoms, fall and hide me in a cloud, so old age will never find me!"

Indeed, I have been looking my best lately. What with all the rich meals I have been eating, I am getting positively fat. A round face and softly dimpled limbs are what seduce men. Instead of stuffing my cheeks with plums, I now line my gowns with soft rolls of silk floss, cunningly doubled in all those places that men like to touch and squeeze. To my utter delight, His Majesty took notice during one of the banquets and sent me a serving of delicacies from His own table with a note that said, "Even hungry ghosts must be fed on the New Year." It was more than I could reasonably eat, but the dear, generous man smiled so lovingly at me that I forced myself.

The change in me has been noted by others. The chancellor himself paid me a compliment the other day. I flirted shamelessly with him before His Majesty and do believe the dearest man was quite put out. I mean His Majesty, of course. The chancellor became frightened and ran off. I suppose he thought he had been caught poaching on a heavenly reserve.

Thus my chances have improved remarkably, while my rival has fallen into disfavor. He rarely sends for her any more. He even dispatched her to court to perform with the circle dancers. When I heard of this, I quickly sent for the court silk merchant and selected a particularly precious figured brocade from his samples. I chose the most striking pattern — brilliant red safflowers against green — and set about making a new robe for His Majesty. Sitting up all night, I used my daintiest stitches and imagined to myself his delight when I presented it to Him. As I sewed the sleeves, I thought of being held in His embrace, and when I stitched the collar, I pressed my face into the fabric in anticipation. The hem . . . oh, dear, the hem! The robe is casual, the sort He would wear in the evening in the privacy of his rooms. It ends above the knees to show off His full silk trousers. I made certain that it opened easily by trying it on when it was finished.

And then I composed a little verse: "Ever since I first glimpsed the realm above the clouds, my love has been as fresh and bright as the safflower."

The great moment of my presentation came after the Oba girl had left for her dancing. She looked quite crushed when any other girl would have been delighted with a visit to the imperial palace. No doubt it was due to having lost His Majesty's favor. As it is, I had no hand in it, though once I almost caught her out. Never mind.

Naturally, His Majesty was surprised when I approached him. Always gracious, he accepted my gift and read the note with the kindest smile.

"Dear Lady Sanjo," He said, "you are a treasure to me. Whenever I am sad, I only have to think of you and I laugh right away. This is a most unusual pattern. How ever did you find it?"

I nearly swooned, but managed, "When it is a matter of giving Your Majesty pleasure, nothing is impossible. I am yours to command, sire. You have but to send for me."

As it turned out, He was too busy that night and the next. I lay awake, my hair and body perfumed, and pictured to myself the moment when we would be together at last. "Eagerly I await his call, but alas, no one appears but the morning star." When He had not sent for me by the time the Oba girl returned, my tears soaked my sleeves. The disappointment might have crushed me "like the waves that pound Nagahama beach," but He did not send for her either.

Besides, by then my plan to discredit her in His Majesty's eyes was beginning to take shape after all. Her dancing for the New Year's guests at the imperial palace had done what I had failed to do: her maid informed me that all the brash young men wanted to get a taste of the emperor's morsel. They soon came, left letters and poems, and waited for replies. Regrettably, she rejected all the notes without glancing at them, but I kept my eye on her suitors and managed to see quite a few of their silly effusions in verse – comparing her to cherry blossoms and themselves to the breeze, talking about how they burned for her like Mount Fuji at night, and endlessly wringing out their wet sleeves.

To my surprise, I recognized the youngest son of the regent among them. I wondered what his father would say if he knew and then realized that the young man was perfect for my plan because he would not dare mention any part of it to anyone.

My heart became "as light as a cloud passing across a mountain peak."

When I took the young man aside, I played the concerned friend. Did he not realize, I asked, what a difficult position the young lady was in.

He admitted it, looking as sorrowful as a wilted cabbage.

Was it kind to turn her poor young head, I asked.

He perked up at this. "Oh? Does she care a little for me?" he asked eagerly.

Poor fool.

"You must not continue this," I said, looking severe. "No matter how much she may pine for you."

He brightened even more at that, then frowned. "But she has not answered my notes," he said.

"I should hope not." I shook my finger at him. "My dear young man, you must stop this nonsense. If you were caught together, it would be the end of her."

"Oh, but Lady Sanjo . . ." he muttered, looking half disconsolate, half hopeful.

I patted his arm in a motherly fashion – he is by no means unattractive – and said consolingly, "Be brave. Put her from your mind. I said the same to her only last night as she lay sleepless in the northern eave chamber."

He stared at me. For a moment, I thought I would have to lead him to the place and show him how to open the shutters. Then he nodded and bowed. "You are right to censure me, Lady Sanjo," he said. "I have been very foolish. Thank you for reminding me of my duty." And off he trod with a little bounce in his step. He is really quite attractive. I'm doing the girl a favor.

Ah, spring!

The Eave Chamber

Eventually, Toshiko returned to the eave chamber. Lady Sanjo was not likely to show her face again after her defeat over the note with the one-eyed cat, and Toshiko felt safe to take it out again. She would sit near a place where the sun slanted through a crack between the curtain and the door frame and carefully unfold the small scrap. Once it was dry, the writing had become more legible. It was very faint, but she recognized the word "come" and guessed that the rest gave directions to his house or a place where they could meet.

Her heart began to beat faster at the thought that he had wanted her to come to him. Oh, if only she had been here when he left the note. Or if at least she had found it right away. She would have run to him then. Now everything had changed, and besides he surely no longer expected her.

She spent much time staring at the smudged words, trying to guess their meaning. One was surely Sumei-mon, a gate in the city. Perhaps he lived near this gate, or in a quarter with that name or near a street called Sumei.

But always she would know that it was too late and, holding back her tears, she would refold the precious scrap and tuck it inside her mother's letter.

In the eave chamber, she felt close to him and had some privacy from prying eyes and from the constant chatter. The emperor only rarely sent for her now that He was preparing for the move to the new palace. She busied herself with writing down the last of the imayo for His collection. Soon He would no longer need her for this work, and she was afraid that He had tired already of her body. There were times when she wondered if her parents would consider Takehira's appointment and a few gowns worth their efforts. Of course, if she were to conceive, that would change everything. Takehira had been quite right about that.

Because of her loneliness and isolation, she wished for a child with all her heart. She would have someone of her own then, someone to care about, and who would care about her. Even if the child were taken from her to be raised elsewhere, she would watch it grow from a distance. She knew that giving birth to the emperor's child would not elevate her to the grandiose heights imagined by her family. Everyone still treated her like the lowliest of His Majesty's ladies, without the slightest recognition of the fact that she was also His occasional bed partner.

But her status seemed to have changed a little the day Lady Sanjo approached her with an invitation to make the eave chamber her own private domain and to sleep there in the future.

Perhaps Lady Sanjo wanted to make amends for her rudeness, but Toshiko was pleased for different reasons. Lately, a few of the ladies had received nighttime visits from men. Toshiko suspected that Shojo-ben was one of them, because her friend was strangely distracted and had a dreamy look on her pretty face. Toshiko was happy for her, but also uncomfortable. When you shared quarters with others, separated only by flimsy screens, and spent much time lying awake in the dark, you could hear every sound, and such sounds as these were all too familiar to Toshiko now. Her closeness to the secret lives of others embarrassed her and reminded her of her own duties in the emperor's curtained bed.

So she welcomed the change and had her maid move her trunks and bedding and a few screens to the eave chamber. Lady Sanjo was there, all smiles and bustling energy, ordering grass mats to be brought in and lamps and braziers to be placed just so.

"You will be quite comfortable now," she said, fluttering her fan. "This room is small but private, and you have your own small garden." She raised a shade and peered out. "Delightful. Nobody ever comes here. You can sit on the veranda if you like. I am sure His Majesty prefers that you keep away from the noisy visitors who seem to plague us lately."

It was, of course, more isolation, but Toshiko was glad of that. There was even a possibility that the emperor had become considerate of her feelings and suggested the change.

That night, she spread her bedding and set her headrest so that she faced the veranda. The weather was still cold, and the shutters were closed at night, but she propped one open a little – finding the catch already unlocked – so that she could watch the pale moon rise above the roofs of the palace buildings. Then she undressed to her under robe, something she had not done for a long time, and lay down beneath a double layer of quilts.

The moon was very beautiful this spring night, a silver disk that floated along the roof ridge in the starry blackness. She remembered how she had sat with her mother and sister, composing poems about the moon. They had not been very good poems, but she had felt cherished and happy then. She let her tears blur both moon and stars. It was a rare luxury, this open grieving. For too long a time she had had to stifle her sadness, always afraid it would be noted, or that the call for her would come while her eyes were swollen from weeping. Tonight it was too late for a summons from the emperor.

After a while, she stopped weeping and dabbed away the tears. Somewhere to the east of her, the doctor would also have gone to bed. Perhaps he, too, was looking at the same moon. Perhaps he thought of her as she thought of him. She imagined their thoughts meeting among the stars like winged fairies or like the herdsman and the weaver maid who met to make love only once a year. Oh, she would give everything for one such meeting.

The emperor had called her His Moon Princess that first time, plying her with pretty stories and pictures like the child she had been until He had taken her in His arms. Sometimes she thought she hated Him.

Her moist cheeks began to itch and she rubbed them dry with her sleeve. Children may cry, but not grown women. She closed her eyes with a sigh.

It was much quieter here than in the great room beyond the door. She was farther from her companions, whose dim shapes, covered with piles of bedding or robes, used to breathe and rustle until the darkness seemed like a huge beehive.

As she dozed off, a faint sound, barely noted, niggled at the remnants of her consciousness. A door closing somewhere? Someone on her way to the privy?

Walking on gravel? There was no gravel on the way to the privy, just the smooth boards of the corridor. Old buildings creaked. Wondering if the new palace would have fewer creaks than this one, she fell asleep.

And dreamed. Some creature hissed and scrabbled in her dream. It tugged at her quilts. The cat, she thought with a drowsy smile. Mikan, the one-eyed cat. The doctor's one-eyed cat. What gentle hands he had. His hand on hers, soothing the hurt from Mikan's scratch –

She came fully awake when the hand – a cold hand – parted her gown and touched her bare skin. A dark shape hovered above her, murmuring, searching with that impatient hand, breathing hotly in her face. For a moment she thought it was the emperor and moved sleepily to accommodate Him, but then the strange scent told her that this was not the emperor and she cried out.

It was only a soft cry and stifled instantly by the man's hand on her lips and his hissed "Ssh!"

She resisted, scrambling away, frightened now, her eyes wide, yet unseeing in the darkness. He snatched at her arm and whispered, "Don't be afraid, Lady Toshiko. I did not mean to startle you."

In her confusion, she tried to account for his presence. Had the doctor sent a message by this stranger? "Who are you?" she managed, pulling her cover closer. "What do you want?"

"I'm Fujiwara Munetada. Don't you remember me?"

She shook her head. "No. What do you want? You're not supposed to be here."

Their furtive whispering made the encounter strangely intimate. Then Toshiko remembered the questing hand on her breasts and was afraid again. But perhaps this Fujiwara nobleman had made a mistake and come to the wrong bed. She said so, and he chuckled softly.

"No mistake, my lovely. Come a little closer so I can see your beautiful face in the moonlight. I have dreamed of this moment ever since I saw you dancing."

Toshiko silently cursed the circle-dancing excursion. "You must leave instantly," she hissed. "If you don't, I shall cry for help. Surely you don't wish His Majesty's anger to fall on you."

"B-but," he stammered, "d-didn't you get my letters? Didn't you w-wish me to come?"

"I have not accepted letters from anyone, and I certainly did not wish this. Go! Now! Before it is too late."

There was a moment's silence. Then, to her astonishment, he said, "No, I won't be tricked." Crawling closer on his knees, he said in a low voice, "You are beautiful, but your manners leave something to be desired. Come, making noise will do you no good. These things are much better carried on in silence. Especially in your case."

There was a touch of menace in his tone. She suppressed her panic. He was right. She could not afford the scandal of being found with a man in her bed.

It struck her that her sudden move to this room had been Lady Sanjo's idea, and that this visit was planned. While she arrived at this knowledge, he was coolly divesting himself of his robe and untying is trousers.

"Don't," she pleaded as steadily as she could. "Please don't do this. It will destroy me."

It did not work. Laughing softly, he slipped under her cover and reached for her. She found herself grasped against a lean and muscular body that was heavily perfumed. Nausea welled up and she gagged, barely controlling the urge to vomit. Using all her strength, she pushed him away. But he was young and much stronger and heavier than she. Chuckling again deep in his throat, he pinned her down and forced a knee between her legs.

Toshiko was seized by a furious and desperate anger. When he positioned himself, breathing heavily now, and then raised himself to enter her, she screamed and struck his face hard with her fist. He fell back and staggered up with a muffled cry.

A moment later, the door flew open, and noise and lights invaded the eave chamber. Women's startled faces, ghostly white in the candle light, peered in at the pair of them. A young man was standing above her, holding his nose and staring in disbelief at the blood that dripped down between his fingers, staining his white under robe, and falling on Toshiko's bare thighs.

Sobbing, Toshiko snatched a robe and crawled away from him.

Lady Sanjo pushed past the others. "What is going on here?" she cried. The answer was obvious – except for the disgust and anger on the young nobleman's face. He glared at the women as he reached for his trousers.

Lady Sanjo was the very picture of shock and outrage. "Lady Toshiko, what have you done?" she demanded.

Toshiko said, "I've never seen him before. I woke up, and there he was." She added angrily, "Is that why you wanted me to sleep here tonight?"

Shocked silence met the accusation.

"What is this?" Fujiwara Munetada had managed to put on his trousers and coat. Now he glared at Lady Sanjo. "This is outrageous!" He mumbled through the wad of tissue pressed to his nose. "One expects better from someone of your age and breeding. I shall not forget this trick." And with that, he flounced out into the moonlit courtyard. The outer gate slammed behind him.

"I . . . I don't understand," stammered Lady Sanjo, taking in the fact that her trick had sadly, and perhaps disastrously, miscarried. "He is the regent's son and must have lost his way. How embarrassing for him. No wonder he blames his mistake on others."

The ladies exchanged glances before drifting away to discuss the incident behind her back.

Lady Sanjo looked after them with pinched lips, then turned angrily on Toshiko. "Well, I assume he's had his way. You might have handled this more discreetly. I'll send a maid to clean up."

Toshiko was at the end of her patience. She rose to confront the other woman. "He has not had his way, as you put it. But I see I was right. You did arrange this visit," she said though gritted teeth. "His Majesty will hear of it. I do not feel safe here any longer."

Lady Sanjo glowered. "How dare you? Go and tell His Majesty and see whom He believes. We saw both of you half naked. Don't think for a moment that His Majesty has regard for every young strumpet that warms his bed. He is tired of you already, my girl. And in your case, He did not think enough of the liaison to set you up in separate quarters. Should you find yourself with child, don't expect Him to acknowledge it. What happened here tonight will convince Him of your low character." And with that, she slammed out of the room.

Toshiko was stunned by her words. The unfairness of her situation filled her with despair. It was not Lady Sanjo who was her most dangerous enemy; it was the emperor Himself. Her sacrifice had been for nothing; she was no better in His eyes than a woman of pleasure. He had brought her here and dressed her up in the *shirabyoshi* costume because that was how He had thought of her. She was no more than a harlot to Him.

As the maid helped her change out of her blood-stained under robe and gathered the soiled bedding, she pondered her future. When she was alone again, she brought a candle closer, took out her writing box, and wrote a brief note, begging His Majesty for an audience. She intended to ask His permission to return home.

But the next day an answer from His secretary arrived, refusing her request with the explanation that His Majesty was too busy with the details of the move. She was referred to Lady Sanjo instead. Naturally, she did not avail herself of this recourse but stayed well clear of that lady and the others.

A servant brought her food to the eave chamber, but otherwise she was left alone. The afternoon after her disturbed night, she heard hammering in the courtyard and peered out. Workmen were doing something to the outside of the gate. After dark, she slipped out to check it. The gate had been nailed shut. She had become a prisoner.

Soon after she fell ill.

Death of a Cat

The illness came on gradually with a slight queasiness after a meal. But this worsened over a number of days until Toshiko took to her bed and was violently ill for three days, vomiting up everything she ate or drank. By the time the vomiting stopped, she was too weak to rise from her bed. She would lie still, looking mindlessly for hours at the dust motes that danced in the rays of sunlight filtering through the shutters, then fall asleep in a shower of stars.

No one bothered her. Her maid crept in a few times to stare at her and to change the stale water in the flask. Now and then one of the ladies would peer in and disappear again. Toshiko gradually became very thirsty but was afraid to drink in case the horrible cramping and purging would start again. It had been so bad that she had brought up blood and fainted after one bout.

On the fourth day, she woke to the sounds of packing and voices, both male and female, and the heavier tread of male porters. They were taking away furnishings and trunks filled with the clothing of the other women. Everyone was moving to the new palace. Perhaps she would be left to die alone here. Illness of any sort frightened people. What if this was the beginning of smallpox? All but the oldest of the palace women must fear the scarring and pitting of their faces more than death itself.

On the evening of the third day, her maid brought a bowl of rice gruel. Toshiko looked at it without interest. On the whole, starvation was not painful. She felt a pleasant languor and lightness she took for the first signs of approaching death. She welcomed this gentle death. Only her thirst troubled her.

The sounds of moving receded that night, and it became quiet. She slept fitfully and, as the first gray light of morning began to fill the room, she woke to find Shojo-ben by her side.

"Toshiko?" Shojo-ben whispered when Toshiko opened her eyes. "Can you hear me?"

Toshiko tried to speak but found her mouth was so dry that her tongue did not move. She managed a soft croak.

"I'm so glad you are better," Shojo-ben continued, trying to sound cheerful, but her eyes were full of tears. "They will surely send a doctor to have a look at you. We are to leave today, so I came to say good-bye. I promise to prepare a nice room for you in the new palace. As soon as you can travel, you will come."

Toshiko croaked again, then managed to mutter, "Fresh water?"

Shojo-ben went out to refill the flask and then supported her so she could sip. The water was wonderful and soothed her parched mouth and throat.

"Thank you," Toshiko said, sounding more like herself, but falling back weakly on her bedding.

"You are a little better, aren't you?" Shojo-ben asked timidly. "I've been so worried."

This contradicted Shojo-ben's earlier optimism, but Toshiko tried to smile. "A little," she said.

The water stayed down.

"Do you want some more food?" Shojo-ben eyed the bowl of gruel. "You did not eat much."

Toshiko made the effort to turn her head and look at the bowl. She did not remember eating any of it, but it was half-empty. Very strange. She looked away, murmuring, "No. I'm not hungry."

They were silent for a little, then Shojo-ben said, "You must try to eat to get better. I want you to be well before I leave His Majesty's service."

"You are leaving?"

Shojo-ben nodded, smiled. "I am to be married."

The light was getting brighter in her room with the rising sun, and Toshiko saw the happiness on her friend's face. "I did not know," she said wonderingly. "How did you manage it?" She remembered the clandestine visits, but it took parental and imperial consent to release a young woman from her service in the palace.

Shojo-ben looked down at her folded hands and blushed. "My husband-to-be will take up his post as governor of Izumi soon and wants me to go with him. He went to my father, and together they went to His Majesty." She looked up and said earnestly, "His Majesty never had any interest in me. He made no difficulties. It is you he prefers."

The knowledge that her misery was due to the emperor's fickle desire for her made Toshiko turn her head away, trying not to weep. "I am happy for you, but I shall miss you so much," she murmured and then could not stop her tears. She felt very weak. Her only friend was leaving and there was no hope for her. It was best to die quickly.

Shojo-ben embraced her and held her.

Outside the eave chamber, someone wailed loudly. Shojo-ben looked toward the door as other voices were raised. "That was Lady Dainagon," she said, releasing Toshiko and getting up. "I wonder what happened. I'll be back in a moment."

Toshiko did not much care. On the whole she was glad to be left alone, though she supposed that she should be happier for Shojo-ben. She dried her face and groped for the water flask, pouring another cup. It was even more refreshing than the first, and she drank a third cup before Shojo-ben returned, looking distressed.

"Mikan is dead. Lady Dainagon just found him," she said, sitting back down. "Apparently he died during the night. You can imagine how upset she is. She loved that cat. He must have eaten something that did not agree with him because he vomited before he died."

Toshiko's eyes flew to the bowl of gruel. She struggled into a sitting position. "The cat's vomit," she asked, "was it rice gruel?"

Shojo-ben looked at the bowl and gasped. "Oh, you think the cat . . . that there was something in your gruel? Oh, Toshiko, are you feeling ill again?"

"No. I did not eat any gruel."

"Oh, thank heaven. That is all right then."

"No," said Toshiko. "It is not all right. The gruel was intended for me. And I ate gruel before I became so ill. Someone here wants me to die."

Shojo-ben's eyes widened in horror. "Are you sure? I cannot believe . . ."

Just then, Lady Sanjo put her head in at the door and said, "Time to get ready, Lady Shojo-ben. Ah, I see you are feeling better, Lady Toshiko. Will you be able to travel with us?"

Toshiko's heart beat wildly. "N . . . no, Lady Sanjo. I'm too weak and feel very sick again."

"Ah." Lady Sanjo nodded. "I shall inform His Majesty. Perhaps he will wish you to return to your family." She bustled off.

"I think she did it," said Toshiko, glaring after her. "I shall not eat anything served to me in the future." She turned to her friend. "Before you leave, would you find me some food, rice cakes or such, something that was meant for the others?"

Shojo-ben looked scandalized. "Oh, you cannot think . . . she would never dare . . . His Majesty would have her exiled. Along with her husband and family." But she saw Toshiko's exhausted face and added, "I shall get you food, but I pray that you are wrong about this." Then she dashed off.

Toshiko did not think she was wrong. The woman hated her, had hated her from the beginning. She did not know why, but everything that had gone wrong for her had been Lady Sanjo's doing. The woman had failed with her plots in the past, but this was too much. Now she was desperate enough to murder her.

Only a short while ago, Toshiko had longed for a quick death. Now she was perversely determined not only to live but to escape from this life. As His Majesty would not let her go, and her family was not about to intercede for her as Shojo-ben's had done, she had no choice but to run away.

Outside she could hear the sound of wagon wheels and the bellowing of oxen. The carriages were being backed up to the south veranda to take the others to their new quarters. Soon she would be alone. Shojo-ben slipped in one final time, her sleeve full of rice cakes. Toshiko thanked her, and hid the food under her bedding. They cried a little over their goodbyes, and then Shojo-ben was gone, the noises receded, and all became quiet.

After a while, the maid came to remove the half-empty bowl of gruel. She looked sullen. Toshiko no longer trusted her and pretended to be asleep. She suspected that the woman had been carrying out Lady Sanjo's orders.

During the long day, she nibbled on a few rice cakes and drank more water. When the maid refilled the flask, she worried that the water might also be poisoned. This time, the woman asked, "Are you feeling better, Lady?" and Toshiko murmured weakly, "No. Go away."

She knew that she must leave as soon as she was strong enough to walk, but her options were few. She could not go to Takehira who lived with other guard officers in his military quarters in the imperial city. She could not go home without money. In any case, neither her parents nor her brother would make her welcome. She would simply be returned to the palace with apologies.

Perhaps she could seek refuge in a temple. But His Majesty would find her there more quickly than any place else.

There was only Doctor Yamada. She wanted to go to him more than anything, but she was afraid. What if he did not want her? This brought tears to her eyes again. Oh, she thought, this weeping must stop.

She tried to stand and managed a few wobbly steps to relieve herself in a bucket behind a screen. Encouraged, she returned to her bed with her mirror. The light was poor with the shutters closed, but she could see enough to know that she looked pale and unattractive. She cried some more and then slept.

Toward evening, the maid brought another bowl of the warm gruel. When she left, Toshiko smelled the food. She fancied it had an odd odor and was grayer than usual. She put it back untouched and ate another rice cake. Her appetite was coming back quickly. The cake tasted delicious.

During the night, Toshiko considered how to get away. The gate to her small courtyard was barred, so she must leave another way. Fortunately the building was nearly empty, and her maid did not seem to be watchful. She thought about her coach journey to the imperial palace. They had passed through a gate, then traveled northward before turning west to the river. It had not taken very long to reach the river. If she could leave at night while everyone was asleep, she should be able to get out of the building unnoticed. But the gate guards would surely stop her. What to do?

Toward morning she thought of a way. Only one more day.

The Emperor's Dolls

With his move to the Hojuji Palace, the emperor decided to break with the past. The world of the senses had become too oppressive, too fraught with disappointment and self-recrimination. He was determined to purify himself of all delusions and walked around his new residence in the first flush of pious enthusiasm.

He would take up his cloistered life here, at peace at last. The new palace combined the best of the two worlds he would henceforth inhabit, directing the nation and treading the eightfold path to enlightenment.

There was the new temple hall, the Rengeo-in, with a thirty-bay-long Buddha hall consecrated to the thousand-armed Kannon. He planned to take the tonsure there, bidding farewell to the world of physical passions.

Soon, very soon now.

He even put aside his collection of songs because it reminded him of his sins of the flesh – troublingly fresh and frequent in his thoughts. Otomae had not returned since the incident of the "Little Snail" song. It was as well, for she, too, made him feel vaguely ashamed and foolish these days.

Only Lady Sanjo was left to remind him of his lapse, and she demanded to see him nearly every day, always claiming urgent business. The urgent business, as often as not, concerned Toshiko.

When he returned to his private rooms, she appeared again. He noticed that she had grown amazingly fat. At the rate she was expanding, it would be no time at all before she looked like that unfortunate woman in his Scroll of Diseases, the one who was so obese she had to lean on two maids to support her as she waddled along.

Lady Sanjo collapsed into an obeisance with a grunt and puff of breath. Really, thought the Emperor, eyeing her cherry-blossom-colored gown with distaste, what possessed her to wear such unsuitably youthful colors at her age?

"What is it now?" he snapped.

She sat up on her knees. "Am I being a bother, sire?" she asked with a simper, blinking her eyes at him over her fan.

"I am busy, as always."

"Oh." She turned her head a little and blinked some more. "I can come back later, when it is more convenient, Your Majesty."

"No," he said quickly. The infernal woman would just continue to pester him the rest of the day. "Is something the matter with your eyes?"

She bowed again with that odd little grunt. "Oh, Your Majesty is always excessively kind. I am afraid I am blinded by the sun whenever I set eyes on you, sire."

Irritating female! It was this sort of adulation that made getting rid of her awkward when he was tempted to do so.

Most recently there had been that unpleasantness of the regent complaining of her rudeness to his son. The young man had been drunk and stumbled into the women's quarters by accident, not an unusual occurrence during the many festivities of the New Year. Lady Sanjo apparently had accused him of trying to rape one of the women. Naturally, the young man and the regent had been offended. But she could hardly be dismissed for being watchful. Frowning, he said sharply, "Make it brief."

She blinked again. "It is about Lady Toshiko."

He sighed. "It is always about Lady Toshiko. What is it now?"

"As Your Majesty may recall, the foolish girl indulged in too much rich food over the holidays and was too ill to be moved with the other ladies." Lady Sanjo paused to wait for his reaction.

He compressed his lips. "I remember. I trust she is better and has joined you?"

"No, Your Majesty. We have tried everything, but she seems worse. Apparently the food here does not agree with her. I suggest that she be allowed to return to her family." She blinked and fluttered her fan nervously.

The emperor stared at her, wondering how sick Toshiko was. In his efforts to cleanse his mind and body from earthly attachments, he had avoided her. But if she was really ill, he should go and express his concern. The image of her, lying amid tangled bedding, her long hair spread around her young body, troubled him. "Hmm," he said. "I did not know it was so serious. What are her symptoms?"

Lady Sanjo twisted her fan in indecision. "Oh, dear," she murmured. "It is not nice to talk of such things in Your Majesty's presence."

"Nonsense. I take an interest in medicine and have seen sickness before," he snapped.

"Yes, sire. She still cannot keep any food down, sire, and earlier she suffered from the flux. I do beg your pardon for mentioning such a dirty thing."

He frowned. "She's not with child?"

"Oh no, sire."

Relieved, he pursed his lips. "Hmm. I should pay her a visit, but at the moment I am very busy. Perhaps my physician can have a look at her."

"Sire, it is not permitted to send a man to the women's quarters," cried Lady Sanjo.

The emperor snorted at such old-fashioned ways. "The man is old enough to be her grandfather, Lady

Sanjo," he said. And so he was, for this was his personal physician and not that clever and handsome young Doctor Yamada who was entirely too knowledgeable about sexual matters to be dispatched to Toshiko. "If she has not been able to eat anything for the past two weeks or more, she is far more seriously ill than you have given me to understand. Or are you exaggerating again just to see me?"

This plain speaking cast Lady Sanjo into such agitation that she forgot to flutter her eyes. "Oh, no, Your Majesty. I would never dream of such a thing. I am merely doing my duty. My report is based on what her maid tells me. Of course, the woman may say things to make herself seem more indispensable as a nurse. I shall go myself and make certain of the facts, and then return to report again to Your Majesty."

The emperor lost his temper. "You should have done this in the first place, Lady Sanjo," he said with a scowl. "It is your duty. In the future you will not trouble me again with unverified reports. When you have investigated, leave a message with my secretary." He saw with satisfaction that he had finally shocked her into comprehension. She gave him a pitiful look, sniffled a little as she prostrated herself, and retreated.

His contentment was gone. He regretted the brief affair with Toshiko – not just for spiritual reasons or because it had brought him little joy, but because it had brought her even less. At least she had not conceived. As soon as she was better, he would let her go. Naturally, in view of their relationship, he would reward her.

She would return to her family a rich woman, endowed with a suitable gift of rice lands, or, if she preferred, she would be married to some provincial official. If neither of those options was to her taste, she could join his daughter's household as one of her attendants. This struck him as excessively generous, considering how her family had tried to manipulate him.

He was saddened by the fact that he had never found a woman who had loved him for himself. There had been so many of them in his life. His childhood was spent in the company of women. To be served by so many women can be a cruel thing for a small boy. To be forever handled, petted, dressed, undressed, bathed, dandled, and made much of may suit a dog but it makes a boy very irritable.

There had been the matter of his dolls. Long before he was old enough to have any understanding, he was given an *amagatsu* doll to protect him. It was made of two crossed pieces of bamboo with a ball of silk for a head and a simple suit of clothes draped over the sticks. It stood at his head when he slept, arms extended protectively over him, and it stayed with him until he reached manhood at age fifteen.

The idea was for roaming evil spirits to mistake the doll for him and possess it instead.

From time to time, other dolls appeared. The paper ones he breathed on and then they were rubbed over his body before being burned to rid him of sins. The *hoko* dolls were mostly toys. They had soft silk bodies stuffed with floss silk and painted faces and black silk hair. They wore fine clothes resembling his own. He played with the *hoko* dolls much the same way the court ladies played with him. He dressed and undressed them, made them walk here and there, made them sit or stand, made them eat and dance, and sometimes he got angry and threw them at one of his ladies-in-waiting.

Now and then, an unstuffed *hoko* would make its appearance. The limp doll was used to exorcise his quarters in the palace. Being hollow, it gathered invisible ghosts and spirits inside it. These evil and jealous phantoms were attracted by his imperial presence. After the priest declared the premises free of them, the doll was ceremoniously drowned in the lake of the imperial gardens after being set afloat in a paper boat. He remembered enjoying this particular exorcism greatly – unlike that other one a few years later.

On the whole, he had regarded his dolls with mixed feelings. He was not sure if they were loving companions and protectors or hollow vessels which hid the very evil he must fear. Once he asked his nurse, Lady Kii, why the *hoko* doll was hollow and why it had to be drowned.

Lady Kii showed him that the *amagatsu* doll also had this "hollowness" because its frame was made of two crossed sections of bamboo. "Bamboo is hollow," she said. "Evil spirits can slip inside. Better inside the doll than inside Your Highness."

Afterwards, he had spent many days watching for the evil spirits and finally he had taken the *amagatsu* apart without finding anything. For his researches he had armed himself with his ceremonial sword to slay any apparitions that might approach.

When his Fujiwara grandfather heard about it, he had laughed. The story had got around. Prince Masahito threatening his *amagatsu* with his sword became an amusing topic for the courtiers and ladies-in-waiting. They came and peered at him as he stood watch, and ran away laughing. One day he crept behind a screen and cried.

Lady Kii found him there. She was a kind-hearted woman and took the trouble to explain the matter further. "You cannot see the evil spirits, Highness," she said. "They are invisible manifestations of the evil in other people. If someone bears you a grudge, that evil intention slips into the doll. If someone is jealous of you, that, too, is trapped inside the doll. In this way, resentment which might turn murderous and kill you, either by poison, or sickness, or possession, cannot harm you. There is no need to watch. The doll does all the watching, you see."

But the next day his brother, the emperor, heard the tale and stopped by to tease him. His Majesty's attendants dutifully laughed as Sutoku, himself only thirteen at the time, made fun of his little brother. This had so enraged him that he had turned his sword against Sutoku. Only the presence of Lady Kii had saved His Majesty from receiving a serious wound.

The incident had painful repercussions. For a subject to raise a sword against the emperor was the ultimate sacrilege. Only the fact that he was a small child saved him. The question of exile was raised and rejected. In the end, it was decided that Prince Masahito must be possessed and would undergo formal exorcism.

Four ladies-in-waiting pinned him to the floor by kneeling on his arms and legs, while the abbot of the Ninna Temple and various celebrated clerics prayed over him.

They reported later that the spirit had spoken through the prince's lips. It had said, "I hate all of you. I hate my brothers and sisters. I hate the emperor," and uttered many dreadful threats. Eventually, the abbot had managed to subdue the demon.

The incident was not forgotten, but things returned more or less to normal afterward. Lady Kii wisely locked the ceremonial sword away, the brothers saw each other only rarely, and then only in the presence of others. But he was not made Crown Prince. His mother found the incident irritating but trivial, but his father expressed his first serious worries about Prince Masahito's intelligence.

He had learned from all this that evil spirits emanated from people, who were as hollow as the dolls, and he believed that he would be safe only as long as he controlled them. Experience had proven him right.

Blaming Lady Sanjo for his glum mood, he rose and walked to his office. His secretary, Tameyazu, jumped up and prostrated himself. The emperor gave him the barest nod and sat down behind his desk. He looked at the arrangement of the furnishings, and wondered where Shinzei would fit in. Then he decided he did not want Shinzei here, not yet, maybe never again. Shinzei had counseled him to bed the girl, as had Otomae. And Kiyomori. He would never be anyone's puppet again.

Flight

The maid snored.

Toshiko had been aware of the irritating habit for weeks. It was probably the reason why this woman, of all the servants, had been left behind to look after her.

Tonight she greeted the rasping sound with relief. As long as she heard it, she was safe. She began by applying her make-up, making it thicker and more garish than usual because she wanted to be taken for one of the professional entertainers. Then she dressed in her *shirabyoshi* costume, adding the small drum, the sword, and the hat. Because she had no one to help her, she was soon out of breath and weak-kneed and had to sit down to rest.

Blessedly, the snoring in the distance continued unabated. Faintly, from outside, came the muffled twanging of the bowstrings of the guards. The sound, meant to scare away criminals and evil spirits, was followed by the calling out of the hour: the hour of the rat. A moment later the temple bell rang, too.

It was time. She got up and took a final sip of water. Then she tied on the tall hat, put the sword through her sash, and slipped the drum cord over her shoulder. She slid open the door to the interior of the hall by tiny increments. The track was well-oiled, but she could not risk the smallest noise. The snoring was louder now. Good. It would cover the whispering of her silk trousers as she glided across to the southern veranda.

She had almost reached the outer doors when the snoring stopped abruptly. Taking the next few steps quickly, she froze with her hand on the shutter. All was silent. Was the woman awake and listening? Toshiko's heart beat so loudly that she was afraid she would not hear her coming. She was about to sink down on trembling knees when the snoring started up again, softly at first, then gaining full power. With a sigh of relief, Toshiko lifted the shutter. It seemed heavy, but she had lost much of her strength during the past days. Gritting her teeth, she managed to raise it enough to slip out and lower it again. The effort left her gasping for breath.

The night was very dark, and a light rain was falling. With a shiver, she pulled the collar of her jacket up around her neck and set off in the direction of the north gate. Her slippers were soon soaked and the hems of her full trousers heavy with moisture.

The unfamiliar grounds of the palace lay empty and silent. She passed several dark buildings she knew nothing about. In the stables were lights, and she could hear and smell the horses inside. Panic returned. Where there were horses, there were grooms. She hurried past. The raised and curving roofline of the north gate hove into sight, and with it more lights and the guards' barracks. Sounds of raucous singing came from the barracks. The thought of being caught by men like those inside almost frightened her into turning around.

The massive outer gate was closed and barred for the night. She must leave that way or not at all. The most dangerous moment had come. She rested a little to gather her courage and strength, then walked quickly toward the gate house.

Iron cressets hung suspended from the eaves of the massive gate. They held burning pine branches to light the area and sputtered and smoked in the drizzle.

The door to the guard house stood open and light fell on the wet gravel outside. Toshiko crept up. Two soldiers in the uniforms of the outer palace guards sat on the floor, playing *go* and drinking warmed wine. The wine pitcher rested on a small brazier. When one of the men turned to refill his cup he saw her outside the door. His eyes widened. He scrambled up. "What have we here?" he said, smiling broadly. His companion joined him in the doorway.

Toshiko looked uncertainly at their wine-flushed, grinning faces. Apprehension knotted her stomach. "Please let me out, honorable officers," she asked, bowing.

"Not so fast, my pretty," said the first guard. "Come in out of the rain. We can use a little company."

Toshiko took a breath and bowed again, with a little flourish, just as a *shirabyoshi* did after her performance. "Begging your pardon, but not tonight, my brave officers," she said, trying to sound regretful. "I'm exhausted. They've have kept me dancing for hours. Please let me out."

"I bet that's not all they kept you for," said the second guard. His companion guffawed.

Toshiko offered, "I'll be back tomorrow. Maybe then?" She smiled and performed another small dance movement.

The second guard shook his head and returned to the game. The first man stepped outside. "A promise? I'll be waiting. Just ask for Corporal Mori at the barracks. I bet I can make you dance all night, and not on your feet either." He laughed.

She hid her disgust. He sauntered to the gate and lifted the heavy bar. Pulling one wing of the gate open just far enough for her to slip through, he waited until she stepped forward, then he snatched her, pressing her against the closed section with his body. He pushed his face into hers. She gagged on the sour fumes of wine. Inserting a hand into her jacket, he squeezed one of her breasts. "Sure you won't stay a little, sweetheart?" he murmured against her lips.

She gasped and slapped his face.

For a moment he looked angry, but then he stepped aside with a chuckle. "Oh, all right, all right," he said. "I can see you're bushed. Tomorrow then. Don't forget."

She did not give him time to change his mind but slipped through the opening and ran.

The road took her straight to the bridge into the city. When she was out of sight of the palace, she slowed a little to catch her breath. The rain still drizzled, but over the mountains to the east the sky was clearing. Moon and stars appeared briefly between ragged clouds and were hidden again. It was no longer so dark now that she was in the open. Ahead lay the city, not quite asleep because lights glimmered here and there. But the road was empty, and even on the bridge were only a few late stragglers. They walked hunched into their clothes against the misting rain and paid no attention to her. The water lapped against the bridge supports and muffled the sound of steps on the wooden planks.

An odd feeling of lightheadedness seized her. She was free – she was truly free. Nobody would find her now. Nobody could ever again force her will and use her body without her permission.

In the city, the storefronts were shuttered and few lights showed in houses. She needed directions to Sumei-mon but there was no one to ask. And there was soon another problem: her costume was a familiar and inviting sight to the night crawlers of the city.

A drunk appeared suddenly out of the darkness and propositioned her, reaching with greedy hands for her sleeves and making obscene demands. She ran, diving into an alley, where she stumbled about and fell over unseen obstacles. A dog charged at her, barking and growling through some broken fencing. She tripped over her sword. When the drum caught on a fencepost, jerking her off her feet into the mud, she tore it off, throwing it, the sword, and the hat into someone's garden before running on.

Her rain-soaked clothing was heavy, and she was out of strength quickly. When the moon came out again, she was alone in a dank corner filled with refuse and broken furniture. She leaned against a wall to rest, then let herself slide down, her legs too weak to hold her.

But the cold and wet soaked through her clothes, and her clammy jacket clung to her body, chilling her to the bone. Teeth chattering, she got up. She must find the doctor or perish in this darkness.

Walking more slowly now and stumbling often, she took her direction by a glimpse of a distant pagoda. Where there was a pagoda, there was a temple, and in a temple, there must be good people who followed the Buddha's way, people who would help her.

Even as she thought this, she stumbled over a sleeping monk.

He was one of those who had taken vows of poverty and wandered the country begging for their food. This one had found a doorway to sleep in, his wide straw hat covering his head against the drizzle, and his bare legs sticking out into the alleyway. Because his legs were so dirty that it was hard to tell them from the mud, Toshiko had stepped on them.

Her heart stopped when the mud-colored creature scrambled up with a curse. It was as if the earth had opened up to spit out an angry goblin. Then she saw the shaven head and the monk's robe, and relief flooded through her. ""Oh, thank heaven," she cried, "forgive me, reverend sir. I did not see you there."

He stopped ranting and peered at her from bleary eyes. "Watch where you're going next time," he grumbled, rubbing his leg.

"Yes, it was my fault," she said meekly. "I am very sorry." Then she asked, "Please, could you direct me? I am looking for Doctor Yamada. He lives near the Sumei-mon, I think."

"You're lost?" the monk asked, his eyes roaming over her shivering figure. "New in town? You look pretty young to be on the game."

Confused, she backed away. He followed, smiling now. Even in the murk, she saw that his teeth were long and yellow and he was no longer young. She could smell onions on his breath and sweat and dirt on his body.

"Come, don't be shy, girl," he said, pushing his face into hers and reached into his robe. He brought out a few coins and rattled them in his hand. "It's your lucky night. I'm in funds."

She swallowed hard and took another step back, bumping into an empty barrel and losing her balance when it toppled. He caught her and tried to kiss her. His onion breath was hot in her face, and his fumbling hand was at her trouser bands.

"No," she screamed, pushing at him. He laughed. "Please," she begged with a gulp, "you're mistaken . . . ." But even though he was a monk, she knew this was no mistake and felt the sour bile rising in her throat. She retched. He loosened his hold and eyed her suspiciously. "What's the matter with you?"

"I'm sick," she mumbled, a hand over her mouth.

"Sick?" He stepped away. "How dare you accost people in your condition?" He spat and abandoned her quickly.

Toshiko gulped in cold, wet air to settle her stomach, then limped away herself.

The alley opened into a road, and this road led to another where she could see lights and hear people. She saw light came from the gently swaying lantern of a wine shop. Customers were leaving. Rain still misted the night air, and across the street several women sheltered under the eaves of a house. When men left the wine shop, the women ran out to talk to them. Their luck was not good. One of the men pushed the nearest woman away so roughly that she fell into the mud. The women went back, calling rude and dirty words after the men.

Toshiko was desperate and by now felt safer with women than with men. Stepping from the shadow into the light, she started toward them, calling out, "Please, can you help me?" At that moment a drunk stumbled from the wine shop and threw his arms around her for support.

"I'll help you, my precious," he promised thickly.

For a moment, they swayed together like a pair of wrestlers. Then Toshiko squealed and, with more luck than design, rammed a knee into the drunk's groin. He sat down hard, doubled over.

One of the women crossed the street, glaring at Toshiko. "What do you want here, bitch?"

Toshiko looked at her, shocked by such anger. The woman was no longer young and her face was plain and marked by smallpox. She wore clothes that were even stranger than her own costume, and much dirtier.

"I am lost," Toshiko said. The woman balled her fist. "Please," Toshiko cried, "all I want is directions." Too late. The fist struck her painfully in the middle of the chest and knocked her back against the wall of the wine shop. Toshiko cried out and wrapped her arms around the pain.

The woman laughed. It was an ugly sound. "I know what you're up to. Get away from here and don't come back! Go on! Run, or we'll teach you manners."

Toshiko just looked at her. She could barely stand, let alone run, so she did nothing, hoping dimly that the woman would disappear and the pain in her chest would fade and all would be well.

Only nothing was well.

The woman seemed to think she was defiant. She called to her companions.

Thinking that they would surely kill her, Toshiko tried to take a step, but her feet would not obey. She sank to her knees and waited hopelessly as the other women crossed the street. The drunk staggered to his feet and looked on with interest.

One of the women came more quickly. "No, Kosue," she said, putting herself between Toshiko and the pock-marked one. "She's just a child." She asked Toshiko, "What are you doing here? Where d'you live?"

The unexpected kindness brought tears to Toshiko's eyes. "Thank you," she said, wiping her eyes. "I was looking for Doctor Yamada's house." Despairing of that purpose, she raised her eyes to the pagoda again. "That temple. I'll go there in just a moment. As soon as I have a little strength."

"Doctor Yamada, is it? You do look bad. Are you sick, poor girl?"

"Yes. No." Toshiko stopped, not sure which answer was correct or useful in this situation.

The woman bent and put an arm around her. "Come, lean on me. I know where he lives," she said, and to the others, "She was just looking for the doctor, you stupid sluts."

The women stepped away then, guiltily, and let them pass.

Toshiko was not sure where they were going or how far. She concentrated on putting one foot before the other. When they stopped, she looked around dazedly. The dark shapes of trees and houses seemed to be doing a slow dance.

"We're here," her companion said, releasing her.

The ground began to sway and Toshiko saw it coming toward her. The woman caught her and propped her against a wall, then went to knock on the door. After a moment, she said, "Someone's coming. Good luck!" and disappeared into the night.

In her black haze, the thought that she had been led into a trap crossed Toshiko's mind, but she was too weak to save herself. When the door of the house opened, she did not bother to raise her head.

A man's voice asked, "What is wrong? Do you need help?"

She took a step away from the wall and fainted.

From Lady Sanjo's Pillow Book

Oh, the injustice of it!

It's all because of that demon of a girl. Why did the fool have to run away? And where was that idiot of a maid? Asleep, she said. Well, she won't sleep well where she is headed.

We searched all day, every nook and corner of our own building and then the palace grounds.

Eventually, I sent the stupid maid to the gates. When she came back, I could see the truth on her face. The misbegotten wench had dressed up in those clothes His Majesty gave her, and the dolts at the gate had taken her for a hired harlot and let her out. In the face of disaster, I was secretly amused: men always know.

But it anything but laughable, though I did not then, in my wildest imaginings have an inkling of the outcome. That night, I had to go to inform His Majesty.

He turned perfectly white at the news and then red with anger. "What?" He demanded in a terrible voice.

"Are you telling me that one of my ladies left the palace after dark and on foot?"

I thought His fury was directed at the girl and replied, "I am afraid, Sire, that she was a most unsuitable person. A country-bred girl. Such people have no idea how to behave among their betters."

He just looked at me. It occurred to me belatedly that my comment was thoughtless, given the fact that He had honored the wench with His favor. But before I could apologize, He said, "Did you not report to me only yesterday that Lady Toshiko was ill? How then could she walk away and leave the palace in the middle of the night?"

I had to confess that I did not know. "That maid must have been drunk," I suggested.

"And who," He snapped, "is responsible for the welfare of the ladies serving me? Who makes the arrangements for serving women and looks after the needs of every lady in my quarters?"

Ah, the unfairness of that!

I replied – by then in tears – that I had been busy with the move to the new quarters and could not be in two places at the same time.

"But you, Lady Sanjo," He said in a tone that cut me to the heart, "left a sick young girl behind, alone and in the care of an unreliable servant."

I murmured an apology. I don't recall my words. The moment was too painful. And then He uttered the terrible words: "Out of my sight!"

I crawled away and hid myself in the darkest corner of the women's quarters where I prayed to Buddha and all his helpers. I made vows to copy the Lotus Sutra five hundred times if only I were forgiven. I wept until all my sleeves were soaked. And I wrote to His Majesty.

Temple Bells

Sometimes Doctor Yamada's patients forced their way into his thoughts and traveled home with him, clamoring for his attention and his pity, begging him not to rest until he had made them better, tormenting him with silent pleas to save their lives.

That night it had been a young girl with a raging fever after giving birth to a puny child that died soon after. He had sat with her for long hours, fretting at his helplessness, changing cold compresses on her head, watching for signs that her young body would win the battle. But toward sunset the familiar veiling had begun to dull her eyes and told him that he could not stop the coming of death. He had seen its approach often in the past, but this time it had touched him especially, because this young mother was Toshiko's age and, while she was not very beautiful, she had had the same smile for him before the coming darkness wiped away all trace of trust.

He had to leave her finally, bone-weary and afraid of seeing her die.

Later he lay on his bed, staring into the fathomless darkness, wondering if he was really any use to anyone. Even those he thought he was helping might regain their health without him, and too many of his patients died.

Sleep does not come when a man struggles with the darkness in his heart. He lay awake, probing his doubts like a festering wound, and counted the times the temple bells called out the hour.

Shortly before dawn, there was a faint knocking at the street door. He got up more wearily than he had lain down. It was probably the father of the dying girl or some other desperate case. They never knocked at this hour unless there was no hope.

The night was still very dark. A faint smell of rain and moist soil filled the air – a scent of spring and growing things. The beginnings of life in the middle of death, he thought bitterly. His visitor was leaning against the wall of his house. It was too dark to see more than a vague shape, lighter than the surrounding night or the plaster of the wall. He was not sure if it was a man or a woman; the clothes look elaborate and formal, a white jacket over full trousers. Dully, he wiped his eyes and realized that it must be one of the street entertainers who sang and danced in the markets in men's clothes.

"What is wrong?" he asked. "Do you need help?"

She raised her head, her face with its garish make-up luminous in the darkness. "Yes," she said softly –

just that – and took a step toward him. Before he could catch her, she crumpled to the stone path.

He picked her up. She was light in his arms, but her clothes got in his way, as did the long hair. Its length astonished him. He stumbled with his burden to his room and laid her down on his bedding. Then he located the flint and lit the wick of his oil lamp, using that to light the candle near his desk, and carried both across the room to examine his patient.

She was struggling to sit up, looking dazedly around the room. "I'm sorry," she said. "I did not know where else to go."

He knew the voice but could not quite believe it. Toshiko? At this time of night? In his room?

He must have said her name aloud, standing there frozen in the utter surprise and joy of it, because she looked up at him and nodded. And began to cry.

He almost dropped the oil lamp in his haste to kneel and take her cold hands, to look in her face, searching for the familiar features under the thick paint. The black paint that ringed her eyes had made streaks down the white cheeks. He melted with love.

"Oh my dearest," he said. His voice trembled. "What happened to you? What can I do?" He remembered her fainting on his door step and asked anxiously, "Are you ill?"

She wiped at the tears with her sleeve, leaving smudges on the white silk, and smiled at him, shaking her head. His heart nearly overturned at that smile. She said, "No. Not now," and squeezed his hands gently. "Not now," she said again and removed her hands from his to reach out for him.

They held each other without speaking. He thought he could feel her heart beating against his and stroked her hair. She was wet, her hair heavy with rain. At some point, he told her that he loved her and made her cry again and clutch him more tightly.

When the first faint gray light of dawn intruded, they were lying naked in each other's arms. They had got there without conscious thought and without volition but with the urgency of an act long overdue.

Afterward they talked. She told him of the poisoned gruel and the dead cat, about dressing in her costume in the middle of the night and slipping past the snoring maid, past the gate guards, of walking through the night, across the river and along the dark streets, asking the people of the night for his house, the one he had written on the slip of paper, and of being shown the way by a real prostitute.

Later he got up, throwing on some clothes, and went to the kitchen for warm water. He knelt and cleaned her face with great tenderness, finding under the mask again the girl he remembered, paler, thinner, and more beautiful.

Only then did she tell him about the emperor, bowing her head, ashamed.

But he had known, had known it when they lay together and their bodies joined – had not wanted to think about it then because of his own responsibility in the matter. It did not affect his love for her, but it would affect their future together.

Otori walked in, having been woken by his excursion into her kitchen. She carried his gruel on a tray and stopped in surprise at seeing a woman in his bed, wearing nothing but her thin under robe. Her sharp eyes took in the disordered bedding and noted his own undress, the embarrassment that was surely on their faces. She stood, at a loss whether to be scandalized or pleased, frowning and smiling and then frowning again.

He was suddenly filled with great joy and took Toshiko's hand. "My dear," he said, "this is Otori, our housekeeper." To Otori, he said, "Otori, you should have brought moon cakes for my bride."

Outside the temple bells began to ring again, and Otori dropped her tray.

Her Husband's Son

Toshiko spent the day after her wedding night in a happy daze. He had been so gentle, so loving. Exactly as she had dreamed he would be. Comparisons to His Majesty made her hot with shame, and she put such thoughts from her mind quickly. But the difference filled her with a deep contentment. She smiled as she walked about her husband's study, admiring his books and pictures, touching his desk just where his hand might have rested, picking up his brush and raising its tip to her lips.

Later, she walked outside, looking at the garden and the small building that was filled with mysterious herbs, hanging from the rafters upside down, like a miniature forest of dead trees and shrubs. Sadahira was a healer. He helped people get over their illnesses. Just as he had helped her the night before. And Sadahira was her husband.

Near the fishpond, she met a small boy. He was a handsome child and seemed kind the way he was feeding the fish. She guessed he must be Sadamu. Her husband had told her about his two sons. They were hers now, too.

She smiled at the boy, who stood still, looking at her, waiting.

"I'm Toshiko," she said. But that was wrong, wasn't it? She was the wife of his father. Would he call her mother? She decided to leave it up to him. "I'm to live here now as your father's wife. You are Sadamu, aren't you?"

The boy nodded. He did not seem surprised at all. No doubt, he already knew.

"I'm very happy to meet you. Will you be my friend?"

Sadamu's face finally relaxed. He nodded and smiled. "You are very pretty," he said. "Would you like to feed the fish?"

And so they fed the fish together. Sadamu told her their names and explained which ones were ill-tempered, and which shy, and who could swim the fastest.

Later that afternoon, she met Sadahira's other son. The one called Hachiro. She was curious about him, because Sadahira had looked unhappy when he talked about him. She had asked if the boy was troublesome, but Sadahira had merely said, "No, but I wish I could trust him. He is gone so much and when he is here, he moves around the house so quietly that he startles me."

"But that doesn't sound so bad," Toshiko said, thinking of her brother Takahira, who was always in trouble and had a very cruel streak.

"I know," said her husband. "I'm doing the boy an injustice. He's a very good student, I'm told. But even so I think there is something not right."

She heard him coming home, though he was quiet. But she had been looking at a book and the house was still. She heard soft steps in the corridor, and a dark figure passed the open doorway.

He had seen her, too, for he slid to a halt and crept back to peer around the corner of the door. She stood at his father's desk, and looked back at him. He was slender and awkward with the awkwardness of a boy who has shot up suddenly. His neck was too long, and his arms hung loosely by his side, bony wrists and long-fingered hands showing below the sleeves of his schoolboy's robe. Unlike Sadamu, he was quite ugly, with a long face and thin lips, and a pair of penetrating black eyes. He stared at her as if she were a butterfly he wished pierce through its body. He made no sound, just looked.

And she blushed. He was not much younger than she. They locked eyes, and she forced herself to smile.

He glared and drew himself up. "Who are you?"

"My name is Toshiko," she said. "Are you Hachiro?"

"Yes. I'm the doctor's son. Are you a patient?"

"No. I think . . . I am his wife."

"He has no wife."

She laughed a little to cover her embarrassment. "I came late last night, and you left very early this morning, before I could meet you. Your father has told me about you."

"Nothing good, probably." Hachiro flushed and glowered.

Before she could answer, Sadahira came. He smiled at her and put a hand on Hachiro's shoulder. "I see you've met my other son, Hachiro. Hachiro, this is my wife."

Hachiro looked at his father and said nothing. He seemed to be waiting for something.

"I'm sorry, this is a sudden surprise, but . . . well, it happened unexpectedly. I hope you'll look kindly on each other in the future, but at the moment we must prepare for a journey."

Hachiro's asked, "What journey?"

It was a rude response on being told of their marriage, but Toshiko could see the boy was upset.

Sadahira told him, "We'll leave today for the farm. I'll rent horses for you and me. Sadamu can travel with Toshiko and Otori in an oxcart."

Hachiro said, "I'm not going."

Toshiko's mind was on the travel arrangements. Her husband proposed horses. She cried, "Oh, Sadahira, I'd like to ride, too. Oh, please, Sadahira. I'm a good horsewoman."

Her husband faltered. "The journey is long and hard, but perhaps you may ride part of the way." Then he turned to the boy with a face like thunder. "I cannot have heard you correctly. Would you repeat your words?"

Hachiro flushed, then paled. "I do not want to leave," he said, sounding desperate. "My school is here. I can live with the monks.

Toshiko said quickly, "I'm sorry, Hachiro. It's my fault." Turning to Sadahira, she asked, "Can he not stay? Surely it will only be for a short time."

"He's too young to live here on his own. It isn't safe."

Hachiro repeated firmly, "I want to stay, Father. I'm old enough."

It was true. She said, "Hachiro is nearly grown. I expect he is older than I am. Surely he has a right to choose his way?"

His father looked at him, distracted by this new complication. "Your sudden love for education is very surprising," he said.

"The monks think I'm a good student," Hachiro said. "They think I might become a monk and serve the Buddha. I'd like to try, Father."

Toshiko was surprised by this. It seemed a pity that he should want to give up the world before he had even tasted it. There was a moment's silence, then Sadahira said, "I never expected this, but if the monks will indeed look after you, and if you find you truly have a desire for this life, I won't stand in your way." He told Toshiko, "I'd better go and make the arrangements then. The wagon and horses will be here soon. We'll leave as soon as night falls."

From Lady Sanjo's Pillow Book

Alas, my fate is sealed.

Oh, how many letters I wrote! Every day I sent a letter in the morning and a second later that day. I sat up by the light of the moon wielding my brush, wetting the ink cake with my tears. There never was a reply.

For a while, rumors went around that His Majesty had ordered a thorough search to be made of the city and had even gone to see the regent about the matter. But she had not gone to the regent's son, and the regent was deeply offended. Then I heard His Majesty had summoned the girl's father. Nobody knows what passed between them, but Oba left in a terrible temper. It was clear that she had not returned to her family.

After that the palace settled back into its normal routine, and I, too, breathed a sigh of relief, thinking that I could surely resume my devoted service to His Majesty and see Him smile upon me again as in the past.

But this morning– oh, ill-fated day! – a servant brought the message that I was to report to His Majesty's office. I went, filled with the most tender hopes. Alas, He was not there. Instead Tameyazu, His secretary and a singularly unpleasant man, received me.

"Lady Sanjo," he said in his cold voice, "you are to join your husband. His Majesty no longer has need of your services."

My heart froze. I am afraid I gaped at him. "B-but," I stuttered, "my husband serves in Settsu Province. I cannot go to him."

"Why not?" he asked.

"It is too far. It is some wild place with rude natives. What would I do there? How would I survive?"

He sneered at that. "Don't be ridiculous. Your husband is the governor of the province. He has been notified that you are coming. You will leave the palace today. Pack your trunks and arrange for lodging until you can set out on the journey." With that he handed me a package with my travel papers.

I don't remember how I got back to my room. When I returned to my senses, I opened the package with trembling fingers. There was nothing from His Majesty, not so much as a scribbled note. And no gift to help defray travel expenses or to recognize my many years of service. I have been dismissed like a criminal and sent into my exile.

My life is over!

Historical Note:

At this time, the imperial power in Japan rested in the hands of retired emperor Go-Shirakawa, who conducted the nation's affairs from his "cloister palace" while a son or grandson sat on the throne. Go-Shirakawa's rule lasted from his accession in 1155 at age 28 to his death in 1192. He managed the affairs of five successive emperors, two of them his sons and three his grandsons.

His tenure was marked by increasingly violent power struggles between the throne and factions among the court and military aristocracies. These disturbances culminated in the Heike Wars and shifted the ruling power permanently from the emperors to military shoguns.

Go-Shirakawa is a shadowy historical figure, considered by some historians too inept to prevent the catastrophe and by others a diplomat and manipulator of complex and powerful interests that were ultimately beyond his control. Whatever the scholarly opinion, Go-Shirakawa appears to have been determined to wrest power from the nobles and return it to the imperial family.

About the rest of the story:

Dust Before the Wind continues the tale of Toshiko and Sadahira as their ill-omened marriage brings problems and the war between the Taira and Minamoto clans tears their lives apart, forcing Sadahira to break his vow against bearing arms and Toshiko to face grief and the struggle for survival.

About the Author

I. J. Parker was born and educated in Europe and turned to mystery writing after an academic career in the U.S. She has published her Akitada stories in *Alfred Hitchcock's Mystery Magazine,* winning the Shamus award in 2000. Several stories have also appeared in collections, such as *Fifty Years of Crime and Suspense* and *Shaken.* The award-winning "Akitada's First Case" is available as a podcast.

Many of the stories have been collected in *Akitada and the Way of Justice.*

The Akitada series of crime novels features the same protagonist, an eleventh century Japanese nobleman/detective. The books are available as e-books, in print, and in audio format, and have been translated into twelve languages. The early novels are published by Penguin.

Books by I. J. Parker

The Akitada series in chronological order

The Dragon Scroll
Rashomon Gate
Black Arrow
Island of Exiles
The Hell Screen
The Convict's Sword
The Masuda Affair
The Fires of the Gods
Death on an Autumn River
The Emperor's Woman
Death of a Doll Maker
The Crane Pavilion
The Old Men of Omi
The Shrine Virgin
The Assassin's Daughter
The Island of the Gods
Ikiryo: Revenge and Justice

The collection of stories

Akitada and the Way of Justice

Other Historical Novels

The HOLLOW REED saga:
Dream of a Spring Night
Dust before the Wind
The Sword Master

The Left-Handed God

Contact Information

Please visit I.J.Parker's web site at
www.ijparker.com
You may contact her via e-mail there. This way you will be informed when new books come out.

The novels may be ordered from Amazon or Barnes&Noble as trade paperbacks. There are electronic versions of all the works. Please do post reviews. They help sell books and keep Akitada novels coming. Thank you for your support.

59603682R00207

Made in the USA
Columbia, SC
05 June 2019